'Tis the Season to be Single

LAURA ZIEPE

ONE PLACE. MANY STORIES

HQ
An imprint of HarperCollins*Publishers* Ltd
1 London Bridge Street
London SE1 9GF

This edition 2018

First published in Great Britain by
HQ, an imprint of HarperCollins*Publishers* Ltd 2018

ISBN: PB: 978-0-00-832105-5
EB: 978-0-00-831848-2

MIX
Paper from
responsible sources
FSC **FSC™ C007454**
www.fsc.org

This book is produced from independently certified FSC™ paper
to ensure responsible forest management.

For more information visit: www.harpercollins.co.uk/green

Typeset by Palimpsest Book Production Ltd, Falkirk, Stirlingshire
Printed and bound in Great Britain by
CPI Group (UK) Ltd, Melksham, SN12 6TR

I would like to dedicate this book to the three loves of my life; my husband Terry and our beautiful twins, Harry and Darcey.

Chapter 1

'Perhaps he's going to propose?' Grace said cheerfully, her eyes sparkling with excitement as she bent down to arrange a drawer of lipsticks.

Rachel frowned anxiously, biting her lower lip as she stared at the twinkly fairy lights and sparkly giant baubles above. The Christmas decorations had just gone up and they usually put her in a good mood instantly, but not today. Her boyfriend of three years, Mark, had called on her lunch break to check she was coming straight home as he needed to talk to her.

'No, I really don't think that's it,' she replied fretfully. 'He sounded really serious on the phone and Mark is never normally like that. It was as though someone had died. Which they haven't, thank goodness, because it was the first thing I asked when I heard his sombre voice.'

'Well, getting married is a *huge* deal,' Grace pointed out, tucking her shoulder-length dark hair behind her ear. 'He's probably just nervous.' She smiled widely. 'You should have seen Simon when he proposed to me. He was shaking so much I thought he was going to drop the ring.'

Rachel gave a light laugh. 'I'm not so sure...' She tailed off, unable to imagine Mark proposing on such an ordinary day.

Firstly, it was a Wednesday and they didn't have plans that evening to do anything special, and secondly, Christmas was just around the corner. Surely if Mark was going to propose he'd choose to do so on Christmas Day? She could just imagine it at the Christmas table, surrounded by Mark's lovely family as they gushed over the beautiful diamond ring. He wouldn't do it on a random Wednesday at the beginning of November, would he? Rachel felt like she'd been waiting forever for him to propose, but try as she might, she just couldn't imagine that being the reason he needed to talk to her.

'Don't look so worried,' Grace told her, in a comforting, caring voice. 'I'm sure if it was that urgent, he would have just told you over the phone.'

Rachel forced a smile and nodded her head. 'Yes, I'm sure you're right. It's probably nothing. I bet it's to do with his work or something along those lines. He's been so stressed over work lately; perhaps he's quit his job? It wouldn't be the worst thing.'

'Has Bianca mentioned anything?' Grace questioned curiously. 'Perhaps she knows what all this is about?'

Bianca was Rachel's best friend from primary school. When Bianca had been made redundant the year before, Rachel had managed to persuade Mark to get her a job at the bank he worked for in London. Bianca had been over the moon and so grateful. Rachel's forehead wrinkled.

'No, she hasn't, and I spoke to her last night. They only work in the same building though. They're in completely different departments so I can't imagine she'd know anything anyway. It's not like they're friends or anything.' Rachel heaved a loud sigh. 'There's no point in me guessing all day. I'll just have to wait and see.'

'Exactly,' Grace said, pulling out a lipstick and taking the cap off. 'Put on a bit of red lippie to get into the festive spirit and everything will be fine,' she smiled, passing the lipstick over.

It was quiet today in Tidemans, the department store they

worked in. With Christmas fast approaching, Rachel knew it was the calm before the storm and she should appreciate the peace and quiet. Right now though, she also knew that she'd welcome the distraction of some customers, as all she could think about was what Mark wanted to say to her. As much as she'd pressed him on the phone, he'd been adamant he wanted to discuss it face to face. It couldn't be anything that bad, could it? A feeling of unease crept up on her. Everything had been fine in their relationship; a little same-old and predictable maybe, but Rachel loved the feeling of being completely comfortable and they were happy, weren't they? Who cared if she no longer had the butterflies like at the beginning? That feeling didn't last forever in any relationship, and Mark was the man Rachel wanted to marry. He was *the one*. For the past year she'd been hoping he was going to propose and she couldn't deny she'd felt a little disappointed after every night out in a restaurant or trip away together when she'd still come back empty handed. What if Grace was right? What if he really was going to propose today? Rachel applied the red lipstick with a brush and puckered her lips together. At least she could make sure she looked nice if he was going to pop the question.

Rachel loved working with Grace on the make-up counter for Pop Cosmetics and they'd become great friends over the years. They knew practically everything about each other, and Rachel was so glad she'd decided to take the job five years ago, despite having reservations about working in retail. There were usually three of them, but their colleague, Amber, was away in Thailand, due to arrive back in a few days' time.

'Good luck,' Grace said, leaning in for a kiss a few hours later when they were leaving. 'Let me know straightaway if you get engaged,' she said, her lips curving at the edges. 'What a lovely early Christmas present that would be.'

Rachel waved goodbye, feeling sick with nerves.

Their flat was empty when she got home, so Rachel put the

kettle on, making a cup of tea for something to do. She was looking forward to decorating their flat for Christmas; they usually drank mulled wine and listened to Christmas songs to get them in the mood. She remembered amusedly how the year before they'd ended up pretty drunk and covered in glitter.

She was pouring the milk into the tea when she heard the front door open and Mark walk in.

'Hi!' Rachel attempted a smile and a breezy tone, swivelling round to face Mark as he walked into the kitchen. Her heart plummeted, as she instantly knew that whatever it was he was going to tell her, it wasn't good news. There was definitely going to be no proposal tonight, of that she was certain.

'Hi. Rach, do you mind sitting down?' Mark asked gravely, walking over to the kitchen table with a slight stoop to his shoulders. His face was white as a sheet.

Rachel swallowed hard, knowing she should have trusted her gut instinct that something was wrong when he had called her that afternoon. Maybe he'd been sacked from his job and they were going to struggle to pay the bills? She could handle that though and would offer to work extra hours at Tidemans and start doing freelance make-up like she'd promised herself she would years ago. Or perhaps someone was sic   k? Rachel was annoyed that she'd allowed Grace to get her hopes up that maybe, just maybe, he was going to propose and everything was going to be amazing in her life. She needed to stop telling herself that if she just had an engagement ring, everything would perfect.

'I've made you a cup of tea,' she said, placing the mug in front of him and sitting opposite. 'Can you tell me what's up now, please? You're starting to scare me,' she confessed, feeling awkward in front of him for the first time since they'd met.

Mark's breathing was shallow and audible as he fidgeted in his seat and stared at his hands uncomfortably. Two red blotches suddenly appeared on his pale neck. He closed his eyes momentarily.

'Look, there's no easy way for me to say this, Rachel, but I'm moving out. I can't be with you anymore,' he stated, matter-of-factly.

Rachel felt as though she'd been winded, her mouth popping open in shock. She was completely speechless, the room spinning round as she stared at him in disbelief.

'I'm so sorry to do this to you, I really am, but I can't live a lie any longer and pretend that everything is okay, when it isn't. You're such an amazing person, Rach, you really are. Someone is going to be so lucky to have you one day,' he said in pitying tones, 'but I don't love you the way I should anymore. You deserve better than me.'

A sense of deep foreboding washed over Rachel like a powerful waterfall. He couldn't be serious? But as she gazed at Mark, praying he was just trying to wind her up, her eyes swept over his guilty, tormented expression, hunched shoulders and unsteady hands, and she knew that her life was about to change forever. This was definitely no joke, and Rachel felt physically sick, her mouth too dry to speak. She blinked several times and squinted her eyes at him. 'But why? What's changed?' she managed to ask, her voice cracking with emotion. 'I thought things were fine. I thought we were happy, Mark. I even, stupidly, thought we would get engaged soon,' Rachel whispered breathlessly. 'I imagined we'd be getting married next year and that maybe we could have a nice Christmas wedding like we'd discussed or…'

'Rach, please don't,' he interjected, looking as though it was painful for him to talk, his eyes trailing to the window like he couldn't bear to look at her. 'It's nothing you've done. You've been great, you *are* great in fact. It's me.' He winced. 'Oh God, I don't want to be the guy that gives you the cliché "it's not you it's me".'

'Then don't be,' Rachel retorted, her voice now razor sharp and unrecognisable. Her heart was beating so fast it felt like it might explode at any second.

'I don't want to hurt you,' he whimpered. 'I don't deserve you, like I said. You deserve so much better than me.'

Even breaking up with her, Mark was being nice about it. He was so well spoken and polite that for some reason it made it more of a slap in the face because she couldn't hate him. How on earth was this happening? How had it come to this? Rachel hadn't gone after a bad boy, trying to tame him unsuccessfully. Rachel had chosen Mark. Mark with the kind, gentle features and smiley face who was friendly to everybody. The type of man to help an old lady crossing the road or to buy the homeless man on the street a cup of coffee. She'd settled for the good guy; the one who wasn't supposed to break your heart after three years together. The one who was supposed to be proposing!

'What's changed?' Rachel asked in a demanding voice. She needed an explanation. Rachel wasn't giving up without a fight. They had so many plans for the future. Rachel had been looking forward to hosting Christmas for Mark's entire family, like she'd done every year since they'd met. She'd been looking forward to playing board games with his sister, Lottie, who was just as competitive as Rachel, handing her presents out, which she'd put a lot of thought into, and pulling Christmas crackers at the table, with Mark's father making them read the terrible jokes inside one by one. She had even been looking forward to Mark's mother getting drunk, mumbling all her words and not making any sense by 9 p.m. Was she really going to be losing everyone in one fell swoop? It was devastating. Brutal.

Mark looked at her then, as though she was a poor little dog he was about to put down. 'I have. Things have just changed. I love you, Rach, you know I do. But I think it's more like a friend.'

It would have hurt less if he'd stabbed her and suddenly Rachel felt angry.

'Right, well that's just great then,' she said, pushing her chair back to stand up, which made a loud scraping sound. 'I'll just get my things and go. There's nothing I can do if you're telling me that you only love me as a friend,' she said, hating the fact that her face was scrunching up and her eyes were filling with tears.

'Please, don't, Rach. I already feel terrible enough,' Mark replied, putting his head in his hands.

'What do you want me to say, Mark? I love you, and not just as a friend. I thought we were going to be together forever, and now suddenly out of the blue you come home and tell me you no longer love me!' Tears cascaded down her cheeks. 'I feel like such an idiot.'

'You're not an idiot. I'm the idiot. I don't know what I'm doing anymore,' he sighed, rubbing his eyes with the palms of his hands.

'You're breaking up with me,' Rachel stated, brushing her tears away roughly. 'I'll leave and make things easier for you,' she told him, making her way into their bedroom to pack a bag.

'No, I'll leave,' Mark said, jumping up to follow her, 'I should be the one to go.'

'No, you won't,' Rachel snapped at him. 'You won't be the one who gets to break up with me and then walk away. I don't want to be here alone, in our flat. There are too many memories. It's all yours.'

'You don't have to go right now,' he mumbled guiltily, his eyes downcast. The dark shadows under his eyes and his blotchy skin gave the impression that the situation was making him ill. Well, good. Rachel hoped he was suffering just as much as she was.

'What shall I do then, Mark? Sleep next to you in bed knowing that you don't love me? Sleep on the sofa knowing that you're next door where I usually sleep? I can't believe you're doing this, Mark. Just before Christmas too.'

'There was never a right time. After Christmas it's your birthday, then Valentine's Day, then our anniversary. When would the right time be, Rach? I could sleep on the sofa,' she heard him say, before she slammed the door to cry alone.

Rachel sobbed, trying to hold it together until she left. She was utterly heartbroken, but she didn't want Mark to see how distraught she truly was. She felt humiliated and foolish. Mark seemed a complete stranger and not the man she'd laid beside for the past three years. Where had all this come from and how had Rachel not seen it coming? If he no longer loved her, there was really no going back now, was there? There was simply nothing she could do about it.

'Where are you going to go?' Mark asked her, his voice laced with sympathy and sadness as she opened the bedroom door with a suitcase.

'I don't know,' Rachel responded honestly. 'Home I guess. Not that it should concern you now.'

'Yes, I suppose home to your parents is best. Rachel, I'm so sorry,' he said pathetically, looking as though he didn't know what to do with himself.

Rachel sniffed loudly, still unable to believe they were breaking up. 'So am I, Mark. So am I.'

She closed the front door behind her, not looking back at him, and made her way to her car before her face crumpled and she cried her heart out.

Fifteen minutes later and Rachel was still crying. She was dreading going home to her parents and explaining what had happened. Her parents would be so disappointed; she could just see her mother's sorrowful expression wondering how Mark had done this to her daughter. Her mother and father adored Mark. They were always telling her what a lovely young man he was and that she couldn't have picked better.

I definitely could have picked better, Mum, the bastard has left me, she thought wryly as she stopped at the traffic lights.

Rachel's mother had been harping on about grandchildren ever since she could remember and now she felt like she'd somehow let her down. She wondered if it would be better going to Bianca's? Bianca lived alone in her flat and had a spare room she could stay in. They'd been best friends since childhood and Rachel felt completely at ease being a snivelling wreck in Bianca's presence. Rachel was always there for Bianca when she was feeling down; she couldn't count the number of times she'd been on the phone until 1 a.m. listening to Bianca ramble on about some guy who hadn't called her back. Deciding this was the best idea, Rachel put her foot down hard on the accelerator and made her way there.

'Rachel?' Bianca looked as though she'd seen a ghost as she opened the front door. Her eyes were open wide with concern and shock as she gazed at Rachel standing there.

'Oh Bee, it's all gone horribly wrong. Can I stay here?' Rachel sniffed, wiping her nose with a crumpled tissue she'd found in the bottom of her handbag.

'Of course.' Bianca opened the door and took Rachel in her arms. 'What's happened? Is it Mark?' she asked gently.

Rachel nodded, her eyes filling with tears again. 'We've broken up,' she croaked. 'He doesn't love me anymore.' Rachel's face wrinkled as she said the words.

'Oh Rachel, I'm so sorry. I'm just so, so sorry. Come through to the lounge. Let me get you a drink,' Bianca suggested kindly.

Rachel let Bianca lead her into the lounge and sat on the sofa. 'It's come out of nowhere. I don't know what I'm going to do,' Rachel said, feeling helpless. The rug had been pulled from under her feet. She couldn't believe she was here, instead of at home making dinner and wondering what to watch on television for the evening. Everything had happened so quickly.

Bianca looked awkward. She felt really bad for Rachel and it was a surprise seeing her in such a vulnerable state. Rachel was the strong one in their friendship. Rachel didn't get upset about the little things like Bianca did. She was the one who was normally comforting and reassuring Bianca for whatever reason. Rachel had been the lucky one. She was the one with the job she loved and the boyfriend she adored. She was the first one to kiss a boy, lose her virginity and get into a serious relationship. It was Bianca who went out on the countless bad dates and struggled to find a nice man to settle down with.

'Can I get you a drink? I can open a bottle of wine if you like?' Bianca offered.

'No, I'm fine,' Rachel exhaled. 'Well, I'm not fine, I'm completely heartbroken, but the thought of eating or drinking makes me feel sick.'

Bianca gave a little nod and sat down slowly opposite Rachel. 'What did he say?' Bianca asked in a small voice, her large brown eyes full of sympathy.

'That he loves me like a friend,' Rachel confessed, rolling her eyes. 'Just what every woman wants to hear,' she said sarcastically. 'There's nothing I can do about that, is there? I can't make it better. I can't say I'll stop nagging him as much, or that I won't be as possessive or whatever other things men hate. Because I don't do any of those things and it's not because I've done anything wrong, it's because he doesn't love me anymore. It's the worst possible thing he could say.' She closed her eyes trying to prevent the tears again. 'I'm just hoping he says he's made a mistake. I'm praying that because I've actually left him, he'll change his mind.' She laughed uncontrollably. 'I'm pitiable, aren't I? I just don't know what's going on anymore. I just want him to want me back.'

Bianca shifted on the armchair and stared at Rachel with a frown. 'Perhaps it's for the best?' she replied optimistically. 'You'll meet someone else, Rach, you know you will. You always do. Maybe Mark just wasn't for you?'

'I don't want to meet someone else,' Rachel moaned, shaking her head and blowing her nose. 'Mark was nice. He was reliable, loyal and dependable. My parents love him. My friends love him. He was *the one*,' she stated firmly, her chin wobbling. 'I thought I was going to be spending the rest of my life with him. I can't explain it…' She broke off. Bianca had never had a long-term boyfriend, so she couldn't possibly know how she felt. Bianca's relationships usually lasted no longer than a month. She had no idea what Rachel was going through, couldn't ever know the pain she was feeling – not that Rachel was about to voice this for fear of hurting her feelings.

'I just keep thinking I should have known,' Rachel continued. 'But I didn't. I honestly thought everything was fine between us. I knew things weren't perfect, but that's life, right? No one's relationship is perfect. The longer you're together the more comfortable and relaxed you get. That's just how it goes. What does he actually want?' Rachel said, raising her shoulders.

Bianca sat quietly looking down at the floor. 'You'll meet someone else,' she practically whispered.

'I'm sure I will eventually,' Rachel nodded, rubbing her nose and desperately trying to find some positivity. She knew this was going to be difficult, but she *would* get through it. She had great friends and family around her for support. She wasn't the first person to go through a break up and she certainly wouldn't be the last. She was aware things could be much worse. Somehow, it would be okay again one day, she did know that deep down. She just needed to get over the shock and hurt. 'I really thought I had the right man,' she explained, shaking her head in puzzlement. Then the thought suddenly hit her, as though a light switch had been turned on inside her head. 'Oh my God. Say he's already seeing someone else? I didn't even ask him. How could I not have asked him? He could be leaving me for another woman. Have you seen him with anyone at work? Do you ever speak to him?'

Bianca's eyes darted around the room, like she was afraid to answer and Rachel instantly felt tension in the room.

'No, I don't see him at work. Well, sometimes I see him. Like occasionally, but it's not often … I … he … we work on different floors,' Bianca replied, appearing a little flustered and uncomfortable.

Rachel frowned, wondering if Bianca was hiding something from her, when her eyes landed on a black jacket hanging up outside in the hallway. A feeling of sheer dread hit her like a tidal wave. She felt sick to the core as she stood up and walked over to it, her hands shaking as she reached out for the jacket.

'Rach? What's wrong? What are you doing?' Bianca asked, watching in horror as she picked up the jacket and opened it.

Rachel prayed that she was wrong. She hoped with every single fibre of her being that it couldn't possibly be true. She opened the jacket and when she saw the pink nail varnish stain inside by the pocket, it took her breath away as though she'd been punched. She knew then exactly why Mark had broken up with her. She pivoted and stared at Bianca in disbelief.

'This is Mark's jacket,' she stated calmly, adrenaline pumping through her.

'No it's not,' Bianca replied quickly, her face turning a shade of pink. She let out a nervous laugh. 'Why on earth would Mark's jacket be here?'

'It's Mark's jacket,' Rachel stated with certainty, ignoring her, her index finger touching the stain. 'I had just painted my nails once when he asked me to grab his phone from the pocket because he was in the bath. You see this mark here?' Rachel pointed to the pink smudge. 'This was because my nails were wet still. I felt really bad about it afterwards, though you can't see the stain from the outside. Mark was always particular about his clothes. He takes good care of them.' She shot Bianca an intense gaze. 'Why is Mark's jacket here?'

Bianca's eyes were as round as saucers. 'Rachel, please let me explain…'

'I got you that job at Mark's firm,' Rachel interrupted. 'It was me, you know. I begged him to get you in there. I told him how down you were and how bad I felt for you getting made redundant. He didn't want to get involved at first; he kept telling me it was a bad idea in case you weren't any good and he'd been the

12

one to recommend you so it wouldn't look good on him, but I kept on about it, singing your praises and persuading him to do it. I've been a good friend to you, haven't I?'

Bianca gave a weak nod, looking away.

'Yes, I have. So I think it's about time you were honest with me, don't you?' Rachel could feel herself growing angrier with every second. All those late nights Mark had been working flashed through Rachel's mind. All the times that Bianca hadn't answered the phone and then made excuses as to why she couldn't meet up, Rachel had just assumed she'd been really busy, and she supposed she had been –

with *her* boyfriend!

'I don't know what you mean…'

'Bee, just cut the crap, okay?' Rachel interjected hotly, rolling her eyes and feeling as if her head was about to explode in rage. 'How long have you been seeing Mark for? How long have you been seeing *my* boyfriend?' She couldn't believe she was even saying the words. She glared at Bianca, feeling the tension emanating from her.

Bianca fiddled with her hair, at least having the decency to look ashamed. She looked at the floor; she'd clearly rather be anywhere else in the world at that very second.

'Rachel, I'm so sorry,' she said finally, tears filling her eyes. 'I never meant for any of this to happen. We both didn't.'

'*We?* So you and Mark are a *we* now?' A loud laugh escaped her lips. 'Tell me, for how long? How long have you both been lying to me?' she snapped, feeling more hurt and betrayed than she ever knew was possible.

'Oh God, I know you're upset, but the last thing we ever wanted was to hurt you. We've both felt so bad, Rachel. Please believe me. It's been going on for about two months, that's all. I told him I wanted to stop. I couldn't carry on until things were sorted between you two,' she sniffed loudly.

Rachel gazed at Bianca noticing her mascara was smudged,

her eyes focusing on the black smear underneath her chocolate brown eyes. She looked around the room at the colourful scatter cushions on the sofa with the sequins which scratched your skin, the full magazine rack with magazines piled messily around it and Bianca's pink fluffy slippers lying in the middle of the room. Mark wouldn't care much for her untidiness. He'd hate it in fact. It would grate on him eventually, but perhaps he didn't even know that side to Bianca just yet. Or maybe it didn't bother him right now because everything was so new, sexy and exciting. She could just imagine the thrill of their sordid meetings, worrying that Rachel may or may not catch them and find out. How could the two of them have got together behind her back? At what point had Bianca become appealing to Mark? He'd never seemed remotely bothered about her before. They'd always gotten along of course, but just on a normal boyfriend/best friend level. There had been absolutely nothing remarkable about their relationship. In fact, she distinctly remembered Mark calling Bianca 'quite the chatterbox,' implying it was a bad thing. So when had the chatterbox become irresistible to him? Nothing between the two of them had ever told Rachel to watch out because, if she wasn't careful, one day they'd hook up and ditch her. They hadn't even flirted in front of her before. Rachel felt as though it was all a bad dream; she was frail and shaky and thought she might pass out from the shock at any second. How could they both do that to her?

Bianca began to weep and Rachel had to stop herself from comforting her out of habit. This was certainly not the time to make her so-called best friend feel better.

'So you've really been seeing Mark then?' she asked, a nasty bitter taste flooding her mouth.

Bianca nodded, her nose beginning to run. 'I think I'm in love with him,' she cried. 'I'm so sorry. It's all just such a mess. We just got chatting at work one day in the lunch canteen. We were talking about you, but there was just this spark between us. I can't explain it. I know you're going to hate me,' she sobbed, 'and I deserve it. I really do deserve it.'

Love? It was as though the word was lodged in Rachel's throat and she couldn't swallow. So it wasn't just a fling then? It wasn't a mistake. Bianca was planning to steal Mark because she couldn't live without him. Supposedly *loved* him. Her Mark. What had happened? Had they started a conversation about her and then realized that actually, they would make a better couple? *How about we both lose Rachel and get together instead?* The world had gone crazy.

'I don't know what to say to you,' Rachel said, filled with a wave of disbelief, her eyes suddenly dry. She was too stunned and hurt to cry at that moment. The shock had dried up her ability to show any emotion. 'I just need to get out of here. I need to be away from *you*.'

'Please just believe that we're sorry, okay?' Bianca pleaded. 'You can't just leave like this.'

Again, the word 'we're', to show that they'd become a secret couple, while Rachel had just been happily living her ordinary little life in ignorance. 'Wrong. I can do whatever the hell I like,' Rachel retorted, her head throbbing like it did when she had a migraine coming on. 'I don't owe you anything, Bianca. You want my boyfriend? You're welcome to him. Don't ever contact me again.'

Rachel marched to the front door, slamming it behind her. She took a deep breath wondering what on earth she was going to do.

What a very merry Christmas this was going to be.

Chapter 2

Grace walked downstairs, instantly feeling irritated at the sight of the damp washing still lying there in the basket. She didn't usually get irritated; people called her 'breezy' and 'laidback'. Grace liked being perceived as a chilled-out kind of person; she simply didn't get people who were always rushing around and stressed out. But, the night before, she'd asked Simon to do just one little thing and clearly it was too much to ask. Feeling a little unwell, Grace had gone to bed early and asked him to put the laundry she'd just washed on the radiators to dry before he came to bed. He'd obviously been too engrossed watching football to hear her, as usual. She couldn't count the number of times he'd agreed to do something, only to not have the faintest idea what she was talking about when she mentioned it again days later. She usually just let it slide. It was just another thing to add to the list of Simon's annoying ways, and normally she told herself it wasn't a big deal. Nobody was going to die.

Grace huffed, the damp smell of the washing filling her nostrils as she picked up the basket. It would have to be washed again now, and she wished she'd just done it herself. Her mother had once told her never to rely on anybody apart from herself, and Grace could see why. As she walked through to the kitchen, she held her breath in exasperation spotting Simon's dirty frying pan, decorated with the remains of crispy fried egg; his plate, cup and cutlery were all just sitting there on the work surface. She didn't comprehend why he couldn't just tidy away after himself. Living with Simon was like living with a child, and if Grace was honest, she'd got to the point where she was fed up of being so relaxed about everything, because actually, it *wasn't* okay. He'd gone to work that morning, and just expected her to tidy up after him. Didn't he understand that Grace had work too? She didn't have time to constantly clear away his mess, but no matter how many times she explained this (in a polite, non-confrontational way), Simon just didn't change. He couldn't quite grasp the concept of sharing the housework. If he was so happy to live in a pigsty then so be it, she thought, deciding to leave his mess sitting exactly where it was, instead of tidying it away like she normally did.

Grace exhaled sharply as she noticed the bin was full to the brim and Simon hadn't bothered to change it that morning, just stuffing his rubbish on top in the hope that she would do it. She wasn't sure what it was about today, but Simon's ways were really starting to get on top of her. She knew it was most likely because it was her time of the month, which was worse for her than normal because they'd been trying for a baby for the past year – and failing. But even if Grace did fall pregnant, how could she have a baby when Simon was like this? What help would Simon be? Over the years Simon just seemed to take her for granted. He didn't appreciate anything she did. She was just Grace, his wife; the woman at home to make his dinners and clean the house, the woman to wash and iron his clothes, and she had just accepted it.

Don't worry, Grace will do it.

It hadn't always been that way, she remembered sadly; when they'd first met ten years ago, Simon had been impulsive and full of energy, often whisking her away for days out with only a moment's notice. She remembered one Saturday when they were both bored, he'd persuaded her to get the Eurostar to Paris; it had been magical and they hadn't been able to look at each other that day without smiling, in their own little secret world. It had been so romantic it was quite sickening and Grace could only imagine the amused and envious stares they had received from other couples who were no longer obsessed with each other because time had disintegrated their passion. *They* were the grinning couple standing on top of the Eiffel Tower taking a selfie. They were the ones holding hands and constantly kissing as though they were never going to see each other again. She recalled how they always had to be touching; just a simple touch of the hand, kiss on the lips or squeeze of the bum and Grace had walked around with a permanent smile because she had a boyfriend who completely adored her. She never once thought that it may not stay that way forever. She remembered one time when she'd been talking to Rachel and Amber, who were both single at the time, about relationships and Rachel had turned to her with a theatrical sigh and said, 'I just want to find what you have with Simon. That's all I want.' Grace had frowned at the time, wondering why Rachel had thought they were so special, but looking back, they *had* been special. How Grace wished she could just wrap up their feelings from the old days in a box and keep them forever. Then as soon as things started to get dull and mundane she could open the box and show Simon. *See how much you used to love me?*

She'd loved his spontaneity. She'd loved how much he *loved* her; now she just felt like an old coat he'd grown tired of but still put on occasionally. She tried to be affectionate towards him, giving him the odd random kiss and cuddle, but she had to admit it felt as though she was the one making all the effort. It wasn't a nice feeling and lately, Grace had found herself wondering if this was really it for her life now. Was this as exciting as things were going to get?

Grace ate her cereal quickly, putting her bowl into the dishwasher. Trying for a baby had definitely made things worse as far as their love life went. Sex had become mechanical, and most of the time, they just wanted the 'job' over with as quickly as possible. Grace would find herself thinking *hurry up* the entire time. It was hardly romantic or fun, and Grace felt frustrated that she still wasn't pregnant. Everyone else seemed to manage it at the drop of a hat, including her sister, Amanda, who'd fallen pregnant six months ago on her first try. Falling pregnant on your first try seemed completely ludicrous to Grace. Just one try! Amanda seriously didn't realize how lucky she was, Grace thought sullenly, as she went back upstairs to quickly brush her teeth. Grace couldn't remember the first time she and Simon tried now, but she did remember how excited they were thinking that they'd soon be parents. How ridiculously naive they were. Grace hated how much hope they'd had. If only she could go back in time and tell herself, *hold tight Grace, in twelve months' time you still won't have got there.*

Grace had always told herself that she wouldn't let the whole trying-to-get-pregnant-thing get her down. It would happen when it happened. She was a relaxed, mellow person, after all. She wasn't uptight about anything and she wasn't about to start changing now, over this. Of course, there was more to life than having children, and she did believe she'd get there in the end. It wasn't the only thing she was focusing on in life. But after twelve unsuccessful months, it was impossible to not worry and feel disheartened and disappointed. It clearly wasn't going to be as easy for them as it was for other couples and she had even started to fear that Simon was losing interest in becoming a father altogether now. The last two times she was ovulating, he'd brushed her off and told her he was too tired. He *knew* the importance of timing in her cycle, but Grace hadn't wanted to push him. She didn't want to be one of those women demanding sex just to get pregnant; she wanted it to at least feel natural. His refusal had hurt though, she couldn't deny that. It had hurt just like his overall lack of interest in her and when she'd recently tried to voice her feelings, he'd just given a loud sigh as though she was trying to create unnecessary issues. Grace didn't create unnecessary issues though! She was easygoing and low-maintenance; how had Simon forgotten that?

Grace turned the ignition on in her car to drive to Tidemans. Her thoughts turned to Rachel and she wondered if she was engaged, smiling for the first time that morning. She hoped she was; Grace knew how much Rachel was dying for a ring. Not that marriage was all it was cracked up to be. She'd never actually voiced her concerns to anybody before about her relationship and she wondered why. Embarrassed perhaps? Did she want them to believe that somehow, despite being together for ten years they were still that same, smitten, giggly couple with their own secret world? Or did she think her moaning about Simon's lack of enthusiasm would simply bore people? She could just see them now, rolling their eyes as she told them Simon had left the toilet seat up *again*. She couldn't resist a giggle at the thought of it; it was just so unlike Grace to complain about things. She'd always been the sort of person to get on with it. She dealt with things alone, but perhaps she was to blame for letting Simon get away with treating her this way for far too long now? Had he taken advantage of her 'no problem' nature? Maybe, if it continued this way, there would be no going back.

Ten minutes later, Grace was walking into Tidemans admiring the beautiful gold and red Christmas decorations and pretty fairy lights, thinking about what presents she was going to buy everyone and knowing she'd have to start soon. They were spending Christmas day with Grace's family and she couldn't wait. Last year had been Simon's turn for them to spend it with his family (they swapped every year so it was fair) and as much as Grace had enjoyed herself, she couldn't help but feel Christmas just wasn't the same when she wasn't with her own parents and sister. It reminded her of being young again and she loved the thrill and excitement when everyone handed out their presents and drank Buck's Fizz with their breakfast. It was the little things. She loved them all being together again and, she had to face it, she felt comfortable enough to just lay and snooze on the settee after her Christmas dinner at her parents' house.

Just as she was thinking about some gorgeous new dresses she'd seen in the kids' department that were perfect for her niece, Poppy, she spotted Rachel at the till. Grace knew instantly that something terrible had happened as her eyes swept over Rachel's hunched shoulders, red, puffy eyes and pale complexion. It was their job to wear Pop Cosmetics make-up and to sell the products, and if Rachel hadn't been able to face applying any make-up that day, then it must be serious. After all, it was a requirement to wear make-up, not an option.

'Morning,' Grace said hurriedly. 'Rachel, are you okay? What's happened?'

Rachel looked frail and fragile, as if she might easily break into a million pieces if Grace touched her. She looked ill. Grace watched in alarm as Rachel's face screwed up and she reached out to hug her, worried that Rachel may crumple into a heap on the floor.

'Mark broke up with me,' Rachel sobbed. 'He's been having an affair with Bianca.'

Grace was stunned and she couldn't conceal it, her mouth hanging open in horror. 'What? You're joking? Oh Rach, I'm so sorry. That's just despicable. How on earth could they do this to you?'

Rachel rubbed her eyes with her fists roughly. 'I just can't believe it and I can't stop crying. I'm heartbroken, Grace. I'm really, truly heartbroken and I'm fed up with crying. I've hardly slept, I've just cried all night long. I wouldn't be surprised if there were no more tears left in me.'

Grace hugged her again tightly. 'I bet you're heartbroken. That's completely understandable. I promise you'll get through this though, Rachel. You're so strong. Everything is going to be okay.'

Grace stood there listening as Rachel explained the story. When Judy, the store manager, came over with a concerned expression, telling them they needed to be at the morning meeting, Grace took control of the situation and asked if they could miss the meeting and just be ready in ten minutes when the store opened. Judy didn't look too impressed, but Grace knew that she trusted her, so she accepted it would all be sorted and left them to it.

'It's just awful, Rach. I really can't believe it. How dare Bianca still try to lie, even right at the end when you found Mark's coat? She's certainly no friend of yours,' she tutted, shaking her head in disgust.

'I just don't know what to do,' Rachel said helplessly. Her eyes were large and round and she looked like a young child who had lost her mum in the supermarket. 'I'm back home with my parents and I just can't believe it. They're gutted for me, tip toeing around and constantly asking if I want cups of tea and I've only been there one night. The fact they're being so nice to me just makes me feel worse; I feel like even more of a let-down.'

Grace frowned. 'You are not a let-down, so stop saying that,' she told her gently. 'You were with the wrong man, that's all. He's shown his true colours. Thank goodness you've found out now rather than in a few years after marriage and a baby or something. You will be happy again, I promise. This pain is only temporary and I really do believe there's someone a million times better out there for you.'

Rachel nodded. 'I know I'll get through this. I have no choice, but it's so difficult. I really believed I'd be with him forever.'

Grace looked into the distance thoughtfully. 'Can I be really honest with you?' she ventured gingerly.

Rachel looked up at her and sniffed, 'Of course you can.'

Grace hesitated, wondering how truthful she really should be. 'It's just, I know you say you loved Mark and I'm sure you do, but I could never really see you two together. I always felt like you hit a certain age, met Mark and just settled. He's a nice guy, well maybe not so much now he's cheated with your best friend—' she snorted '—but I find him a bit … well … boring.' There, she'd said it.

Rachel gave a light laugh, 'Yes I suppose he is really, but he's what I want. What I thought I wanted anyway.'

'Exactly. He's what you *thought* you wanted. But I don't think he was ever *the one* at all. You've never really seemed that happy or excited with him. I remember what you were like with that guy Justin before you met Mark…'

'Great, so now you're reminding me of Justin who completely pied me after our date. Another rejection,' she replied in mock annoyance with a glimmer of a smile.

'Come on, you know what I'm saying. You've always talked about Mark like he was an old friend rather than your boyfriend and deep down, I think you know you weren't really all that happy with him. Being happy with someone is what life is all about,' Grace told her boldly. 'Life is too short to be anything but.' As Grace said the words, she thought of her own marriage. Was she happy with Simon? She hated to think it, but she wasn't sure she really was anymore. He didn't make her feel special. He completely shut her out when she tried to talk about it as though she was an annoying wasp buzzing round his head. How could she be giving this advice to Rachel, but living unhappily with her own husband? She was a hypocrite and she hated herself for it. A complete fraud.

Rachel looked down at the floor. 'Perhaps you're right.'

'I am right. Let Mark and Bianca have each other! What a wonderful relationship they're going to have, already built on deceit and lies. She's actually done you a favour. Now come on, let me put some make-up on you. It'll take time to feel better, of course it will, but I'm going to make sure you don't scare off any of the customers in the meantime,' Grace said, deadpan.

'Cheeky cow!' Rachel laughed loudly, softly punching Grace's

23

arm. 'Thanks Grace. I didn't have the energy to get ready today. I was scared I would cry all my make-up off. Talking to you has cheered me up though. Maybe I was just desperate to settle down? It's all so confusing at the moment.'

'Just no more crying,' Grace reprimanded her like a school teacher. 'I swear to you, you're going to be fine.'

The day went by quickly, and Grace was pleased to see Rachel chatting enthusiastically to customers by the end of the afternoon and applying their make-up. She still had a sadness about her, her watery eyes gave it away, but the customers were completely oblivious which was the main thing. They were unaware she'd just had life turned upside down, and Grace admired her for it.

Grace's own situation had been playing on her mind all day. She definitely still loved Simon, but she didn't love their relationship. He'd changed towards her and no longer made her feel special and loved. He simply couldn't be bothered with her, and Grace had finally decided that enough was enough; she wasn't going to accept it anymore. As much as it killed her and broke her heart, they needed to separate. Grace feared their relationship would only get worse if she didn't do something about it. The thought of being alone seemed much more pleasant than being constantly taken for granted. There was a lot to think about still. Where would she stay? Or would he move out? But Grace had made her mind up. Everything she'd said to Rachel had been a wakeup call to herself.

Simon was already home from work when Grace walked through the door. She loved their house and felt sick at the thought of not living there should she be the one to go. She remembered when they'd seen it online and Simon had turned his nose up.

'Needs loads of work done. Can you imagine how long it would take to get that place looking nice?'

But Grace *could* imagine, and there was something inside her

24

telling her that the two-bedroom cottage was for them. It was such a reasonable price too, and Grace knew how much she'd love decorating and renovating it. Simon had thought she was crazy at first when she told him she wanted to go for it. She'd told him they could knock the wall down between the kitchen and dining room so it was open plan, and change the back door into bifold doors opening out into the garden (which was a complete mess, but they could fix it!). She could just imagine them hosting barbeques in the garden with their friends and family in the summer whilst pouring jugs of ice-cold Pimm's.

When Simon had listened to her ideas about what to change, he'd turned to her and said, 'How can I say no to that little happy face?' and kissed her on the nose. Grace could remember it like yesterday, but the idea of Simon looking at her in that way again seemed like a lifetime ago. It just never happened anymore. Now, it was easy for him to say no.

Grace walked into the lounge where Simon was sitting watching the television.

'Oh, there you are,' he said, quickly glancing up and then looking straight back at the television, 'I was going to call you earlier, but I must have been distracted at work. Look, I know we're supposed to be going to your sister's for Christmas, but I was talking to Mum today and she said she can't see us Boxing Day as they're going out with June and Charlie. God knows where, some restaurant I think she said. So I said we'll go there instead.'

Grace sighed. She was angry that he thought it was acceptable to change Christmas Day plans without consulting her, especially when it was her family's turn to spend Christmas Day with them and he knew how much she'd been looking forward to it. Not that any of it mattered now with what she was about to do, but still. This was so *Simon*. Years ago, he'd never have said something like this. Years ago, Grace had been the most important person to him. Her feelings had come first. Now he just seemed to do what he liked without a second thought for her.

25

'Simon, I really need to talk to you. Can you please turn off the television?'

He glanced up again. 'Is it urgent? I'm listening to this.' He nodded towards the news showing on the screen. 'What do we have for dinner by the way? I'm starving.'

Grace calmly picked up the remote control next to him and switched it off.

'Alright, there's no need to do that,' he huffed loudly.

'I need to talk and yes, it's urgent,' Grace stated authoritatively, her heart beating ridiculously fast.

Simon sat up, looking at her in confusion as she sat opposite him on the sofa with her head in her hands. This didn't feel real. Grace felt silly being so serious, as though she was pretending to be the kind of woman to break up from her husband. Grace was the type of woman to say she loved an awful haircut to the hairdresser, she drank her cold coffee in Costa and she got nervous returning items back to the store, even though they were poor quality and had fallen apart after one wear. It just wasn't like Grace to do something this drastic, but it was about time she stood up for herself. She had no choice. She *had* married for life; it hadn't been a decision she'd taken lightly, but this wasn't the marriage she'd signed up for.

'I don't feel happy anymore, Simon,' she told him, staring at him intently.

The room was quiet and still.

Grace cleared her throat and continued. 'I don't feel appreciated, or even loved by you. You used to be all over me, and I felt like the luckiest girl in the world, but it's changed. *You've* changed. I feel like you just expect me to cook and clean for you, you never offer to help with anything. You never want to go out with me either, but you have no trouble going out with your friends. There's no passion between us anymore. It's like you're bored and complacent, and it doesn't feel nice for me. And I've tried to talk to you—' she played with her hair awkwardly '—but you just roll your eyes. You won't ever discuss anything. You just tell me I'm creating unnecessary problems and I'm not.'

Simon exhaled sharply. 'I'll change, okay, I'll do my best. I'm not perfect, I know that. I do love you and maybe I don't show it enough. I'm sorry. Can we not just move on from this?' He looked at her as though she was being unreasonable distracting him from the news. He didn't grasp quite how serious Grace was about this.

Grace shook her head. 'No, Simon, we clearly can't. We've had this discussion before and it's just not getting through to you, is it? I don't know what I want anymore, but I know it's not good for either of us to continue in this marriage the way it is. I want to split up,' she announced confidently. Now her mind was made up, she wasn't going to change it.

Simon raised his eyebrows and looked at the floor in disbelief. 'You want a divorce?' he questioned in surprise. 'Things aren't that bad, for God's sake.'

'They are to me,' Grace replied sadly.

'Oh, come on Grace, it's not like I beat you or treat you badly.' He clicked his tongue as if she was going over the top. Making a fuss over nothing.

Grace frowned. 'You don't treat me well. I shouldn't have to stay in an unhappy marriage just because you don't beat me.' She shook her head, focusing on a tiny black stain on the grey fabric sofa.

'I'm not saying that…'

'I need to be alone, Simon. I'm sorry. I've made up my mind. Things haven't been right here for ages, and you know it.'

Simon took deep breaths as it finally dawned on him that she truly meant it this time. 'I do love you, Grace.'

'If you love me then you'll let me go,' she told him, her eyes burning with tears. She felt like someone was strangling her, all hot and clammy. She removed her cardigan.

Simon remained silent, looking at the floor and Grace stood

up and walked towards the kitchen, feeling relieved that she'd been brave enough to tell him.

Grace couldn't believe she'd really said it. What would they do now? It was terrifying thinking of a new life without him. But as she gazed at Simon's mess from that morning, still sitting on the kitchen work surface, she knew, for certain, that she'd made the right decision.

Chapter 3

It was Amber Houghton's favourite time of year and though she'd just returned to the chilly UK weather after spending three weeks in Thailand, the brightly-lit, festive high street was enough to put a smile on her face. The constant snippets of her favourite Christmas songs as she walked past the open shop entrances made her feel excited for the holidays ahead. It hadn't felt like it was almost Christmas when she'd been abroad and it was nice to come home with something to look forward to.

As Amber strutted towards Tidemans, she felt a warm glow admiring their beautiful gold and red décor. They got it right every year, she thought in approval. Gone was the tacky tinsel and garish ribbons from years ago, replaced with only the finest, elegant decorations; the shop looked truly stunning giving her inspiration for her own flat. It was about time she bought some new Christmas lights, wreaths and garlands.

She was looking forward to seeing Grace and Rachel again. The three had become really close over the years and Amber couldn't wait to tell them all about her trip. She frowned deeply as she spotted them both standing at the counter arranging the make-up looking miserable. Grace usually had a warm, smiley face, but she had dark circles under her eyes that showed she'd had trouble sleeping, and Rachel looked pasty and thin, her hair lank and lifeless. Immediately, Amber could tell something was wrong. Something had changed. Amber had always had a good instinct and she recalled the time her mother had asked her to sit down so they could talk when she'd been only six years old. Amber had known without her mother saying a word, that something very serious had happened and her life was about to change. She could see it in her mother's eyes and feel it in her pained expression and tense atmosphere. She'd somehow guessed that it was about her father and her mother had confirmed that he'd left them. Gone off without even a goodbye. Amber had never seen him again.

'Hi.' Amber smiled and gave Rachel and Grace a hug.

'Amber, how was your holiday?' Grace asked.

'You look amazing,' Rachel added. 'I'm so jealous of your tan.'

Amber stepped back and looked them both in the eye. 'Are you going to tell me what's happened? What's wrong with you both?'

They glanced at each other sadly before turning back to her.

'You first,' Grace encouraged Rachel.

Rachel breathed out audibly and Amber couldn't help but notice that her usually impeccable make-up looked sloppy and rushed. Her foundation was a shade too dark, not blended in properly along her jawline, her mascara was smudged under her left eye and her lip liner was all over the place, making her lips look large and wonky. She looked like she just didn't care. This wasn't Rachel. Rachel never normally had a hair out of place.

Amber stood open-mouthed as Rachel and Grace explained what had happened. She couldn't have been more surprised if she'd tried.

'I've only been gone for three weeks. How can it be that all this has happened?' she questioned, flummoxed.

Rachel and Grace looked at each other blankly as if they were both wondering the same thing.

'We're still living together,' Grace stated, looking ashamed as though she'd been caught doing something she shouldn't. 'Which I know is bad, but I've hardly seen him. He's staying in our spare room. He's tried to talk to me to change my mind a few times, but I know if I give him another chance, things will go straight back to how they are now and I won't allow that to happen. I'm going to move out soon, but it's just the cost of renting...'

'Why don't you find somewhere together?' Amber suggested, realising it made perfect sense. 'Halve the cost and bills?'

'That's a good idea actually,' Rachel replied chirpily. 'If you want, that is?' she asked hopefully, her eyes flicking to Grace.

'I'd love to live with you,' she responded, an expression of pure delight creasing her face and making her look like the old Grace for a few moments. 'I hadn't thought of that.'

'I'm quite excited now.' Rachel grinned. 'I've felt utterly rubbish since I found out about Mark and Bianca, but this is something for us to look forward to. We can even spend Christmas Eve together if we move quickly. Do the place up all nice and Christmassy. There's some gorgeous new decorations upstairs.'

'I hope there's room for one more on your Christmas Eve gathering?' Amber flashed them a smile, feeling more upbeat about her friends' situations. To say she was stunned was an understatement. *She* was usually the single one. Rachel and Grace were the two in relationships. That was the way it was. The way it had always been. It would be strange getting used to them both being free and unattached, but it would be fun, Amber would make sure of that. Amber was happy to be the single one while the other two spoke about marriage and children; being in a relationship brought nothing but drama that Amber could do without, and she knew she was somewhat of a commitment-phobe. She just didn't trust men, it was as simple as that. Eventually they let you down and disappointed you; Amber only had to think about her own father to know that, and now Simon and Mark were also proving her theory to be right. She was perfectly fine on her own. That was the way she liked it. She certainly wasn't bothered about getting married and she didn't want children either. She didn't care that people looked at her as though she had two heads when she said she wasn't bothered about having a family. She didn't feel the pressure of her age like Rachel did, and she was glad she was that way too. She remembered how Rachel and Grace had gushed over her last boyfriend, Frankie, the year before.

'He's gorgeous and so nice,' Grace had beamed after he'd dropped by in the store to say hello. 'I think he's *the one*, you know.'

Amber had rolled her eyes.

'He's such a catch, Amber,' Rachel had joined in.

Amber thought they were probably more disappointed than she was when she broke it off six months later. Yes, Frankie was handsome and had a great personality to match, but he started to get too keen, constantly asking Amber's whereabouts and dropping hints about moving into her flat. Before she knew it, she had the 'icky' feeling she inevitably developed over a period of time in a relationship. The feeling where everything they did started to make her want to run for the hills. And she had.

'So tell us about your holiday,' Rachel asked.

'I'll tell you all about it after work,' Amber replied with a smirk.

'After work?' Grace frowned, looking confused. 'I'm going home after work. I'll probably have an early night.'

Amber's eyes opened wide. 'Don't ever let me hear you say a thing like that again,' Amber scolded her in mock offense. 'We're going out for drinks. It's about time you two learnt what single life was all about.'

'I can't even remember what it's like being single,' Grace said plaintively as they sat at a table in a busy bar. 'I don't know how to chat to men anymore. I'm not sure I'm ready after Simon. It's all so recent and raw. I'm still married.'

Amber took a sip of her prosecco wondering what it must feel like to be single for the first time in years. It made her more certain that relationships weren't for her. Her friends looked truly miserable and deflated; all because two men had made them feel this way. 'I'm not asking you to remarry tonight,' she laughed dryly, 'but it will do you the world of good to just be out and not stay cooped up at home trying to avoid your husband in your own home. It's time you both enjoyed yourself and had some fun. If you end up chatting and having a little flirt with the opposite sex then what's the harm in that? You're single after all. There's no better time to be single than at Christmas. 'Tis the season to be jolly.'

"Tis the season to get drunk,' Rachel said morosely, raising her eyebrows and downing a shot.

'That's the spirit!' Amber said, lifting her glass in the air. 'Now come on girls. I know you're both in a lot of pain, and no, I probably don't understand what you're going through, but Mark is a complete twat who can't keep his dick in his pants and Simon is blind if he can't see that he has the most amazing woman in the world and hasn't appreciated her. They're both the losers!'

'You know what, Amber, you're right,' Rachel said with sudden confidence as though the thought had only just dawned on her. 'I was a good girlfriend to Mark and I would have made a great wife too. I've always been honest with him, put up with his snoring without complaining and even sat there massaging his back for hours when he needed to wind down from work. It *is* his loss! Simon's too. Let some other fool wait on him hand and foot without so much as a thank you,' she said, turning to Grace.

'Exactly.' Grace nodded in agreement. 'We don't *need* them. We chose to have them in our lives and we will be perfectly happy without them. We're strong, independent women.'

'Oh, I'm so relived you two are being more upbeat,' Amber said brightly. 'I was thinking it was going to be an evening of doom and gloom tonight. I even tried to get Kirsty from womenswear to come along with us when I was looking at dresses for the Christmas ball on my lunch break just in case you two bailed and went home early,' she admitted.

'Oh no, the ball,' Rachel sighed, like it was the most important thing in the world. 'We won't have dates, Grace. Pervy Michael from menswear won't leave us alone,' she said worriedly. 'You know what he's like. The minute he gets wind of our breakups he'll be on our cases, breathing down our necks and asking for dances.'

'You're right,' Grace agreed, now appearing slightly dejected, with the merest little nod of her head.

'Oh, for goodness' sake, who cares if you're both single attending the ball?' Amber threw her eyes upwards. 'It's hardly the end of the world, is it? There will be plenty of dateless people there.'

'Like who?' Grace questioned gravely.

Amber hesitated thoughtfully. 'I don't know … pervy Mike?' She squinted her eyes and clenched her teeth as she said the words, waiting for them to chastise her.

'Very funny,' Rachel replied with a stern expression. 'It's okay for you, you go with Jack every year. You already have your handsome date.'

She was right that Amber always took Jack, but he didn't count as a date. Not really. He was a friend, perhaps even her best friend. Her mother and Jack's mother were best friends and had been since Amber could remember. Amber and Jack had gone to nursery together, primary school and secondary school too. They'd spent the summer holidays together, both their families going on camping trips to France. Well, Jack had the proper family, Amber thought, having a father and an older brother, Michael, too; Amber and her mother would just tag along, but it was fun, and Jack was like the brother she never had. He was the only guy to have ever seen her without make-up. The only one she would openly pick her spots and clip her toenails in front of (much to his disgust). She was completely comfortable in his company and always had been. She didn't have to defend herself to anyone that their relationship was purely platonic. Everyone knew what they were like. They accepted how close they were. There had been only one occasion when they were sixteen and Jack had tried to kiss her. He'd just broken up with his girlfriend and if she remembered rightly, he'd been drunk. Amber had brushed him off, mortified, and he'd laughed it off the next day and apologized. They were such close friends that the encounter hadn't changed a thing. Jack hadn't known what he was doing, and Amber had quickly forgotten all about it.

'You'll both go and that's that,' Amber told her firmly. 'Now get a grip and listen to what I have to say. This year we'll go to the ball together. So what if we won't have men with us, who cares? As Grace said, we're single, independent women,' she stated decisively, her head held high, 'and I think we should make a pact to stay single and be *each other's* dates. To hell with what anyone thinks. I bet we'll have more fun than the boring work lot anyway.'

'What about Jack?' Grace asked.

'Jack won't care about going to the ball. I swear he only goes for the free booze. I'll be doing him a favour letting him off the hook for the year. He's constantly telling me it's about time I got myself a real date, and now I have, with you two.' Amber smiled. Of course, they wouldn't be real dates either, but who really cared so long as she cheered her two friends up? Amber didn't *need* a man to make her happy, and she was determined to make her friends feel the same. Christmas time was a cheerful time, there was no place to be wallowing in self-pity.

'I agree with Amber. We don't need dates. We'll have more fun together anyway and I'm certainly up for it if you are?' Grace's eyes swept from Amber to Rachel, a relieved expression on her face as though she'd been handed a lifeline.

'I guess it will be a good evening if we're all going alone,'

Rachel shrugged and then added chirpily, 'I'm quite looking forward to it now.'

'That's sorted then,' Amber replied with authority. 'Look at all the handsome men around here you can flirt with. I think that's Jonathan from menswear over there in the far corner; we'll get him over here soon. It's time to have fun! 'Tis the season to be single.'

Chapter 4

Rachel opened her eyes, confused at first about where she was until her gaze fell on the familiar lilac curtains, which she remembered picking out when she'd been at college living at her parents' house. Her heart plummeted and the familiar sick feeling washed over her as the betrayal hurt just as much as the moment she'd discovered the affair. The same thing happened every morning. When would she start to feel better? She knew it had only been a week and she was doing her best to focus on moving on, but she couldn't ever imagine the heartache easing. She wondered what they were both doing now. Had Bianca moved into her flat? Was she lying in her bed with Mark, the place Rachel had been not that long ago discussing Christmas plans and holidays next year? Were they wrapped in the bedding that Rachel had picked out, costing them a fortune, their bodies entwined as they gazed into each other's eyes with sheer joy that they could finally be together? Or did Mark find it easier going to Bianca's flat, where there were no memories of Rachel to remind him that he was a deceitful, conniving bastard? She wondered if he knew how untidy Bianca was yet, or if he'd discovered that sometimes before bed she wouldn't stop chatting when you just wanted to go to sleep. Mark loved his sleep. He'd detest her chatting all night. Or was it all so new, fresh and exciting that he'd rather stay up talking to Bianca, thoughts of his 6 a.m. alarm the last thing on his mind? Rachel hoped he was tired. He deserved it. The pig.

Bianca had tried calling Rachel several times, but she'd ignored her. How dare she think she could try to explain herself? Rachel honestly didn't want to know at what point Bianca had decided to steal her boyfriend. It was like a storyline from a film or a book; it wasn't supposed to happen in real life, and certainly not to her. She felt so stupid. Humiliated. She didn't want to know anything whatsoever about their affair. How they just couldn't help it, the connection between them too strong to fight and how the last thing they wanted to do was upset her. The usual bullshit clichés. Of course she was upset; all her life plans were now in tatters. Everything was ruined.

She held the palms of her hands over her face. She had a headache. She'd drunk far too much wine the night before and couldn't remember getting home. The thought depressed her; she had really thought drunken, wild nights were behind her. She had been settled, grown up even, and behaving irresponsibly was supposed to have been a thing of the past. Something to fondly look back on. She'd been in a secure relationship and was supposed to be getting married, yet here she was, single, hungover and doing the exact opposite of what she thought she would be doing just over a week ago. She was back to square one.

She heard a light knock on the door and her mother's head peered round.

'Morning,' she said delicately, in case she'd woken her up. 'Cup of tea,' she added, walking into Rachel's bedroom and putting a mug next to her bed.

'Thanks Mum,' Rachel replied, the words sounding more like a croak.

'You were back late,' her mother said, sitting on the end of the bed. 'Good night?'

Rachel sat up feeling like a little girl again when her mother would sit at the end of her bed reading her a bedtime story. Her mother had aged without her noticing over the years. Her dark hair, which was clipped back, was now peppered and streaked with grey and her skin had the look of tinfoil, too baggy round her eyes.

'What time did I get back? Sorry if I woke you,' she apologized, feeling guilty that her mother now had the worry of her daughter going out all over again.

'About 1 a.m. it was, I was already awake. You know I can't sleep until I know you're home,' she replied helplessly.

'Oh Mum. I'm 29 years old,' Rachel rolled her eyes, knowing deep down it wouldn't matter if she was 49; her mother would still worry.

'How was it?' her mother asked hopefully.

Rachel felt like a let-down. She shouldn't be putting her parents through all this concern, not now. She knew her mother wanted to see her happy and settled and would most likely be crossing her fingers that she met someone every time she went out.

'It was a good night,' Rachel replied as brightly as possible, wanting to show her mother she was okay.

Her mother nodded, watching Rachel closely and Rachel focused on the small lines around her mother's thin lips that she hadn't seen before, afraid to look into her eyes.

'It's okay to feel down, you know, darling,' her mother said caringly.

Rachel contemplated saying she was fine. She was over it and had moved on already, but her nose began to tingle and her eyes became blurry. 'Oh Mum, it's so hard,' she replied. 'I keep thinking about how much they must have lied to me. I keep picturing them together and what they're doing now.'

'They deserve each other,' her mother said, in an unusually abrupt manner. 'I, for one, am glad they both showed their true colours before you and Mark got any more serious. Thank heavens there were no children involved. You may be hurting now, darling, but they've actually both done you a favour.'

'But you loved Mark,' Rachel stated weakly. 'You all thought he was wonderful.'

Her mother frowned. 'I never loved Mark. I loved how he made you happy of course, but if you want the truth, I always thought there was something off about him. I felt like he put on an act in front of us. Your father felt the same.'

Rachel felt confused. 'Really? I thought you adored him.'

Her mother shook her head. 'Heavens, no.' She jutted out her chin. 'I've always thought you could do much better.'

'But I'm 29…'

'Which is still young,' her mother interjected quickly. 'Tracey Harper next door didn't meet Martin until she was 38, and just look how happy they are. She even had two children, one in her forties.'

Rachel bit her lip. Her mother was right, just like Amber and Grace were; she was being silly worrying about her age. Why had she planned her life so meticulously, feeling disappointed when she hadn't met the targets on time? First it was find a boyfriend, then it was move in and get engaged before 30, to then have her first child by at least 32. Rachel was learning that you couldn't plan life. Nobody knew what was around the corner. Everything could change when you least expected it and she was just going to have to go with the flow. Relax a little and perhaps be more like Grace.

'And as for Bianca, your so-called friend…' Her mother inhaled sharply. 'She'll realize one day what an amazing friend she's lost. She's *always* been selfish, looking out for number one, but this really takes the biscuit. I've always said she was jealous of you, even when you were little.'

Rachel nodded in agreement. Her mother was right. Looking back, Bianca had been selfish in their friendship. Rachel remembered how she'd helped organize Bianca's 21st birthday party alongside Bianca's mother, to make sure it was perfect with everything she knew Bianca wanted. Bianca had been thrilled when the limousine turned up to take her to her black and white themed party. Yet when it came to Rachel's 21st birthday party, Bianca had told her at the last minute she couldn't come, saying her boyfriend at the time had bought her a ticket to the theatre, and she couldn't get out of it as they were staying in a hotel in London overnight. Rachel had been gutted, but she hadn't said a word. Perhaps she wanted to believe Bianca that there was really no way out of it, but deep down in her heart, she knew how simple it would have been to sell the tickets or for her boyfriend to have taken a friend instead. Rachel was supposed to be Bianca's best friend, but as her mother had said, she always put herself first. Rachel was often dropped last minute if Bianca had a better offer elsewhere. It was about time Rachel started to see her for who she really was, rather than constantly making excuses for her. Who cared what she and Mark were up to? She didn't see Mark in the same light anymore and could never get back with him, knowing he was capable of lying and cheating, and she didn't want to know Bianca either.

'I think I'll be fine you know, Mum,' Rachel said honestly. 'It will just take a bit of time. But you're right, this is all for the best.'

'Most definitely. You're welcome to stay here for as long as you like too.'

Rachel smiled and gave her mother a hug. 'Thanks. I'm going to start renting a flat with Grace soon though,' she explained.

'What a good idea. Grace is lovely,' her mother said happily. 'Such a shame about her and her husband though.'

'I know. It's strange we're both single at the same time after all these years.'

Her mother nodded and said she was going off to get ready and when Rachel looked at the time she realized she should be doing the same. The chat with her mother had made her feel better again, she thought as she jumped in the shower. Maybe, just maybe, she really was going to be okay.

'Hey,' Amber smiled widely as Rachel approached the make-up department. 'How are you feeling this morning?'

'Ill. Dreadful. Sick. Just to name a few.' Rachel half-smiled. 'Please don't let me drink that much on a work night ever again. Just stop me. Grab my shots and tip them on the floor. Give them away or something.'

'Oh, come on,' Amber giggled. 'It's more fun getting drunk and it's Christmas time so it's *allowed*. I actually quite love drunk Rachel.'

'Amber, I don't even remember getting home!' Rachel laughed heartily. There was that feeling again as though she'd gone back in time and was a teenager doing silly, childish things she'd normally frown upon. 'That hasn't happened for years.'

'Really?' Amber appeared confused, narrowing her beautifully made up, almond-shaped, dark grey eyes. 'Then you don't remember speaking to…'

'Morning,' Grace interrupted as she walked over. 'How is everyone feeling?' she asked amusedly.

'Like death warmed up,' Rachel told her. 'Please say you were as drunk as me?'

'Probably not as bad as you, but I wasn't drinking shots. I still feel rough though. I honestly don't know how you do it, Amber. Going out and partying all the time and then going to work the next day isn't as easy as I thought.'

'Oh girls, you get used to it.' She chuckled as she sat down and began filing her nails.

The girls chatted about their evening and Rachel felt her spirits lift as they laughed and joked about the people they'd chatted to, not that Rachel remembered half of them. Tidemans had already started playing their Christmas music, and Rachel decided she was going to cheer up as much as she could this year. She'd always loved Christmas and wasn't going to let Mark and Bianca ruin it for her.

Amber coughed as Jonathan from menswear approached the counter, then she grabbed Grace softly by the wrist and pulled her aside much to Rachel's bewilderment.

'Hey.' Jonathan shot Rachel a smile that seemed to hint they shared some kind of secret.

'Hi,' Rachel replied, her forehead wrinkling as she wondered what he wanted. She vaguely remembered Amber saying he'd been in the same bar the previous night, but nothing after that, and she'd only ever seen him a few times In Tidemans seeing as he was fairly new.

'Good night last night?' he said, resting his chin on his palm as he lent over the counter confidently, like he'd known her for years.

Rachel looked at him, puzzled. He must have seen them there too. Was he about to laugh about something she had done? The not knowing was awful. 'Yes,' she said the word slowly and carefully waiting for some kind of trap.

'You don't remember, do you?' he grinned, clearly enjoying the baffled expression on her face.

Rachel felt as though the top button on her blouse was choking her and she imagined her neck was becoming red and blotchy, the blush quickly making its way to her face, which was feeling hotter with every second. It reminded her of how she used to feel when she was picked out in university lectures to answer a question or give her view on something when she hadn't been listening. 'Erm…' she stuttered. What had she done?

'I was chatting to you last night for ages,' he smirked amusedly, gazing at her intensely. He had lovely dark blue eyes, she'd give him that. 'I was just double checking you were still on for tonight?'

Rachel's frown deepened as she felt like a fly trapped in a

spider's web, a sense of panic washing over her. 'Tonight?' she said a little shakily. Why was she feeling so nervous?

'Yes.' He gave a light laugh. 'You agreed to go to dinner with me. Of course, if you can't, I understand...'

'Of course she can,' Amber interjected hastily much to Rachel's surprise. 'You were just telling me how much you were looking forward to it, weren't you, Rach?' Amber eyed her encouragingly.

Rachel stared at Amber with a *just you wait* expression. 'Yes,' she finally replied forcing a grin. Her mouth was dry and her heart was beating dramatically.

'That's great then.' Jonathan returned the smile. 'I'll come meet you here after work. I was thinking of booking a table at Mario's. Italian okay with you?' he asked.

'Italian is just fine,' she responded, unable to believe that she was really going on a date so soon. She didn't know Jonathan and certainly didn't recall talking to him the previous evening. The thought of sitting and eating dinner with him terrified her. She'd never been fond of dates. Even her first date with Mark had scared her half to death, but now after what she'd been through, she felt less confident in herself. But what choice did she have when she'd been put on the spot? How could she say no without feeling more humiliated?

Rachel turned to Amber and a giggling Grace as Jonathan walked away. 'I cannot believe that just happened!' she said putting her face in her hands. 'I am *so* embarrassed. He must think I'm such an idiot! And, you—' she poked Amber in the arm playfully '—thanks a lot for that. Now I'm going on a date with him. I hate dates. I don't even know Jonathan.'

'But you soon will,' Amber chimed in cheerily. 'It's only a date. What are you so afraid of? Enjoying yourself?' she teased.

'I don't know,' Rachel chewed her bottom lip. 'I just can't believe I'm here, about to go on a date when it was only days ago I thought I'd be marrying Mark.'

'I know,' Grace replied tenderly, 'but you should go on the

date: You need to move on, sweetie. We both do. Even if it's so soon afterwards, a date can't hurt.'

Rachel inhaled slowly. Grace was right. Was she ready to move on with someone else so soon? Absolutely not, but she needed a distraction from her thoughts of Mark and Bianca. The quicker she stopped feeling sorry for herself the better. Besides, Jonathan was quite nice looking. She didn't know him well enough to judge him entirely, but he was fairly attractive, so it was a good start she guessed. He didn't make her weak at the knees, but then, Rachel was certain that Mark hadn't either. He'd just been there when she decided it was time to get into a serious relationship. He'd ticked the majority of her boxes.

'I'm going to go out with Jonathan,' Rachel gave a little nod of her head, listening to how the words sounded out loud. She felt like laughing hysterically. What on earth was going on in her normally, quite monotonous, drama-free life? The words sounded strange, like someone else had said them. Quickly planning what make-up to put on and promising she would dash upstairs to womenswear on her next break to purchase a new outfit, Rachel smiled. There was nothing to be afraid of at all.

After all, what did she have to lose?

Chapter 5

Amber was smiling as she thought of Rachel going on her date with Jonathan. It was a good thing, and she knew Rachel would see that in the end, despite reminding her of a lamb being led to the slaughter as she'd walked off with him. Rachel didn't need Mark. She just needed to relax and let her hair down. She needed to stop planning and organizing and just go with the flow a bit more. Rachel was the type of girl that planned every single outfit for her two-week holiday. She kept up to date with her washing and ironing, she labelled jars for miscellaneous items in her house (spare buttons, safety pins, elastic bands), everything had a place in her home. There were no junk drawers.

'You don't have a junk drawer?' Amber had asked in shock when she'd visited for the first time.

Rachel had looked slightly dazed, squinting her pale blue eyes and cocking her head to the side as she asked, 'What's a junk drawer?'

She didn't even know what a junk drawer was for goodness' sake! It was kind of self-explanatory. Amber recalled the weekend she'd gone away to Rome with Grace and Rachel several years back. Amber's jaw had almost hit the floor when Rachel's alarm went off at 7 a.m. on their first day.

'What's going on?' Grace had groaned as Rachel had opened the curtains allowing the sunshine to blind them.

Amber had been too tired and confused to speak.

'We need to get up!' Rachel had enthused, much to their disgust. 'There's so much to do and see. I've printed off an itinerary for both of you so if we quickly go downstairs to breakfast we can head straight to the Colosseum to beat the crowds. Then there's the Vatican museums and this gorgeous little place for lunch I've seen that has excellent reviews on TripAdvisor…'

Amber's lip curled upwards as she thought back to it. The trip had been fantastic despite the early starts. Sometimes you needed a friend like Rachel. The planner. The organized one. Amber was the complete opposite. She hated planning. If it had been down to her she would have laid in bed most of the morning and wouldn't have seen half of the amazing sites they'd managed to in the short time they were in Rome. Amber was impulsive; she liked excitement and to not know what was coming next. She loved having fun and letting her hair down. But at times she was reckless, wild even, not doing herself any favours. How many times had she lost her mobile phone on a night out because she was drunk and careless? She couldn't seem to help it though. It was just the way she was.

Amber wrapped her scarf tightly round her neck as she made her way to the coffee shop. She exhaled, watching her breath form in a cloud in front of her. It was freezing and she wondered if it might snow soon. She hoped so; there was nothing better than snow at Christmas time to get you in the mood. That, and a nice hot chocolate, which she vowed she was going to order as soon as she met Jack.

Jack was already in the coffee shop, punching away on his mobile while he waited for her. Amber smiled fondly as she spotted him; he was so familiar and comfortable, yet she always felt excited to see him. Jack was part of her happy childhood

47

memories. She was completely at ease in his presence. She felt like she hadn't seen him in a while because he'd been busy before she went to Thailand. They hadn't seen each other in just over two and a half months because he'd been away before she had. It was too long.

'Hello stranger,' she grinned, bending down to give him a big hug. 'Ooh nice aftershave,' she complimented him.

'You look well,' he grinned back at her revealing his straight teeth. 'Nice tan. How was Thailand?'

'Amazing,' Amber replied. 'You should have come. We'll have to go another time together as I'd definitely go back. There're some islands I didn't have time to visit, but my favourite was Ko Tao; scuba diving there was out of this world. You would have loved it.'

'I'm jealous,' he said, standing up. 'Let me get the drinks. What do you want?'

'Large hot chocolate with cream please.'

'That sounds good. I'll make that two,' he responded as he walked to the till.

Amber noticed a couple of girls sitting on a table close by look in Jack's direction and then over to her disappointedly, obviously mistaking them for a couple. Amber couldn't deny that Jack was incredibly handsome. If he wasn't like a brother to her, she would most likely be checking him out too. It wasn't just his dark hair, olive skin and blue eyes, it was his confidence along with the fact he was completely unaware of how attractive he was, which was incredibly appealing. Not only that, but he was a nice guy. He had a great sense of humour and didn't take himself too seriously. He had respect for women. He was a loyal boyfriend; though it was very rare he was ever in a serious relationship. He liked to be single just like she did. They both agreed life was easier that way. Amber knew that someday a girl would be very lucky to have him. He was a keeper and they were both very protective over each other.

'Thanks,' Amber said, spooning some of the sweet, fluffy cream into her mouth as Jack brought over the drinks.

'So, are you all depressed now you're back home in the cold?' Jack asked.

'Not at all. You know how much I love Christmas,' she replied honestly. 'I've missed you too. We need a night out soon. With alcohol instead of chocolate.'

'I think you're coming over to us this year on Christmas Day, aren't you?' Jack enquired.

Amber nodded. Their families took it in turns every year and they always had such fun. They usually had a big breakfast together and played games all afternoon before watching a nice Christmas film. 'Yes, I'm sure that's what Mum said. I'll be buying you fake tan this year seeing as you're so pale next to me,' she giggled, holding out her tanned arm.

Jack laughed good-naturedly. 'I've just been busy with work. You know I'd have gone with you if I could have. Drinking and partying with you in Thailand sounded a lot better than staring bored out of my office window.' He looked up at her, 'Meet any nice men while you were away?'

Amber grinned mischievously. 'A few. I met one guy I really liked, but he was from Perth in Australia. Not exactly around the corner.' She raised her eyebrows. 'I've always wanted to go to Australia though. It's definitely next on my list.'

'Shame,' he said genuinely, taking a sip of his hot chocolate.

Amber turned up her nose. 'Not really. He was a nice guy, great body too, but I wouldn't have met up with him again. You know me. I'm not after anything serious.'

'You don't give people a chance,' Jack pointed out, 'and you should. You deserve to find someone to make you happy.'

'Coming from you,' Amber replied with a light-hearted laugh. 'You're the same as me. You never give girls a chance. What about poor Jenny?'

Jack raised one eyebrow curiously. 'Jenny?'

'See, you don't remember her,' Amber said in mock outrage. 'She was such a sweet girl. Pretty in a girl-next-door type of way, medium height, always wore a denim jacket. She was in love with you, but you brushed her off. Remember?'

'The girl I met at that London conference last year? That Jenny? There was no spark between us,' Jack defended himself.

'You never allow a spark to develop, that's why,' Amber told him, trying to prove that he was exactly the same as her. 'You're seeing a new girl every time I see you.' Not that Amber ever liked any of them. None of them seemed good enough for Jack. Jack was a catch; he had a great job in the City working in banking and she knew he was earning a very good salary. Most girls seemed to latch on to him the minute they found that out.

'That's another reason why I wanted to meet you today,' Jack half-smiled, but became serious suddenly.

Amber's heart plunged, taking her by surprise. She frowned. 'Why's that?'

His face exploded into a smile and his eyes sparkled. 'I'm getting married Amber. I'm engaged.'

Amber felt dizzy suddenly as though she was dreaming. 'What? Engaged to who?' She felt breathless, like someone had punched her hard in the stomach. How was Jack engaged and she didn't even know about it?

'Her name is Natalya. I told you about her last time we met up, remember? I'm not sure you were listening. You're going to love her Ambs, you really are. I think you two are going to get on like a house on fire. I've told her all about you. She may even be coming Christmas Day now so you'll get to know her properly. Mum and Michael love her too.'

Amber twisted her fingers feeling awkward and left out for some unknown reason. She racked her brains. She vaguely remembered him talking about a Natalya last time they met, but she hadn't paid much attention. She had thought Natalya was just *another* one of Jack's girls. There had been nothing he'd said to make her think otherwise, she was sure of it. Her eyes swept over Jack's joyous expression and she forced herself to smile back. 'That's amazing news,' she told him. 'Wow, I can't believe it. What made you propose so soon?' she wondered. She'd never been so astounded. They'd always discussed how marriage was bullshit. They'd shared the same views. How had Jack changed his mind in just over two months and found the girl he wanted to marry so quickly? It was surreal.

'I've been with her for four months.' He smiled gaily. 'I know it's not long, but when you know, you know, right?'

Amber shrugged, discomfited. 'I wouldn't know.' She knew she was being pathetic, but she hated the fact that Jack had made such a huge decision and she was only just finding out about it now. 'When did this happen?' She was unable to hide the shock in her voice.

'A week ago.' He raised his shoulders casually. 'We didn't want to announce it on social media or anything cheesy. I wanted to tell you and your mum in person, though your mum's meeting my mum tonight so I think Mum's probably beaten me to it.' He gave a slight laugh.

There was a long pause. 'Well, congratulations,' she finally said, attempting brighter tones.

He tugged at her hand across the table. 'Hey, you're happy for me, right?' He gave her a hopeful expression and it melted her heart.

How could Amber not be happy for him? He was the closest person to her and she didn't know what she'd do without him in her life. Jack was everything to Amber; if he'd found love and was only just telling her now, she needed to get over it and wish him the best, despite feeling a little out of the loop. A little left behind. She hadn't met Natalya, but as Jack had said, they'd most likely get on like a house on fire. They had to if Natalya was going to be Jack's wife. 'Of course I'm happy for you,' Amber squeezed his hand back. 'I'm just shocked, that's all. I never thought you'd

51

get engaged at all, let alone after four months to someone I don't even know. It's just a lot to take in, but if you're in love, then that's great news.'

'I am, Amber. I really am in love. Miracles really do happen,' he laughed. 'I'm meeting her and her parents for dinner after this. I'll arrange a get together for the three of us as soon as I can, I promise.'

Amber stood up to hug him. 'Congratulations again,' she said, holding him close and taking in the scent of his citrus and sandalwood. She closed her eyes as she held him tightly, still unable to believe that Jack was really getting married. No matter how hard she tried she couldn't erase the feeling of hurt, yet she knew she was being ridiculous. He'd gone back on his word and decided that actually, marriage was right for him. What next? Children? It was laughable, yet now he was engaged, it didn't seem so weird at all. Jack would make a great father. It all just seemed such a shock. A big surprise to take on board. How had Natalya changed his mind so quickly? *She must be some woman*, Amber thought sourly. But as Amber gazed at Jack's beatific expression she knew it was love.

She just didn't know why she felt so sad about it.

Chapter 6

Grace exhaled as she heard the front door close. As she'd heard Simon fumbling with his key outside a few moments ago, she hadn't realized she'd been holding her breath. How silly. She was awkward and uncomfortable living with her own husband like he was a stranger. It reminded her of when she'd started university and had to share a house with ten other people she'd only just met. The tiptoeing to the bathroom in the middle of night, careful not to wake the others up. The uneasy feeling when someone spotted her in her pyjamas with no make-up on. It had taken a while to feel relaxed and get to know the others. But with Simon, things were only going to get worse. She already knew everything about him. She was only going to feel more anxious being in his presence. He hadn't been out much since they'd split, but how would she feel if he started dating? She couldn't imagine seeing him making an effort, dressing up and splashing on some aftershave to impress another woman. But one day he would. Yet another reason she needed to change her living arrangements as soon as possible. Simon most likely felt the same, she thought worriedly.

It was Simon who had offered to sleep in the spare room, so Grace would be kind enough to read or just browse online in her bedroom for the evening and let him have the front room.

The spare room didn't have a television, and besides, Grace felt guilty seeing as she was the one to call their separation on. *Sorry I don't want to be with you, oh and no television either,* seemed a bit harsh.

'Hi,' Simon stood by the door to the front room at the same time Grace switched off the TV.

Grace looked up at him, feeling saddened by his appearance. He looked well and truly depressed, the dark circles under his eyes suggesting he hadn't been sleeping properly. He was such a tall man with broad shoulders, something that had instantly attracted her, but he seemed to have shrunk lately. Like he was a balloon that someone had deflated slightly.

'Hey,' Grace replied. 'You're back late. Everything okay?' She smiled at him, concerned about how he was feeling. She may not want to continue with the way things were in their marriage, but she still cared for Simon deeply. Loved him even. She just didn't love the way he made her feel anymore.

'Just working, that's all,' Simon replied distractedly.

'I hope it's all going well,' she told him caringly. It would be awful if he was having problems at work too. Talk about bad timing.

'Yeah, just really busy,' he said sighing heavily.

'Well, I'm going to go upstairs,' Grace told him in formal tones, standing up. 'Give you some space down here.'

He looked pained. 'No, please don't Grace. It's your house too, and you shouldn't have to keep running off up there, holed up in the bedroom. I wanted to talk to you.' He cleared his throat, his expression grave as he stood opposite her.

Grace's brow wrinkled and she prayed he wasn't about to beg her for another shot again. It would never work, and she wasn't going to be one of those women that fell for the 'I'll change' garbage, only for things to return to normal after a month or so. She'd told him that. He knew she was too intelligent for that. *Not for me, thank you very much.*

'I'm going to move out,' Simon said in melancholic tones.

Grace had never seen him so serious before – like someone had died. 'Right,' she replied bravely, pretending she'd been expecting him to say it. Even though she knew they couldn't continue their living arrangements, she hadn't expected it to come from him. She genuinely thought he would happily stay with the way things were, though they were no longer together.

'If you don't want to be together, I just feel like it's unhealthy for us to be living in the same house. It's too hard to see you every day.' His lips twitched showing he was discomfited and Grace had to stop herself from putting her arms around him. 'I'm sure you agree it's a bit ... odd. You shouldn't have to shut yourself away. So I'll move out. You stay here. I'll still pay half the mortgage until we decide what we want to do about the house and everything...' He broke off.

Grace swallowed hard, her throat feeling as though it was closing up. 'Thanks,' she managed wanly. The thought of him going felt so final. It was finally dawning on her that they would no longer be a couple. The idea of selling their dream little house made her feel wretched too. They'd saved for almost a year to modernize their grey and cream kitchen, paid for new cream carpets and bought the perfect sofa, made especially to fit the bay window. They'd made it their own. She loved her house. 'It's very kind of you to offer to pay half the mortgage, but I was actually planning to live with Rachel so perhaps she can just live here and pay towards it,' she suggested. 'If she wants to, that is.'

Simon frowned. 'Isn't she with Mark?'

Grace realized she hadn't got around to telling Simon that Rachel and Mark had split up. Normally she would tell him everything and it felt weird that he didn't know something so important about her friend. Grace shook her head, 'They've split up. He was cheating on her.'

Simon exhaled slowly as he studied her in astonishment. 'Wow. I can't believe it.'

Grace thrust her hands into the pockets of her trousers. 'I know. It's really awful. With Rachel's best friend too.'

Simon shook his head. 'Idiot. And he seemed like a nice guy to me.'

Grace nodded, recalling the times they'd met in the past. Last year's Christmas ball had been hilarious. Mark had been so drunk that Simon had to carry him out; they'd laughed about it for days afterwards. 'I'm sure Rachel will be fine about living here. Saves us looking for somewhere new.'

'Yes, it makes sense,' Simon agreed.

'Where will you go?' Grace asked him. There was that feeling of guilt again.

'Paul has a spare room at his I'm going to rent.' He attempted airy tones, but she could see from his tired looking eyes he was struggling with the situation. He definitely wasn't okay with it. 'I was going to go tonight. No time like the present. So please, stay down here and relax. No need to go upstairs now.'

'No, I guess not.' Grace could only stare at the floor awkwardly. 'Do you need help packing your things? Remember to take a few towels and some bedding from the airing cupboard; I'm not so sure Paul will have any spares.' She couldn't help herself. Grace had always done everything for Simon. Even when they went on holiday she packed his case for him. She remembered their last holiday to Malta.

'Didn't you pack my white polo shirt?' Simon had huffed, going through the clothes in his bag.

Grace had thrown her eyes upwards in annoyance. 'Simon, you can pack your own suitcase, you know. If you care so much about what you have then do it yourself!'

That had shut him up. He much preferred Grace doing everything for him. She pretty much took care of all the housework, his washing, his ironing and she cooked for him. Perhaps she was partly to blame for this? Her mother had done everything for her father so it was all Grace knew. The women took care of their men. The problem was that Simon didn't appreciate anything anymore. She didn't know how he'd cope without her, and despite knowing that it was probably a good thing, and he'd finally see how much she really did for him, she couldn't help but worry about him. She told herself off, knowing that it was nothing to do with her now. She had to let him get on with it. He was a grown man and soon enough he'd work it out for himself.

'Don't be silly, I'll do it. Thanks for the offer though.' He shot her a strained smile.

'If you need help, just shout,' Grace responded kindly.

She couldn't concentrate on the programme she was watching after that. It was the kind of programme Simon hated watching, about a man that was given away for adoption trying to trace his family.

'What's the point in watching something that makes you so emotional?' he would usually say.

Grace couldn't focus on what the man on the screen was saying now. All she could think about was the fact that Simon was leaving and she was now going to be alone in their house.

Forty minutes later he started bringing suitcases downstairs. 'Obviously I've probably left a few things by accident,' he explained, 'but I think I have most of it. Just collect anything you find and I'll pick it up another day. I have all the important things I need.'

'At least let me help you take it to your car,' she offered considerately.

'No honestly, I'm fine.' He smiled graciously. 'Thanks though.'

It all felt so strange seeing Simon doing something on his own. He normally wanted Grace to do everything for him. He'd become lazy, expecting everything to be done for him. He'd normally have asked her to help before she even had the chance to offer. Grace felt as though the world had gone mad as she heard him heave the second suitcase out the door. She couldn't watch him; it was far too painful and strange. *He'll probably change now,*

Grace thought wryly; she'd shown him his errors and he'd turn into the perfect man for the next woman he met. His new woman would most likely think that Grace was crazy for splitting up with her loving, kind and helpful husband. As if that had been the case! Regardless, it was much more difficult letting Simon go than she'd first anticipated.

'I guess I best say goodbye then,' Simon said in a lowered voice a few moments later.

Grace gulped. She'd been dreading this moment the whole time he'd been packing. Her chest felt tight, like someone was sitting on it, restricting her breathing. 'I don't know what to say, Simon,' she replied helplessly, feeling incredibly sad.

Simon cleared his throat again, unable to look in her direction. 'Maybe it's easier if I just go. Don't come out, stay there. It's too hard.'

Grace nodded, a tear falling down her cheek. 'If that's what you want,' she told him obediently, frozen in her seat.

When she heard the door slam, she broke down. This was what she wanted, so why did she feel so down about it? She'd given her marriage her all, yet despite telling Simon time and time again how she was feeling, he had never tried to change once. Did he not care enough to bother trying to make her happy? Now it had come to this and it was heartbreaking. He'd gone. Would they end up getting a divorce? Then it really would be final and Grace didn't think she was ready to accept that just yet. It was all well and good agreeing with Amber and Rachel that she would be single and do her best to start dating, but Grace just couldn't do that. She wouldn't do that. She needed to be alone – to be surrounded by her family and friends and the people that loved her. She wasn't close to being able to date yet and she knew that was okay. She was grieving for her marriage still. But she had to give up fighting for it, didn't she? She'd been fighting a losing battle for too long.

Deciding there was no point in pretending to watch television,

Grace made her way upstairs to their bedroom. She was surprised to see a note on the bed. Memories came flooding back to her once more.

'You write like a child,' she'd giggled coquettishly the first time she'd seen Simon's handwriting.

'Hey, I do not!' Simon laughed merrily back. His eyes scanned the writing on her Valentine's Day card. 'Okay, maybe I do a bit. When we write joint cards, you'll have to be the writer,' he grinned.

'Joint cards?' Grace smirked, one eyebrow raised. They'd only been together four months at the time.

'Yes, joint cards,' Simon had said confidently, and she'd been glad, because she felt it too. She also knew this was the start of something meaningful and serious.

Grace picked up the note, reading Simon's familiar writing.

Grace,

I know there is nothing I can say to change your mind, because talk is cheap and actions speak louder than words. I've had time to think about everything you've said. I honestly do understand how you feel and I'm sorry if you feel I don't appreciate you like I should. I guess I'm guilty of just believing you'll always be there. This has been a huge wakeup call to me and I cannot lose you. I'll do anything to get you back, and that's why I think this break will do us the world of good and I'm going to prove to you that I really can change. I have to. So please don't give up on us just yet. Let me show you how I can make you happy again. I promise you, I will. I don't care how long it takes. I love you, though I know I don't tell you enough. I've always loved you and that will never stop.

Simon x

Grace brushed a bit of hair away from her face.
Maybe there was a little bit of fight left in her after all?

Chapter 7

'So any brothers or sisters?' Rachel asked Jonathan in upbeat tones, filling the awkward silence again. He'd seemed so chatty and confident when he'd come to chat to her at Tidemans, but the truth was, she was finding this date hard work. Dates weren't supposed to feel like job interviews. When they were good they were relaxing and exciting as you discovered things about each other. Jonathan was actually quite quiet, and when he wasn't sitting in silence Rachel found his negativity quite draining and depressing. They were sitting in a beautiful cosy Italian, which was romantic with pretty white Christmas lights hung in the window, the room dimmed with candles on the tables. It could have been quite lovely with the right company.

'A sister,' he answered blankly, as though he was bored.

Don't worry about asking if I have siblings, Rachel thought caustically. Getting him to ask her a question was like trying to get blood out of a stone. 'I have a brother,' she said quickly.

That was the end of that conversation, she thought frustratedly.

'So Christmas is coming up,' she attempted to sound excited, but sitting with Jonathan was making her feel anything but.

'I hate Christmas,' he replied matter-of-factly, wiping his hands on his napkin, making Rachel flinch.

'You *hate* Christmas?' she asked, incredulous. This was never going to work.

He wrinkled his nose. 'It's too commercialized now. It's all about buying presents with stores blasting out annoying Christmas music, Tidemans included. How many times a day can we listen to that snowman song, seriously? I just hate all the advertising and the special offers and deals rammed down people's throats tricking them into feeling like they have to spend a fortune on their loved ones. I don't like spending time with my family for an entire day either. I just look forward to January when it's all over.'

Rachel was horrified. 'January?' Everyone knew that January was the worst month of the year. When people had a birthday in January there was that look. That sympathetic look that said, 'what a shame, you poor thing'. Everyone was too skint to celebrate in January. They were too fat to go to dinner, often dieting after they'd overloaded on Christmas cake the month before. It was wet and cold and the magic had just gone. The last of the Christmas lights were being turned off. How could anyone possibly look forward to it? 'Right,' she said, looking at the happy couple on the table next to them and changing the subject. 'So, do you enjoy working at Tidemans?' she asked, thinking it was a safe subject.

He itched his nose. 'Not particularly. It was hardly my dream job to work in a menswear department,' he snorted like she'd asked a silly question. 'I'm sure you feel the same working in a shop doing make-up. Hardly a successful career working in retail, is it? I don't plan to stay there long.'

Rachel was insulted and she knew the frown on her face was conveying this, but he didn't seem to notice. 'I actually really like working there,' she announced defensively. 'It's not just about make-up, it's about transforming women and making them feel better, more confident even...' She tailed off. 'I work freelance too, so it's not the only job I do,' she added hotly. This was true, but Rachel hadn't been doing as much freelance work as she wanted to lately. She hadn't done a wedding in months and it was a reminder she needed to update her make-up social media pages to get more work.

'You probably don't have a choice.' He shrugged casually. 'It's not as though Tidemans pays good money, is it?'

'Well, it's enough for me and I enjoy it,' she declared, affronted, wondering how he could be so obtuse. 'Perhaps you *should* leave if you hate it so much.'

His gaze swept over her wintry expression. 'Oh come on, no need to get in a mood about it,' he chuckled to himself amusedly, making her feel even more irritated. 'I didn't mean to offend you.'

Rachel smiled tightly, taking a large gulp of her wine. 'Let's just change the subject, shall we?'

'By all means,' he replied, taking another bite of his fish.

Rachel couldn't bear the silence, and she was discovering that if she didn't ask the questions, then he wouldn't talk. It was unbearable. 'So, what were we chatting about last night?' she asked, deciding to come clean. 'I'll be honest, I don't really remember,' she smiled sheepishly. 'Slightly drunk.'

He gave a little laugh. 'I thought so. I could tell by the look on your face when I came over to you this afternoon.'

Rachel clenched her teeth together. 'Sorry.'

'Don't worry,' he said, blinking a few times. 'We were talking about the fact that you're newly single. You mentioned something about your ex and your best friend,' he told her in serious tones, 'until one of your friends said the subject was off limits.'

'Mark and Bianca?' Rachel questioned, her heart sinking a little that they had been her topic of conversation. Would she always be one of those girls who got drunk and rambled on about the time she was so brutally betrayed? She thought she'd been doing so well. She wondered what she'd said, feeling a little glad he knew about them so she could tell him the story. She'd been dying to complain about it all day but wanted to show she was moving on in front of Grace and Amber like she'd promised.

'I didn't catch their names,' he replied politely.

'Yes, that's what he's called. What *they're* called. I thought I was going to marry him. We met through a mutual friend over three years ago. I thought he'd be the perfect husband,' she laughed a little manically. 'Three years I wasted on him. *Three* years,' she emphasized again, because he didn't look that shocked about it.

'You said last night…'

'And as for Bianca,' Rachel was feeling angrier just mentioning her name, 'she was supposed to be my best friend. I've been friends with her since I was about five or six or something ridiculous. Can you imagine someone you'd been friends with for so long running off with your fiancé?'

Jonathan appeared puzzled, 'I didn't think you were engaged?'

Rachel flapped her hand, 'We weren't. But as good as,' she said hurriedly. 'I used to sit up for hours on the phone to her when she was upset that some loser hadn't called her back. I used to change my plans with Mark if she didn't have anything to do at the weekend to keep her company. And *this* is how she repays me?' she said, exasperated, shoving a forkful of pasta into her mouth. She watched as Jonathan's eyes flew to a bit of pasta she'd flicked onto the table by accident. 'She was lying to me until the very end. Until she got caught out. I don't even know who I'm most angry with,' she said, shaking her head, incandescent at the thought. 'Some moments I think they deserve each other and I'm better off without both of them in my life and then other moments I'm angry. I have so much to say to them but I don't want to speak to either of them.'

Jonathan cleared his throat and looked at his watch. 'Yeah, it can't be nice.'

'*Nice?* There's absolutely nothing nice about either of them, Jonathan. But I'm moving on, just look at me. I'm dating already. I'm single and I'm absolutely fine about it. Amber says Christmas is the best time to be single. I don't need them. I'm perfect just on my own.'

Jonathan downed the last of his drink. 'That's good.'

'Do you know how I found out about them? Did I tell you that part?' she asked him, really wanting to get it all out.

His brow furrowed. 'Something about his jacket?'

'That's right!' She nodded, impressed that he'd remembered as though he was a student at school who had just answered with the correct answer. 'He left his jacket at her house. I mean, just imagine if I hadn't seen it? She probably wouldn't have told me, the coward that she is. He's just as bad as he never said a word to me either. After being in a relationship with me for over three years.'

She watched as Jonathan signalled to the waitress for the bill.

Rachel's mouth popped open. 'Are we going?'

He flashed her a sympathetic smile. 'Yes. Rachel, you're a lovely girl, but if I'm honest, I really don't think you're over your ex-boyfriend.'

Rachel opened her mouth to protest. Of course she was over it. She was ready to be single and have fun. Meet new people. She had to tell him he'd got her all wrong. Instead she sighed loudly, deciding against it. 'It never would have worked anyway,' she told him truthfully in morose tones that echoed his own. 'I mean, how can anybody not like Christmas?'

Chapter 8

'So how did the date go?' Amber asked Rachel optimistically as soon as she arrived at work.

'Yes, tell us everything,' Grace probed excitedly.

Rachel smiled and Amber was certain she was going to tell her she'd loved it. She knew with a little push in the right direction, she could meet someone really great. Someone that wasn't Mark.

'Does that smile mean you like him?' Grace asked, clearly thinking the same thing.

Rachel gave a dry laugh. 'It was awful.'

Amber's face fell. 'It can't have been that bad.'

'Oh believe me, it was,' Rachel replied, her eyes widening. 'We were completely incompatible. He was full of negativity when I actually got him to speak; it was completely draining. Then we got on to the subject of Mark and Bianca and…'

'Oh, don't say you spoke about them the entire time?' Amber rolled her eyes feeling disappointed. She thought back to a previous date when a guy she liked had rambled on for hours about his ex. It had been so off putting; like finding a delicious looking cake, but then noticing it was past its sell by date and the best time to eat it was back in the past. He had bored her to tears by the end of the evening, and it had been clear that he still had feelings for his previous girlfriend. Complete waste of time, even if she did get a lovely free dinner.

'Not the entire time, no, but maybe more than I should have. I just knew he wasn't for me so I guess I didn't care that much.'

'How come you seem so happy about it?' Grace asked, looking as confused as Amber felt.

'Because I realized that perhaps I'm not over Mark and Bianca yet. That's what Jonathan thinks too…'

'Why is that a good thing?' Amber interjected.

'I don't know, but I've accepted that I can't just forget about them and move on as easily as I'd hoped. But it's a process and I just *know* that as time goes on, it will get easier to date and meet new people. I'm certainly ready to try. Not Jonathan again, but someone new,' she declared, putting her hands on her hips, ready to take on the world.

'Good then, I guess,' Amber responded. 'Perhaps you'll meet someone else on Saturday night,' she added mischievously.

Grace frowned. 'What's happening on Saturday?'

Amber thought back to the conversation she'd had with Jack the night before. It was his work Christmas party. They always had it earlier than other companies and Amber was always his plus one, just like he was hers.

'They book the venue late November to save money,' Jack had told her. 'All the money everyone makes them, and they're still tight,' he'd explained in disapproval.

'I'll be there,' Amber had replied eagerly. Despite Jack believing his work was tight, she knew there would be copious amounts of champagne on offer and they usually had such fun. 'What about Natalya? Doesn't she want to go?' she asked curiously, surprised she was still being asked now Jack had a fiancée.

'She can't make it,' Jack had replied, sounding regretful.

'So you'll have to make do with me for the night.' Amber had smiled on the other end of the phone, even though she couldn't deny she felt slightly hurt that she would no longer be Jack's first choice to take anywhere anymore. His fiancée would always come first, as she should of course. It would just take a lot of getting used to.

'So you'll come?' Jack said ignoring her comment. 'I'll get you a ticket then.'

'Do you have room for two more?' Amber had wondered, intrigued. She could guarantee Rachel and Grace would be sitting home eating pizza otherwise, probably curled up in bed by 10 p.m.

'Seeing as you have to buy tickets this year, I can't see it being a problem. I'm close with my boss too, so I'm certain he'll do me this little favour. I'll double check with him, but I'm sure it's fine. They seem pretty relaxed this year.'

'Great. I'll bring Grace and Rachel if it's possible then.'

Amber was brought back to the present by Rachel.

'Well?' Rachel asked her questioningly.

'You're both coming to a Christmas party with me in London,' Amber grinned.

'Really? Whose?' Rachel asked, tucking her hair behind her ears.

'Jack's,' Amber announced. 'It's going to be fun and great for the pair of you. You'll be surrounded by hot city men in suits all nights.'

'Sounds good to me,' Grace smiled good-naturedly; she was so easygoing that Amber knew it wouldn't be difficult to get her to agree, though Grace had never really been a big partygoer. She was a homebird, happier in her pyjamas and slippers than her little black dress and stilettos, and there was nothing wrong with that. But if she stayed home all the time she'd only become more depressed about her failed marriage; Amber was sure of it.

'It does actually. I'm looking forward to it. Are you sure we can just go along?' Rachel wondered, before muttering to herself,

'Oh goodness. I'm going to need a new dress; then I'll need shoes and a bag to match. I wonder if I'll have time to go out on my lunchbreak and find something tomorrow?'

'Jack is tight with his boss,' Amber explained knowledgeably. 'He's said he can sort it. So it's all planned then. We'll meet at mine and get the train together.' She paused for a moment and then added as brightly as she could, 'Oh, and you may want to congratulate Jack. He's engaged.'

Grace's jaw dropped open. 'Engaged?'

'To who?' Rachel asked hastily.

Amber tried to sound casual about it, as though she wasn't too bothered by his huge news. She was still unsure as to why she cared so much that she hadn't been told sooner about it. 'Oh, just some girl named Natalya he's been seeing for four months. Apparently he just knows she's *the one*. I can't believe I haven't even met her yet, but he seems really happy.'

'Oh wow, amazing,' Grace grinned.

'Ah that's so lovely for him. I wonder if you'll be bridesmaid?' Rachel said thoughtfully.

Amber frowned, disliking the thought of being bridesmaid. She hated being told what dress to wear and how to have her hair. She'd do it of course for Jack, but there was something bothering her about the idea. 'He hasn't planned ahead that far yet, I don't think. I mean, I'm really happy for them both, though it *has* only been four months.'

'He must really love her to propose so soon. My cousin got engaged after two months and they've been married ten years now. I think it's sweet,' Grace replied, rummaging through some blushers.

'I haven't even met her. It's weird; I usually know everything about Jack and what's going on his life.' Amber bit her lip feeling uncomfortable about the situation.

'Oh, I'm sure you're going to love her,' Rachel responded, as she was cleaning some make-up brushes. 'You and Jack are super close so I'm sure you and Natalya will be too when you get to know her.'

'Yes,' Amber replied forcing a smile feeling silly, 'that's what he said and I'm sure we will.'

Grace then changed the subject and told them about Simon moving out.

'Oh gosh Grace. How are you feeling?' Rachel asked her, a concerned expression etched on her face.

Grace breathed out slowly. 'It was so strange being all alone in the house last night and he looks like a broken man. I feel so guilty, but things just couldn't have carried on the way they were. I'm just going to have to get used to it. We've separated and I don't know what the future holds for us. I was actually going to ask you if you'd like to move in, Rachel?' she said, looking in her direction.

Rachel dropped the brush she was cleaning. 'I'd love to,' she beamed. 'Only if you wouldn't mind though. Obviously I'll pay rent and at least this means we won't have to find anywhere now. Perfect location for work too,' she said happily. 'Don't worry about me leaving any mess around either; I'll help clean everything and help with all the chores. We can have a rota for cleaning.'

'I don't doubt you for a second,' Grace replied, knowing how organized and spotless Rachel's home had been. 'The house is ready as soon as you are.' Grace smiled back. 'I'm looking forward to having some company.'

Amber was glad their living arrangements were finally sorted. It would help Grace move on without seeing Simon every day.

Amber prepared some make-up for a client that was booked in for a makeover. She had called the previous day to book the appointment, specifically asking for Amber, which had been nice to hear. It felt good when clients recommended you to their friends. It was partly the reason she loved her job; making women feel happy and more confident was an amazing feeling. Ten minutes later Amber's client walked into the store. She was a pretty girl in her early twenties, with long blonde hair and striking turquoise eyes mixed with flecks of yellow and orange.

'I'm here for an appointment with Amber,' she stated with a warm smile to Amber who was at the desk.

'Ah yes,' said Amber, 'Miss Watkins?'

The girl nodded.

'I'm Amber,' she replied, pulling out a chair by the make-up counter and large mirror. 'Take a seat.'

'Thanks,' she replied, sitting down.

'So, how can I help you today?' Amber asked in a professional, upbeat voice smiling widely.

'I'm getting married,' the girl announced, the happiness radiating from her. 'I wanted some new make-up. I'm still unsure whether to do it myself or to get a make-up artist for the big day. My make-up bag needs a total overhaul anyway,' she explained.

Amber nodded. 'Okay no problem,' she said, used to hearing this kind of thing all the time. She knew if she did a good job, she could be the one actually doing her make-up on her big day and she was determined to make the girl look stunning, not that it would be a difficult job. Her bone structure was incredible.

'Your make-up looks amazing. I wish I could do it like that,' the girl told Amber kindly.

'Thanks,' Amber smiled. As she listened to how the girl wanted to be both glamourous but natural at the same time she couldn't help but notice her long, slender legs and tiny waist. Oh, to be that young again. Amber was by no means big, but once she'd hit 30 it had become much more difficult to keep the weight off. She could no longer get a McDonalds for breakfast after a heavy night out. She only had to look at a sausage and egg McMuffin and she'd put on a pound.

As Amber cleansed, toned and moisturized the girl's face, she also found herself admiring her flawless, creamy complexion. Was

Amber's skin once this wrinkle-free? She couldn't remember. 'So how did you hear about me?' she wondered inquisitively. 'Have I done someone you know's make-up before?'

'Not quite,' she gave a little girlish giggle, 'I believe you're friends with my fiancé, Jack? He told me to come here. He said if anyone can do make-up and help me with tips that it's you.'

Amber was stunned and felt like she'd been electrocuted. She could feel her face becoming hot and felt ridiculous for it. 'Oh my goodness. So you're Natalya?'

'Yes. So pleased to meet you,' she replied in shrilly, excitable tones. 'I've heard so much about you. I had a day off work and decided yesterday I should come in and introduce myself. I've asked Jack when I can meet you, but he seems too busy to arrange anything.'

Amber swallowed hard, her mouth suddenly dry. She couldn't believe that this was Natalya who she'd just been telling the others about. She was so *young*. So pretty. Amber felt taken aback by the surprise visit. She had wanted to be prepared when she met her, not caught off guard. Not that it mattered of course.

'Glad to meet you too,' Amber said finally. 'I only found out about you yesterday. I was quite surprised to hear that Jack was engaged,' she revealed honestly.

'Oh, I know. He's just so romantic. We've literally just fallen head over heels in love,' she gushed in a sickly sweet voice.

'So I hear,' Amber replied in polite tones. It was unnerving her that this was Jack's fiancée. She seemed so confident, energetic and nice. It was easy to see how Jack had fallen for her.

'I can't wait to spend Christmas with him. You'll be there too, won't you? I was wondering if you had any idea what I could buy him. I want it to be really special. Something he'll love,' she said hopefully.

Amber felt her heart sink, dreading spending the day with this girl. This perfect, young, beautiful girl who was somehow making her feel old and dull. She felt like last year's Chanel bag in comparison to this shiny, new, glossy one. Amber instantly disliked her. She knew she was being harsh and it was her own problem, but she couldn't help the way she felt. She knew immediately that she *had* to make an effort for Jack's sake. She didn't want people thinking she was jealous because Natalya was going to marry her best friend. Jealousy was such an unattractive trait. Amber remembered when she was younger watching her friends' fathers pick them up from school or attend assemblies and sports days. How she'd wished her father had been there to watch her or collect her from school! To remind her that she was loved and cherished. To show her she was worth it. There was this one girl called Jodie, whose father had been the perfect parent. Amber remembered during one assembly Jodie's father attending and telling them all about his job as a policeman. Amber had sat there feeling envious. Her father had never had a proper job when he'd been at home. He hadn't been a normal, loving dad like the man before her. Jodie's father never missed a single thing Jodie participated in; right down to terrible choir performances they did. Amber had hated Jodie for it deep down. She'd never been unkind to Jodie, but she could never engage in any conversation or allow herself to be friends with her. It was too painful to watch the beautiful relationship she had with her father.

'Don't be jealous,' Amber's mother had told her crossly one day after Amber had mentioned it. 'It makes people ugly.'

'I'm not jealous,' Amber replied indignantly. She didn't really understand the meaning at the young age of 10.

'Don't be,' her mother had repeated sternly. 'Jodie's father is ill, Amber. He has terminal cancer.'

The words had astounded her and Amber had felt dreadful. Jodie's father had died two years afterwards and Amber had become friends with her within those two years, feeling guilty for the ill thoughts she'd had previously. She could see how jealousy made you bitter and twisted and vowed to do her best to be happy for people in the future.

Amber forced a smile and a merry voice, applying foundation to Natalya's velvet, glowy skin. 'I know just the thing to buy him and of course I'll be there at Christmas. I can't wait.'

Chapter 9

Grace walked into the hotel room pulling along her heavy vanity case. They hadn't told her she'd have to carry it up two flights of stairs and it weighed a tonne. Trust the lifts not to be working the day she came, she thought wryly, wiping her brow.

The room was chaos. Girls were everywhere, drinking prosecco, tapping away on their mobiles and gazing into any mirrored surface they could spot. The room was foggy with hairspray and perfume with flashes of bright white light coming from the photographer every few moments, and Grace smiled, loving every second. The build up to a wedding was like no other. She could almost feel the nerves in the air and it was her job to make the bride and bridesmaids feel more relaxed and confident. She couldn't deny though, that today, she felt a little sad. It brought back memories of her own wedding day. It was the first wedding she'd done since her break up.

'You look absolutely stunning,' Simon had told her as soon as they got a moment alone on the day they'd married. His eyes had been twinkling with adoration and she could really tell he meant every word. She felt like the luckiest woman in the entire world and she recalled looking at him, unable to

74

believe that now, she really had a husband. She felt so grown up. So mature.

'You don't look so bad yourself.' She'd grinned back, all nerves from before the ceremony now just replaced with joy.

'I'm so lucky,' he'd told her sincerely. 'I love you, Grace. More than you'll ever know.'

It had brought a tear to her eye and she'd playfully punched his arm. 'Stop or you'll ruin my make-up,' she'd laughed before kissing him tenderly on the lips. Nothing could ever come between them, she had thought. They were legally bound together as man and wife and they were solid, strong and so very happy. Everything would be okay with Simon in her life, she'd been sure. She wasn't entirely sure how long it was before he had changed, but things just seemed to go downhill and it was heartbreaking thinking back. Grace had to stop thinking about how they once had been. That Simon had long gone; nowadays he wouldn't even notice if she had six inches cut off her hair. She felt invisible to him. Undesired. It was a horrible feeling that she never wanted to feel again.

'Are you the make-up artist?' A bridesmaid walked over to her, interrupting her thoughts.

'Yes,' Grace replied cheerily. 'Where do you want me?'

Time seemed to fly as Grace applied make-up to the wedding party. She now just had the bride left to do as soon as the hairdresser had finished her hair. She thought about going out that night to Jack's work Christmas party and felt a little nervous about it. She really wasn't used to going on nights out and she hadn't bought a new outfit like Rachel had. She'd left it too late and was just planning to wear something she already had – not that she could think of anything.

It had really surprised Amber when Jack's fiancée had turned up at Tidemans the day before. Grace could tell that Amber seemed a little taken aback about it and she wondered why. Amber and Jack were close family friends, exceptionally close, but every

75

time she or Rachel had quizzed Amber if their relationship was more than friendship, Amber had laughed it off. So what was she bothered about? She guessed Amber felt quite protective over him; as though he was her younger brother or something. Grace was sure she'd come round to Natalya eventually.

The bridesmaids had a gift for the bride and they all went to another room next door. 'We won't be long,' the bride, Sally, informed Grace. 'They just want to give me a gift before my make-up gets done. In case I cry,' she chuckled.

'No problem,' Grace told her warmly. She only had an empty house to go back to so she was in no rush. Rachel had planned to move in the following week and she couldn't wait for some company. After living with Simon for so long, however unhappy she'd been, she missed the presence of someone else being in the house and knowing she wasn't alone.

'Wow, it's awfully quiet in here,' came a man's voice behind her.

Grace pivoted round to be greeted by a tall man in a smart, black suit carrying a gift. He had short dark auburn hair, a protruding Adam's apple and a kind face. He looked confused to see her standing in the room alone.

'I'm the make-up artist,' she informed him. 'They've just gone next door to give Sally a gift.'

'Oh right,' he smiled at her, 'I'll just wait here then. I'm Sally's brother, Steve. I have a present from the groom,' he explained, holding it up to show her as proof.

'That's nice,' Grace returned his smile. She'd normally feel a little awkward being stuck with a stranger, but there was something about Steve which made her feel at ease. She could see the similarity now between Steve and Sally as she glanced at him. They both had bright blue eyes and a petite, straight nose.

'Is she still nervous?' Steve enquired.

Grace nodded. 'A little, yes. To be expected.'

His eyes trailed down to Grace's wedding ring, which she still

76

hadn't taken off. Her hand felt bare without it. Like she was naked. 'I see you've done this before. You must know the feeling.'

Grace immediately felt her diamond ring self-consciously. It symbolized another lifetime. Another Grace and Simon. 'Yes,' she replied, 'though I'm probably not the best person to talk to about marriage.'

He looked intrigued. 'Oh?'

'We've just separated,' Grace said reluctantly, feeling a little embarrassed for no apparent reason. Should she have told a complete stranger such personal news? It was most unlike her.

'Oh, sorry to hear that,' Steve replied looking genuine. 'Were you married long?'

'Four years,' she told him, tucking her hair behind her ear.

They stood in an awkward silence.

'So, make-up,' Steve started in light tones, clearly attempting to change the subject, which Grace was grateful for. 'How long have you done that for?'

'Since I was about two,' Grace said with a little giggle. 'I used to steal it from my mother's make-up case. My lipstick skills have improved a great deal since then though. I now manage to get all the lipstick inside the lip line.'

He laughed good-humouredly. 'I expect they have. Especially if Sally picked you. I know how she's been after the perfect every-thing for the wedding. That includes make-up artist.'

'I'm glad,' Grace replied, smiling. She wondered how long the others were going to be, but realized she was quite enjoying their chat. There was something incredibly warm about Steve she hadn't felt in a while. 'What do you do?'

'Teacher,' he replied looking rather guilty.

'What do you teach?' Grace asked interestedly.

'What would you guess?' he asked, looking curious.

'Maths?' Grace answered after staring at him intently.

'You got it,' he grinned, as though he'd been caught out. 'What gives it away?'

'I can just imagine you as a maths teacher, I don't know,' Grace said, narrowing her eyes, unsure why she'd thought it. She guessed it was because he looked smart. Intelligent. He didn't look the creative or arty type. 'Do you enjoy it?'

'I do,' he nodded. 'A great deal. Some of the teenage students give me a hard time, but hey, I've got used to it,' he said, just before the sound of chatting and laughter came from the corridor outside the hotel room. He looked serious suddenly. 'Do you have a card or anything on you?'

'Erm, yes I do,' Grace replied, her heart thumping furiously in her chest as she fished around in her bag for her business card.

'My friend has recently become engaged,' Steve explained, as she handed it over, 'I'll pass this on to his fiancée.' He flashed her a pleasant smile.

'Thanks,' Grace said, feeling a little flustered, wondering if it was more than that, or if she had misread the signs. She felt so out of touch in the dating game. It felt alien to her to be talking to a strange man and questioning whether he liked her or was just being polite and friendly. She'd felt safe being Simon's wife. She hadn't had to worry about things like this because she was married. Taken. Completely off limits. She'd never envied her single friends or longed for the days when she'd flown solo. She was a 'couple' person. Much happier in a relationship than traipsing round bars and clubs eyeing up potential eye candy. But who knew; maybe that was the old Grace? She hadn't been alone for so long that she couldn't really remember how it felt.

Sally and the bridesmaids came into the room then, laughing about something and then gushing over the gift Steve had brought from Sally's husband.

'Are you ready?' Sally asked Grace, looking up at her a few moments later.

Grace caught a glimpse of Steve and he smiled and waved

goodbye silently. She took a deep breath before answering Sally, 'I think so, yes.'

Amber waved to Jack as she made her way through the crowd to the bar where he was standing with Grace and Rachel following closely behind her. It was already really busy and the party had only started thirty minutes ago. Jack was deep in conversation with a work colleague, so Amber helped herself to three glasses of champagne from a tray sitting on the bar and turned to the others.

'I wish Tidemans Christmas ball was as nice as this,' she said, admiring the huge dance floor and trays of canapés being handed out by the waitresses wearing black skirts and white blouses.

Rachel was busy eyeing up Jack. 'Is it just that I'm noticing now I'm single or has Jack been working out?'

Grace was gawping too. 'Has he had his hair cut? It looks nice.'

Amber looked over at him, feeling happy to be in his presence as always. He was looking rather gorgeous in his pale blue shirt and grey trousers, but no different to how he usually looked. He'd always been a catch. Perhaps she'd just never really thought about it before. 'He looks the same,' she replied insouciantly. 'I wouldn't get too excited anyway, we know he's engaged to Natalya now,' she said sulkily, unable to hide her discomposure. 'There's plenty of good-looking, single men here tonight to keep you both occupied, don't worry, and if we don't like any of them then who cares? We'll still have fun and there's always the next night out.'

Amber watched as Jack shook hands with the man at the bar and walked over to them. He smiled widely. 'Alright girls? You're all looking beautiful,' he complimented, kissing their cheeks. 'You okay for drinks?'

'Fine,' Grace smiled back, 'We've just got these,' she lifted her glass.

'How are you?' Rachel asked him. 'Congratulations on the engagement. Amber told us about it. We met Natalya yesterday; she seems lovely.'

Jack nodded, 'Yes she told me she went to see you.' His eyes flicked over to Amber. 'She loved the make-up by the way, so thanks. I knew you'd do a good job.'

'It wasn't difficult to make her look pretty,' Amber told him honestly. 'She's beautiful.'

'I know. I'm a lucky man,' he replied merrily.

Amber couldn't help but suddenly feel that Natalya was the lucky one. Jack was her best friend and she hadn't realized how much she cared about him until now. It had been the two of them for so long. The thought of him doing everything with Natalya now made her feel sad and left out.

They chatted for a short while between them before Jack excused himself. 'I'll catch up with you in a bit, I just want to chat to someone over there,' he explained.

'He's nice over there,' Rachel said, her eyes glittery in excitement.

'Which one?' Grace asked.

'The one with dark hair. Quite tall,' Rachel replied, sneakily looking over at him. 'No wedding ring too, which is good.'

'Go over and chat to him,' Amber persuaded her.

'And say what?' Rachel frowned, looking doubtful.

'Just ask how his night's going,' Amber suggested casually. 'Smile at him, flirt, I don't know.'

'I can't.' Rachel gave a nervous laugh as though the thought of approaching someone was ludicrous.

'Follow me,' Amber instructed them, wanting to show Rachel that there was no need for being shy or bashful. Ever since Amber could remember she'd always been confident approaching men. She genuinely didn't see what the big deal was? What was the worst that could happen? Her friends needed to understand that you couldn't just wait around and hope that someone was going to talk to you. Sometimes men felt intimidated too. Sometimes they were just as shy.

'You've got to go for what you want in life,' she told Rachel when they were only a few feet away from him, 'or you'll never get anywhere.'

Rachel looked mortified. 'What are you going to say to him? Amber, please...'

Amber ignored her and tapped the man that Rachel had said she liked on the shoulder. She shot him a bright smile when he turned around with a baffled expression on his face. 'Hi. My friend here was saying she thought she recognized you from somewhere. Whereabouts do you live?' she asked him. 'Is your name Chris?'

'No, it's David. I'm from Wimbledon,' he replied, glancing back at Rachel.

Amber pivoted round to Rachel. 'He's from Wimbledon, Rach. It can't be who you thought it was.'

'Why, where are you from?' David asked Rachel, taking a few steps closer to her.

Amber smiled at Grace. *That's how it's done.*

Another suited man David had been chatting to turned his attention to them. 'You don't work with us, do you? I've never seen you before if you do.'

'No, we're friends with Jack Wyatt,' Amber explained.

'Ah yes, I know Jack. Good guy. I'm Duncan.' He put his hand out for Amber to shake it.

'Amber,' she smiled back.

'Grace.' She shot him a natural smile.

'I'm just going to find Jack,' Amber said quietly to Grace, thinking it was the perfect time to leave her newly single friends talking. She wandered through the sea of people looking for him when she heard her favourite Christmas song. Amber remembered when she was sixteen sitting upstairs in her bedroom with Jack on Christmas day and playing it on her CD player full blast, over and over until he'd begged her to change it. She'd found it hilarious and played it every year after that. She even hunted it down a few years ago on a CD and wrapped it up for him as a present for a joke. Whenever she heard it she thought back to that time in her room. Being young and happy, her only worries being about school exams and how they were going to sneak some cider past their parents.

She had to find him before the song finished and drag him to the dancefloor.

She felt a tug at her hand and Amber's face exploded into a smile as she swivelled round to see Jack.

'Our song!' she shouted happily over the music.

'Dancefloor?' he questioned, seeming to read her mind.

'Of course,' she answered excitedly, following his lead.

They laughed together as they danced, Jack spinning Amber round in circles until she became dizzy.

'This song will always remind me of you,' Jack told her affectionately.

'Of us,' she corrected him, with a huge smile as she thought back all those years. She loved it being just the two of them, she realized. She got on well with Jack's brother too, but no one made her feel as comfortable as Jack did, and they'd often gone off when their families met up, just the two of them.

'Fancy a shot?' Jack asked when the song was over.

'Do you really need to ask me that?' Amber quizzed him, raising an eyebrow.

They downed a shot and Amber felt the warmth of the alcohol burn her throat, making its way down into her stomach. 'I still need to buy tickets for the winter market,' she mentioned to him. It was a Christmas event in London they attended every year together, walking round stalls and picking out gifts for their families as they drank mulled wine. 'You need to text me with dates you can do,' she added. 'Once I know that, I'll book it for us.' Amber was looking forward to it. They usually had dinner nearby afterwards and a few drinks. It was a little tradition.

'Ah I was going to ask you about that,' Jack said, 'I was telling Natalya about it and she was saying she'd love to come along. That's okay, isn't it?' he questioned innocently. 'You can get to know her better and she'll probably be better at helping you pick presents than I am,' he laughed.

Amber's heart sank, but she smiled stiffly. 'Of course. More the merrier,' she said, unable to help feeling incredibly disappointed. It wouldn't be the same with Natalya there. It was something they did together. Just the two of them. Couldn't he see that she would feel like a gooseberry? The odd one out. The little tag-along.

He looked shocked suddenly as he stared at something behind her.

'Speak of the devil!' His eyes were aglow with delight.

Amber turned round, unable to believe that Natalya was making her way towards them. She looked amazing, her blonde hair bouncing as she walked sensuously in her little black dress.

Natalya ran into Jack's arms, kissing him hard on the mouth.

'You said you couldn't come,' he said to her, looking thrilled that she was there.

Natalya was grinning from ear to ear, 'I didn't think I could. But here I am,' she squeaked, looking pleased with herself, kissing him again 'I had to sweet talk my way in as I didn't have a ticket. Apparently being your fiancée has its benefits as the doorman let me straight past.' She looked completely smitten as she stared at him. She glanced at Amber quickly. 'Amber, hello again,' she giggled, shooting her a smile.

Amber made herself smile back, but imagined it appeared like more of a grimace. 'Hi.'

'I was just talking about you coming to the Christmas market,' Jack explained.

'Oh, I hope you don't mind, Amber,' Natalya said in saccharine tones. 'It's just Jack was telling me about it and I'd love to come along. I've never been to one before.'

'Perhaps you two should just go alone?' Amber suggested stubbornly. There was no way she was playing piggy in the middle with the newly engaged couple.

'No way!' Natalya looked mortified. 'I know you two do it every year and I wouldn't want to get in the way.'

It was irritating how nice she was. It would have been easier to dislike her if she'd been a bitch.

'Don't be silly. You won't be in the way,' Jack reassured her. 'If anything, I will. I was just saying how you two will enjoy the shopping a lot more than I will. I'll probably just sit in a bar somewhere. We'll all go.'

Amber nodded, her lips pressed into a line. 'Course we will. It will be fun,' she managed to reply as convincingly as possible. It wouldn't be the same though. Amber wanted to go with Jack. Alone. She hated that Natalya would be joining them.

'I'll introduce you to some work colleagues now you're here,' Jack said, linking arms with Natalya. 'They've been dying to meet you. You don't mind, do you Ambs?' He asked, oblivious to how sick to the stomach Amber was feeling inside.

'Course not,' Amber responded after clearing her throat. She stood frozen on the spot, watching the two of them walk off together.

A voice came from behind her then. It was Grace. 'I got away from that Duncan. Thanks for leaving me with him; he wouldn't stop asking me out on a date. He's completely not my type either. I felt so awkward trying to come up with reasons why I couldn't.'

Amber was hardly listening, still gazing intently at Jack and Natalya through the crowds.

'I thought I'd come and see if you wanted a drink. What are you looking at? Rachel is still speaking to that David bloke. He seems quite nice. Oh *no*, Amber,' she heard Grace say, making Amber shift on the spot to face her.

'Oh no, what?' Amber asked feeling puzzled.

Grace's eyes were wide in surprise as she too, looked through the crowds to where Amber had been staring. 'You're in love with him, aren't you? You're in love with Jack.'

Chapter 10

Rachel was in a good mood as she made her way to work. She'd done all her Christmas shopping the previous day, despite her slight hangover from Jack's Christmas party, and when David had sent her a text message asking if she wanted to meet up for a quick coffee, she'd accepted. David was a nice man, and she'd enjoyed spending a bit more time with him, despite deciding on her way home she would prefer him as a friend. There just hadn't been that spark for her, and though he ticked all her boxes, Rachel was determined to only settle with someone who made her feel excited and alive. A man that made her heart flip over just at the very thought of him. Still, she felt happy. She was looking forward to meeting new people, enjoying the thrill that she didn't know what would be happening and who she would be going out with in the future. Being single wasn't too bad at all.

'Hi,' she greeted her friends as she made her way over to the make-up counter.

'Morning,' Amber replied, looking a little depressed.

Rachel felt sorry for her. Ever since Saturday night when Grace had said she was in love with Jack, Amber had appeared beaten. As if she only now understood her true emotions towards him. She hadn't realized it, mistaking her strong feelings for those of

86

an overprotective friend. Rachel had never seen Amber act like this over any man before. She was usually so casual and in control. So blasé. Was she surprised about Amber's feelings? Perhaps Rachel was in a way. Amber always went for any man she liked without batting an eyelid. She was assertive and confident, so to see her like this was strange to say the least.

Grace smiled as she applied some pink lipstick in the mirror. 'Good morning. All packed and ready to move?'

'I sure am. I should be over around eight o'clock this evening,' Rachel said cheerfully. She was really looking forward to moving into Grace's place that night. It was a new start. A little adventure. She turned to Amber, 'So how are you feeling since the weekend?'

Amber exhaled slowly, thrusting her hands into the pockets of her trousers. 'My head is a complete mess,' she muttered despondently. She looked confused. 'I mean, growing up, we were often teased about being more than just friends, but we laughed it off. I've always cared so much for Jack. He's such an important person in my life, I guess I've been terrified to imagine anything other than friendship between us. Just imagine if it didn't work out? I couldn't lose him as a friend and I couldn't bear for things to be awkward between us.'

Rachel frowned, not able to imagine how Amber must be feeling. What was the right thing to do? Not say anything and let Jack live happily ever after with Natalya? Or should she tell Jack how she felt? At least then he would know and she'd have been truthful about her feelings. 'What are you going to do?' Rachel asked delicately.

Grace put her arm around Amber and rested her head on her shoulder. 'If only you'd realized before he got engaged.'

Amber groaned. 'I know, I know. Nothing with me is ever simple,' she sighed. 'I'm not going to do anything. How can I? Jack seems happy with Natalya. What kind of a friend would I be to suddenly just drop it on him that I'm in love with him? I've probably always been in love with him; I've just been too blind to see it for all this time. I don't even know what I want either. Yes, I love Jack, but do I want a serious relationship? I've been so happy on my own. It's easier that way. It's what I'm used to. Even if I told him I liked him as more than a friend, I still don't know what I'd be offering him. I'm so messed up.'

'But say he feels the same?' Rachel questioned seriously. 'I'm not so sure you should keep it a secret. It will eat you up for the rest of your life, the not knowing. How can you watch him get married and spend time with him and Natalya when you're in love with the guy? Your feelings could change everything if you tell him.'

Amber looked into the distance deep in thought. 'I just can't,' she explained, her mouth twisting awkwardly.

Grace nodded. 'At the end of the day it's up to you, but I think I'm with Rachel on this. Jack should know how you feel.'

Amber shook her head with more certainty. 'No, I won't do it. I could ruin everything. I'll just push my feelings away, to the back of my mind. I don't have a choice.'

They stood in silence for a few moments.

'Changing the subject,' Rachel began, 'I went out for coffee with David yesterday.'

'David from Saturday night?' Amber perked up. 'That guy from Wimbledon?'

Rachel nodded smiling widely. 'Yep. He's a lovely man, but I can only see us being friends. Still, aren't you proud of me?'

Amber's face lit up. 'Of course I am! I knew it wouldn't take you long to embrace being single. It's nice to see you enjoying yourself.'

'Yes, well done. I'm still yet to do it,' Grace said, clenching her teeth as though it was going to be painful.

'It's actually not all bad, you know,' Rachel told her sagely with a smirk. 'I'm quite enjoying myself. I'm even thinking of trying dating online too.'

Later that afternoon, Rachel made her way outside on her

lunch break for a wander around the shops. All her Christmas shopping was already done; she could never leave it until the last week like Grace did. The thought brought her out in a cold sweat. Rachel liked to start buying gifts from August onwards; that way she had plenty of time to find the perfect gifts for everyone. Still, it didn't hurt to have a browse for herself now, did it? She was bored of her wardrobe, hardly ever buying new things when she'd been with Mark because he always commented that she had enough already and what a waste of money it was. He'd made her feel guilty for any purchases she made. She smiled; she was single now, so to hell with what Mark thought. It was her money and she would do what she liked with it! She needed some nice new winter clothes and a few going out tops and dresses wouldn't hurt either. After all, she wanted to look nice if she had any new dates in future.

Despite the sun shining brightly on Rachel's face, uplifting her mood, it was freezing outside and Rachel searched in her bag for some gloves, pleased when she found a soft, leather pair that Mark had bought her for Christmas the previous year. She looked ahead at the busy shopping parade, people darting in between each other, frantic expressions etched on their faces as they attempted to buy gifts ready to hand out on Christmas morning. It would be like this every day now leading up to Christmas, she thought, and then just as manic after the New Year when the sales were in full thrum.

Rachel spotted a beautiful black dress on a mannequin in the window and decided to go in and try it on. She left thirty minutes later with two jumpers, a top, two dresses and a scarf, pleased with her purchases. Things were really looking up.

As Rachel turned the corner to head to another little boutique she'd been meaning to have a look in, she stopped dead in her tracks, her body frozen to the spot as blood pulsated loudly in her ears. Her heart was crashing in her chest as she gazed at the couple before for. Standing in front of a shop with their backs to her were Mark and Bianca. She could tell by Mark's tall stature and Bianca's long, wavy black hair that it was them from a mile off. She even recognized Mark's red jacket. She remembered he'd bought it in a shop in Brighton when they'd gone away for the weekend.

'Practical, lightweight and waterproof,' he'd said sensibly in satisfaction. 'And good value too,' he added, looking at the price tag.

Rachel stared at the pair of them holding hands and looking in the shop window and immediately she felt sick. She'd pictured them together countless times, often forcing the image of them to the back of her mind; to a place she didn't allow herself to go. Seeing them here in person, her whole world came crashing down all over again. She wanted to forget about them both, to pretend they didn't exist, but seeing them together was definitely going to set her back. It made it all seem so fresh and new again. She'd been doing so well the past week, she thought sourly, getting on with her life, only looking forward and attempting to remain optimistic about the future. She hadn't expected to see them. She hadn't been prepared for this at all.

Rachel watched carefully as they moved on to the next shop, chatting away together. As though someone had taken over her body, she found herself following behind them, as far away and inconspicuously as possible. She felt the anger well up inside her. How dare they be out shopping together, acting like everything was perfect in their lives when they'd treated her so badly? To look at them you would think they were just an ordinary, happy couple; no one would ever know how deceitful and disloyal they'd been in order to be together or all the heartache they'd put her through. She knew that she should look away and leave, but she couldn't help herself. It was like watching a horror movie that you knew was going to give you nightmares, but you couldn't take your eyes away.

Mark would never normally have had a day off work to go

shopping. It was so unlike him; work had been one of the most important things in his life. He was always striving to get a promotion and Rachel usually struggled to get him to take a day off if they were going away at the weekend. She remembered when it was his birthday a few years back and she'd booked a short break in Croatia. Mark had loved the present, but seemed put off when she told him he needed to take three days off work to make the trip worthwhile.

He'd huffed, looking really put out. 'Three days? Rach, I'm so busy at work,' he'd said, shaking his head as though she just didn't understand.

'I spoke to your boss and it's all sorted,' Rachel had replied enthusiastically. She'd been so excited about giving him the gift; she couldn't believe he was being negative about it.

He sighed. 'It's a lovely idea and I'm sure we'll have fun, but maybe just run it by me first next time, eh?'

Yet here he was with her oldest friend, Bianca, *shopping*. Happily taking a day off for *her*. The thought really stung. He was still continuing to hurt her without knowing it.

They stopped suddenly outside a café and were obviously discussing whether to go inside. As Bianca led the way in, Mark pulled her arm back and span her round, putting his arms round her.

He'll never kiss her, Rachel thought, *Mark hates public displays of affection.*

To her surprise Mark leant forward kissing Bianca softly on the mouth, completely oblivious to the people around them. Not caring because they were clearly in their own little, joyful world.

Rachel's nose tingled, her eyes clouded over and her chin began to wobble. Did she even know Mark at all? She couldn't deny that she'd hoped, deep down, that they would split up now the thrill of being caught had been taken away. She'd prayed they'd get bored of each other and realize they'd both made a huge mistake, begging for her forgiveness. How ridiculous she was.

Though they'd both contacted her, and she'd ignored their calls, watching them now gave the impression that they really couldn't care less about her and the fact she hadn't spoken to them. All they needed was each other. It hurt in a way that Rachel didn't think it would. She was certain she'd been getting over it. In fact, she *knew* she was getting over it; she could see now that Mark had never really been right for her. She didn't want either of them in her life ever again now she'd taken time to think about the situation, so why was seeing them together bothering her so much? All her happiness from earlier had evaporated in one fell swoop, as though someone had burst a bubble. Three years she'd wasted on bloody Mark! Rachel was furious. Bianca too, who was her oldest friend; how could she be standing there, as cool as a cucumber kissing Rachel's ex-boyfriend? What kind of person was she exactly? Rachel would never, in her wildest dreams have betrayed her like that.

Rachel marched away feeling devastated and enraged at the same time. She couldn't possibly go back to work after this; she could feel herself getting worked up into a state. She didn't want to talk about it and she knew Amber and Grace would know something was up immediately. Just one look at her face would tell them that something was wrong. Deciding she had no choice but to call work and say she felt too ill to come back in after lunch, Rachel made her way to the car park where she'd parked her car.

Tears flooded her eyes as she drove and once again, Rachel sobbed her heart out. She felt annoyed with herself for feeling the way she did. She was irritated that she couldn't be strong and positive twenty-four hours a day, but she was only human. Tomorrow was a new day and she'd do her very best to pick herself up again from where she left off this afternoon when things were looking bright. She was bored of crying about the same old thing and feeling sorry for herself. But it was agonizing; she actually felt physically in pain, her chest aching and her head pounding like she had a tight elastic band round it. Damn the pair of them!

Her eyes were blurred yet again and her eyes filled with tears and Rachel gasped when she heard a loud thud and felt the car jolt as she whizzed past a parked car on the street. What on earth had just happened? Rachel looked in her wing mirror to see a man shaking his head and getting out of the car. She quickly wiped her face feeling mortified, as she knew she would look a complete state with mascara running down her face, but she had to stop and get out because she'd just hit the other car.

'Shit, shit, shit,' she muttered under her breath, wondering if her day could get any worse.

She looked in the mirror trying to clean her face up, knowing it was obvious she'd been crying. She had no choice but to get out the car, apologize and sort this mess out; panda eyes or not. Taking a deep breath, Rachel lifted her head high and walked towards the angry looking man inspecting his car. He looked like he was in his mid-thirties and was smartly dressed in a suit and tie, his blonde hair swept back, not a strand out of place. He looked just as pristine as his car had been before Rachel had hit his wing mirror clean off, which he was holding in his hands.

'I am so sorry,' Rachel sniffed, tucking her hair behind her ears. 'I don't know how I just did that. It's really not like me; I'm normally such a good driver,' she mumbled, feeling embarrassed. 'I didn't realize I was so close.'

The man sighed impatiently. 'I really don't have time for this,' he told her, exasperated. He was looking at the wing mirror and holding it up to his car as though it would stick back on, huffing and puffing as he did so. 'I need to be somewhere so I'm just going to have to take your number and sort it out later.' He appeared stressed out and in a rush, making Rachel feel more guilty and stupid.

Rachel frowned feeling terrible. 'Is it just the wing mirror? I can buy you another one. You just tell me how much it comes to and I'll give you the money. I really am ever so sorry. I didn't realize how close I was,' she repeated wanly.

'So you said,' he replied, appearing unamused. He took his mobile out of his jacket pocket. 'Here, put your number in and call your phone.'

She obeyed his orders, wondering how much a wing mirror cost. He was driving a black Mercedes so she guessed it wouldn't exactly be cheap. She could have kicked herself for being so careless. That would teach her for continuing to drive when she was crying over her ex. This was just what she needed after spending a fortune on clothes for herself, she thought wryly. Her mobile rang as she dialled her own number. He looked at her then like she was an interesting creature that he couldn't work out.

'Name?' he asked abruptly.

'Oh, it's Rachel,' she replied. 'What's yours so I can put you in my phone too?'

'Nick,' he said, eyeing her suspiciously. 'Nick Cunningham.' He paused for a few moments. 'Is everything okay?' he asked curiously, staring her in the eye. 'You're not upset about the accident, are you?'

Rachel sniffed again and wiped her eyes again, humiliated that she looked such a mess. 'Oh no, not that,' she explained, flapping her hand. This is just the icing on the cake, she wanted to add, but didn't.

'Right. Good,' he said airily, as though he didn't actually care but felt he had to ask if only for his own conscience, checking his watch.

He looked like he was someone of importance and Rachel wondered where he was in such a rush to go. 'Just let me know how much I owe when you get the chance,' Rachel told him. 'I can't apologize enough.'

He ignored the remark. 'Just watch where you're driving,' he scolded her in sharp tones. 'It could have been a lot worse and you could end up getting hurt. I'd say you were pretty lucky this time.' With that he was in the driver seat, slamming his door and leaving her standing there, on the spot, feeling more alone than ever.

Chapter 11

Grace didn't know if she was more surprised that he'd texted her or about the way the text message made her feel. She was grinning. Really grinning. She felt like a teenager all over again when she would sit on the sofa texting a boy from school and her parents would give her that look. *What are you so happy about?* She'd forgotten that a feeling like this existed. Steve from the wedding had liked her. At least she wasn't going crazy and misreading signs. It was only a short message, but he was asking her for dinner that evening and Grace felt a mixture of nerves, excitement and guilt. Simon and his sad little face was never far from her thoughts though. She was about to text Steve back saying that she couldn't because Rachel was moving in with her that night when her phone beeped again and it was a message from Rachel.

Still not feeling great, so is it okay if I move my things in tomorrow night? X

Maybe it was a sign? She remembered a bride saying once how it was fate how she met her husband. Her husband hadn't wanted to go out the night they met, but had left his house keys at a friend's house and they'd persuaded him to go out when he got there. She had also planned to go to a different bar but the queue had been too long so they'd reluctantly gone to the place where she and her husband had met. His friend had been drunk and fallen over, making him bump into her, spilling her drink.

'The universe was pushing us together that night,' she remembered her explaining. 'We were just meant to be. If his friend hadn't got drunk or he'd had his keys on him, we never would have met. Sometimes things happen for a reason. I really believe that.'

Maybe this was all happening because she was meant to go out with Steve? Was that what this was? Grace shook her head, tutting to herself, unable to believe she was considering that the powers of the universe were pushing them together. Grace was a very black and white person; she didn't believe in karma or fate normally. But she did like Steve, even though he was a stranger. Grace hated feeling weird and uncomfortable around someone, especially at dinner. She relished the stage where it was okay to rest your head on the other person's shoulder. When you could hold their hand and not feel uneasy about it. She didn't know if she was brave enough to date just yet, but when would be the right time? Say Steve was supposed to be her next boyfriend and she was too shy to get up and go out with him? She had to do it, didn't she? The thought of staying home in her dressing gown sipping hot chocolate with marshmallows was alluring, but Grace made the decision to embrace the single life like Amber kept telling her to. Even Rachel had started dating. She texted Steve back saying that she was free and a message pinged back almost instantly.

Great. What's your address? I'll be round at 8 x

She couldn't believe she was actually doing this, but on the plus side, at least she didn't have to cook herself dinner, she thought amusedly. After putting on some fresh make-up, slipping into a mid-length black dress and spraying herself with perfume, Grace didn't know what to do with herself. Her stomach was dancing with nerves and she couldn't concentrate on her favourite television show, as she constantly checked the time and wondered what Steve would be like. She hadn't been on a date in years. This was scary stuff. It didn't feel real.

Grace heard a knock at the front door and her heart skipped a beat. She was surprised that Steve had arrived fifteen minutes early. Taking a deep breath, Grace picked up her bag, put on her coat and walked to the front door. As she opened it, she was stunned to see Simon standing in front of her. Her shock mirrored his own as he stood there gaping at her, his mouth slightly open.

'Oh, hi...'

'Sorry, I should have called you to let you know I was coming over,' Simon stuttered quickly, looking her up and down and making Grace feel self-conscious that she looked so glamourous. She didn't know the last time she'd dressed up and gone out somewhere special with Simon. He was used to her in her work attire or casual clothes at the weekend, her face usually make-up free to give it a break. 'I didn't realize you were going out.'

'Well, yes,' Grace replied biting her lower lip, feeling incredibly uneasy. 'Did you need to get some more things?' she guessed. 'I've found a few bits of yours and put them all down here as Rachel is moving in tomorrow.'

'You look nice,' he said kindly. For once, Simon looked like he genuinely meant it. He was looking at her as though she were a new person he hadn't seen before, reminding her of when they first met.

'Thank you,' she replied, her mouth twisting awkwardly and her eyes downcast, wondering how he'd feel about her going on a date with another man. She really didn't want him to know and needed to get him out of the house fast.

He cleared his throat. 'Did I leave my black trainers here by any chance? I can't find them,' he said, scratching his head.

'Yes. I've put them in a bag along with some other things I thought you may need. It's under the stairs if you want me to get it?' she offered hastily, not wanting him to come in the house in case he ended up staying a bit longer and chatting.

'Thanks,' Simon replied, still standing by the door much to her comfort.

Hopefully she could give him the bag and he would go. Steve was due to arrive soon and Grace felt terrified that Simon was going to see him. Imagine if he came to the door when Simon was still standing there. Would she introduce them? The last thing she wanted to do was hurt Simon; he may not have been the best husband, but she didn't want to upset him.

Grace handed the bag over and smiled, hoping Simon would get the hint to leave.

'Off anywhere nice?' Simon asked her curiously, looking a little afraid of the answer.

Grace felt the heat begin to rise up her chest creeping its way up to her face, like she'd just stepped out into boiling sunshine. 'Just out,' she replied reluctantly, hating how bad she felt about the situation.

He nodded, looking defeated. 'It's okay, Grace, you don't have to tell me what you're up to. I no longer have the right to know now we're not together…' He tailed off and coughed a few times, looking like he needed time to work out what he was saying. 'It's just so weird not knowing what's going on in your life, you know? It's not been that long, but I miss you.'

Grace's eyes welled up with tears seeing Simon so vulnerable. Simon, who was tall and strong and usually emotionless. She hadn't seen this side of him since his grandfather passed away five years ago. He was right. It was weird not knowing what he was up to. Didn't he realize that she was constantly thinking about him and hoping he was okay? Didn't he understand that although she was trying to move on, this was just as tough for her? Despite not being happy in their relationship, she missed him too. Seeing him right now in front of her looking so sad only made her realize how much she still loved and cared for him. Perhaps those feelings would never really go away? Maybe she would always love Simon?

Simon broke the silence. 'I'm sorry, Grace, I shouldn't have said that. Have a lovely evening wherever you're going. Thanks for my stuff,' he smiled gratefully, lifting the bag.

'That's okay,' was all Grace could manage to say.

Simon gave a little nod and walked out of the front door and down the street.

A few seconds later, Steve's car pulled up.

Grace struggled to concentrate during the dinner with Steve, despite him being a lovely, friendly man. He was just as nice as she remembered. She couldn't stop thinking about Simon. Did he guess she was going out on a date? It must have been so strange for him if he had. Grace would hate to see Simon about to leave for a date. Dressing up and putting on aftershave for *another* woman. It didn't seem possible. Grace couldn't imagine him with anyone else. She simply didn't want to either. She recalled once when they'd been on holiday to Greece and met another couple, Kimberly and Scott, and he'd really laughed at Kimberley's bad jokes over dinner. It had been so weird to see him even remotely flirtatious with another woman, despite it being innocent and him denying it until he was blue in the face. Kimberley had been a gorgeous brunette, and only seemed to ever wear plunging dresses showing off her ample cleavage; it had been no wonder Simon had acted like a silly schoolboy in front of her, she practically had every man's tongue hanging out every night. Grace hadn't cared that much either – she wasn't the jealous, insecure type – but it had just seemed really odd and out of character. Simon just wasn't usually a ladies' man.

'How's the tuna?' Steve questioned, interrupting her thoughts.

'It's good,' Grace replied, cutting off a piece. 'Would you like to try some?'

Steve shook his head. 'Oh no, that's not necessary. Thanks though.'

Christmas music was playing softly in the background and the restaurant was covered in gold and silver tinsel. It reminded Grace of a place she and Simon went to years ago on Christmas Eve. Their meals had been terrible but they'd had such a fun night, drinking copious amounts of alcohol to make up for the bad dinner. The restaurant owner had looked irritated with their loud laughter and even more so when they'd left and Simon knocked over a large Santa Claus figure, but they'd found it hilarious.

'Sorry Santa,' Simon had guffawed, picking him back up and rubbing his head fondly. 'I hope this doesn't mean I won't get any presents?'

He'd then looked at Grace and they'd cracked up together, stumbling outside into the bitter cold.

'So how did your sister's wedding go?' Grace asked politely. She knew she had to make some effort, though it was a struggle when her mind was elsewhere.

'It was great, thanks,' Steve answered, taking a sip of beer. 'I was just disappointed you couldn't have stayed for the day.' He smirked coquettishly.

Grace gave a brittle laugh. Steve was a lot more handsome than she recalled, not drop-dead, stop-in-your-tracks gorgeous, but she found him attractive. He was so very different to Simon though, and she couldn't stop comparing them. There was a long pause. 'Have you had any serious relationships?' Grace wondered.

Steve wiped his mouth with his napkin and placed it on his lap. 'I was in a relationship for eight years,' he explained.

'Wow, that's a long time.'

'Yes, it was. We were young though. I think I was nineteen

when I met Jasmine. It just suddenly dawned on me one day that we weren't at all right for each other. It was a habit being together.'

Grace nodded slowly deep in thought. 'Yes, I know what you mean by that. It's sometimes easier to stay with someone than be brave and break away. Go into the unknown.'

'How's the unknown treating you?' Steve said, intrigued.

'It's not easy,' Grace replied, unsure what to say.

'I can't imagine it is,' he replied considerately. 'I'm having a lovely evening though, Grace. If you'd like to do this again some time, I'd love to see you again.'

She inhaled, feeling as though Steve deserved the truth about how she was feeling. 'Listen, Steve, you seem like such a nice guy and I feel really bad saying this when I've come out with you for this lovely meal. The truth is, I just don't think I'm ready to date yet. I've just come out of my marriage, and it's not fair on you, or anybody else for that matter, that my head isn't in the right place. Do you understand what I mean? It's all a bit too soon for me. I didn't realize I'd feel this way until I've actually ventured out and gone for it. You're the first man I've dated since the separation. I'm so sorry.'

Steve shot Grace a kind smile, his eyes giving away that he was disappointed. 'I understand. Please don't worry or feel bad. I've had a great evening regardless, and hey, whenever you are ready, you have my number,' he told her sweetly.

'Thanks Steve. I probably shouldn't have come tonight. I hate to think I've wasted your time…'

'You haven't, I promise. It's been really nice to meet you. I enjoy taking beautiful women out for dinner so again, don't apologize.'

'Well, at least let me pay the bill,' Grace offered.

'I won't hear of it,' Steve said, putting his hand up on protest. 'I'm a gentleman. I'd never let a woman pay. I appreciate the offer though so thank you.'

Grace flashed him a gracious smile. 'Thank you too. You really will make someone very happy one day.'

She followed Steve outside to his car, feeling relieved that she'd told him where he stood. She worried she would feel discomfited after telling him she wasn't ready to date, but Steve continued to make her feel completely at ease. Who knew; if things had been different, perhaps things could have worked out between them? But the one thing Grace had learnt tonight was that she wasn't ready to move on just yet with Simon still firmly in her thoughts.

Grace couldn't wait to get into her pyjamas and into bed. It was freezing outside and she was certain it was going to snow soon. There was nothing she loved more than the snow. Simon had always been like a child about it too in the past, waking her up early just to tell her it was snowing outside. She used to moan at him that it was a silly reason to wake her up so early but she'd enjoyed it secretly. It was one of their things and it would seem really strange not getting woken up by his excited, shrilly voice telling her to look outside.

The following morning Grace stretched out in bed and yawned. It was so difficult getting up when it was wintertime, but she always left her alarm to the last minute so she had to start getting ready straightaway. She quickly checked her phone, her heart in her throat as she saw there were two text messages from Simon. She read the first one.

Look outside! x

She smiled immediately, jumping out of bed and pulling her blinds up. She was stunned not only to see a blanket of white on the grass in the back garden, but also to see two snowmen holding hands with great big smiles made from black pebbles. Had Simon really been round that morning and made them for her? He had to get up early for work anyway, but what time had he been there to create two snowmen? She laughed out loud, unable to believe what she was seeing. They made a snowman every year it snowed, but he'd never made two before; one clearly a girl and one a boy.

Grace clicked on the next message happily.

Once, we were just as happy as these snowmen. I want you to be that happy with me again, Grace. Let's go back to the very start, even if it means just going out as friends. I'll do anything to change into the old Simon you once loved. I can't live without you. Please meet me Friday night. I've bought tickets to a Christmas show at the theatre and I'd love you to come. Simon xxx

Grace beamed. Simon *cared*. He was really willing to try to change for her, happy to take things slow and go back to the beginning. She had thought he didn't have it in him to fight for her. For their relationship. She hadn't been certain he cared enough anymore and it was a nice feeling, knowing that he did. Had this been the wakeup call he needed? Would she be making a mistake if she gave him another chance? Would things just go back to the way they were? Could people really change?

Grace wasn't certain of anything, but she knew from the smile on her face and the warm feeling in her heart that for the first time in ages, she felt happy.

Chapter 12

Amber was on edge. It was the least comfortable she'd felt in a very long time and the thought irritated her; going to the Christmas market with Jack was something she usually couldn't wait for. It was their little thing they did together every year. But now here she was, waiting for Jack and Natalya at the tube station, feeling as though she'd rather be anywhere in the world. She'd wondered that morning whether she should tell them she was unwell; too sick to get out of bed. It was snowing after all – a likely time for someone to come down with the flu or a virus. They would have easily believed her. But she knew what Jack was like and he'd probably have popped over with some medicine and soup or something. He was caring like that. The perfect boyfriend, and Amber had been too blind to realize until it was too late. It was so typical of her to recognize her true feelings at the wrong time. She was like that with everything. She thought back to when she'd been viewing apartments and how she'd seen her dream one straightaway. The estate agent had told her to get in quick with an offer, as it would be snapped up quickly, but Amber just assumed it was his sales spiel and continued to look at others. Of course, by the time she came to realize that the first apartment was in fact the best one, it was already sold. She did love the apartment she lived in now, but not like she had with the first one she'd viewed.

Was this what it was going to be like with men she met now? Would anyone ever compare to Jack? Was she going to get married one day (unlikely, but still) and wake up every day to a husband who she thought was nice, but not as nice as Jack? The one that got away. It was such a depressing thought. How had Amber not known that she was in love with him? Looking back, she knew she'd always loved him; she just hadn't wanted to admit it in case she ruined their friendship. So she told herself that he was like a brother. You couldn't fancy your brother, could you? It had been safe. The relationship they had was incredibly important to her, too special to spoil with confessions of love, so she'd simply denied it, even to herself. But now, it was all she could think about. He was the only thing on her mind, night after night, and today was going to prove incredibly difficult. It was now she understood that she loved Jack as more than a friend, she felt awkward around him. Every little touch from him made her skin tingle and heart flip over. It was so much easier when she had told herself she only loved him as a friend.

She wrapped her scarf around her neck a little tighter to shield herself from the cold. The snow had settled and the houses looked so pretty around her, everything sprinkled in white.

Amber spotted them walking towards her and tried to smile, hoping it was appearing natural and friendly. Praying it wasn't revealing that seeing them together, her heart was breaking a little bit more.

'Hey,' she greeted them, wondering if something was up as the pair of them didn't look in particularly good spirits.

'Hi Amber,' Natalya leaned in and planted a kiss on her cheek, but her voice wasn't as chirpy as usual. She was normally like an excitable puppy and her despondent expression appeared as though her owner had left her alone for the day.

'You okay?' Jack asked, giving her a hug. He smelt delicious as usual, as she took in his familiar aftershave.

'Yes, freezing, but it's perfect weather to go to a Christmas market I guess,' Amber replied.

They both seemed pretty tense and Amber guessed they'd had some sort of argument before they'd met her.

'Everything okay?' Amber mouthed the words to Jack as they walked to the train, without Natalya seeing.

He shrugged and rolled his eyes. 'I'll explain later,' he mouthed back.

It wasn't the best of journeys into London. It became even more clear that something was up as the pair of them wouldn't talk to each other and only seemed to answer Amber. Still, Amber was thankful they weren't all over each other making her feel like the odd one out. She'd take an argument any day of the week, however selfish that made her.

They walked around the market together browsing the stalls and buying presents and Amber was delighted when Natalya said she wanted to go back to the entrance to buy something she'd seen when they'd first arrived.

'We'll wait for you in the pub, shall we?' Amber said, turning to Jack.

Jack nodded.

'You didn't need to buy anything else, Amber?' Natalya asked hopefully, clearly not wanting to go back alone.

Under any other circumstances, Amber would have told Jack to go alone and she would have gone with Natalya. But Amber wanted to speak to Jack and find out what had happened. She wanted to be alone with him. This was normally their day out after all, and she still wasn't happy the day had been gatecrashed by Natalya.

'I'm all shopped out,' Amber fibbed in weary tones, looking at the cosy pub in the distance. 'I'm sure you won't be long. What drink do you want?'

Natalya looked a little vexed as she looked at the busy market. 'A white wine would be lovely please.'

'A white wine it is then,' Amber replied cheerfully. 'We'll see you in a bit.'

Amber followed Jack as they made their way to the pub. 'Right, can you please explain now what is up with you two, please? Talk about making me feel in the middle today,' she said, pretending to feel uncomfortable when actually she was hoping they were having problems and the wedding would be called off.

Jack sighed heavily as he lent on the bar. 'I went out last night with work. Christmas drinks,' he said, looking up with an unreadable expression. 'I was supposed to be seeing her but she texted me at nine telling me it was too late and I should just stay out. So I did. She wasn't impressed. Started saying that I must be chatting up other women or something.'

Amber nodded, her brow wrinkled. 'Well that's just silly. Why would it mean you were chatting up other women just because you were out late? So you've had a bit of an argument?'

Jack nodded. 'I adore her, I really do, but it's hard to adapt to being in a relationship when I'm used to being single, you know? I go out a lot with work networking and building relationships with clients. I don't think she understands that. She expects me to be home at six every night to see her and I've told her, that's not going to happen. I was still intending to see her last night, but the time just went before I knew it. I didn't do it on purpose. My job means I have to work late sometimes. Not all the time, but a few times a week.'

'Of course,' Amber said, gazing at her friend lovingly. She would understand if she was his girlfriend. She wouldn't kick up a fuss. 'So what now?' Amber wondered. A break up? She was hoping that Jack would see that clearly this wasn't going to work. Jack needed someone less needy. He needed someone more understanding. He needed *her*.

'Oh, we'll be fine,' he said nonchalantly. 'We don't argue a lot, this is one of our first ones. I guess I'll just have to sit her down and explain that I'll make more of an effort.'

'But she needs to see that it's Christmas and you're working…'

'Yes, but I can see where she's coming from,' Jack interjected, sticking up for Natalya, much to Amber's annoyance. 'Maybe I need to change a bit. I suppose you have to compromise when you're in a relationship. Everyone has issues and bumps in the road. It's not a big deal.'

'I'm not saying it is,' Amber replied slightly defensively. Why was he telling her any of this if he didn't want her opinion and was going to stick up for Natalya anyway? Why was he arguing with her if he agreed with what Natalya thought? 'I think it's silly that you're not talking. When Natalya comes back, you should talk to her and sort it out. I don't mind going off for a bit to give you some space,' she said considerately, hoping he would tell her that her going off wasn't necessary.

'Would you mind?' he asked, rubbing his stubble with an awkward gaze. 'I feel bad that we haven't spoken today. You're right, it's ridiculous. I hate arguing with her. I'm just used to being single and only ever having to think about myself.'

'Of course I don't mind,' Amber replied, squeezing his hand, not wanting to let go of him.

'You're a good friend, you know that?' he said fondly, staring into her eyes.

'I know, I know,' she said, looking away. 'It's freezing outside and I'm enjoying my mulled wine. Instead I have to go back out into the cold to look at all the same stalls again just so you can make up with your girlfriend.' She rolled her eyes in mock exasperation.

'Fiancée,' he corrected her. 'Though I'm certainly not in a rush to get married anytime soon.'

It was music to Amber's ears. She'd been terrified he was going to give her a wedding date. That would make it more real. It would make Jack seem even more unobtainable than he already was. Not that Amber had any intention of ever telling him her true feelings. How could she? He seemed really keen on Natalya, upset by their silly row. Amber didn't feel like she'd ever be able to say anything bad about her, even if she thought it; Jack had made it quite clear just a moment ago that he would be on Natalya's side. It was just another stab in the heart. 'I couldn't agree more,' Amber replied. 'You shouldn't be rushing into marriage. Especially after only meeting not so long ago.'

Jack took a sip of his pint. 'That's the thing though. She wants to get married next year. She doesn't want to wait.'

Amber nearly spat her drink out in shock. 'But why?'

He shrugged casually. 'She says she knows I'm *the one* and doesn't see the point in waiting. She wants children straight after the honeymoon.'

'Wow,' Amber said in a quiet voice. She didn't trust herself to say anything else. She could just imagine blurting out that he needed to stop this right now. He couldn't marry Natalya and he definitely couldn't have children with her. She could imagine his confused expression as he asked her why and then she would grab his face like they did in films and kiss him.

That's why.

'I know, it's crazy, right? I still feel too young to have kids. But my dad had two by my age.'

Amber swallowed hard. 'You'll make a great father.'

'Do you really think?' He looked ecstatic at her words, a huge grin on his face and Amber couldn't believe that they were actually seriously talking about this. When had Jack grown up without her? Six months ago, he would have laughed about becoming a parent, but now, here he was, unable to wipe the smile off his face at the thought of it. 'I've always thought I'd be a bit of a pushover as a parent. A bit like my dad I guess. I swear he used to turn a blind eye to us when we used to steal cider at Christmas. He must have known,' he laughed.

The time when Jack had tried to kiss her flashed into Amber's mind again. If only she'd known back then how she was going to feel at this very moment. She'd have kissed him back. To hell with how they both felt the next day. Life was about risks. It was a risk Amber had wished she'd taken. But she had only been sixteen and too young to know what she wanted in the future.

Natalya walked through the entrance to the pub at that moment, her eyes roaming the sea of faces until they landed on the pair of them. She looked truly miserable and vulnerable walking in all alone and Amber knew it was her time to leave so Jack could make amends.

'Just call me when you've finished and I'll either come back or meet you at the tube station so we can go back together,' she told him, standing up. She looked up at Natalya who was now looking puzzled that she was leaving. 'I'm going to quickly have another browse around,' she said quietly. 'Let you two talk.'

'Thanks Amber,' Natalya replied.

It was thirty minutes later when Amber's mobile rang. Amber was bored stiff and ready to leave, so was pleased they'd finally sorted things out.

The journey back was completely different to the way there. Gone were the awkward silences and icy stares between them. It was exactly how Amber had feared as she watched the couple all over each other, stealing kisses and touching hands whenever they could. Amber could tell that Natalya was insecure though. There were a few times that she felt Natalya was kissing him just to show the world that Jack was hers and she even caught her telling him off for looking at another woman on the train for too long. Jack seemed genuinely confused by Natalya's sulky expression, denying he'd been looking, and Amber felt sorry for him. She had to bite her tongue to stay out of it and not get involved. She didn't want to be the interfering, jealous friend, but she couldn't see why Natalya was acting so anxious about what Jack was doing. Jack wasn't that kind of guy. He wasn't the creepy man eyeing up girls on trains. If anything, he was the guy helping out the woman on the train being hit on by someone sleazy. Jack was a gentleman. He could be trusted. How didn't Natalya see this?

'Thanks so much for letting me come along today, Amber,' Natalya smiled, leaning on Jack's shoulder on the train. 'I'm all tired now.'

'Don't be silly. You're more than welcome,' Amber replied, wondering if she'd asked to go along because of her insecurity. Was she worried about their friendship? Amber wasn't sure. She was so friendly towards her, but she was now starting to wonder if it was a case of her keeping her enemies close. The more she watched Natalya, the more she questioned whether this was the case. 'Anyway guys, this is my stop,' Amber said, standing up. Jack stood up and hugged her quickly and Natalya copied.

'Lovely to see you as always,' Jack told her. 'We'll have to meet up soon and go to that new Italian restaurant in Manor Street.'

'Definitely,' Amber replied, her stomach growling at the thought.

She waved goodbye to them, watching as Natalya cuddled up to Jack and closed her eyes, exhausted. Was she trying to show Amber that he was hers now? Or was Amber imagining it? Not that Amber would ever say a word. There was no way she'd want to upset Jack and lose him as a friend entirely. But if there was one thing Amber would lay money on, it was that all was certainly not well in paradise.

Chapter 13

Rachel exhaled sharply when she saw Nick calling her, but she clicked on the button to accept the call. She was already late to work and really didn't have time to chat. The sooner this was over with the better.

'Hello?'

'Hi Amber, it's Nick Cunningham,' came the sharp tones down the phone, 'about the car.'

'Oh hi, Nick. Sorry again about what happened,' she apologized, a little breathlessly as she raced to Tidemans.

He ignored the apology. 'I've had the car looked at and it's going to cost around £200 to repair,' he said hurriedly.

Rachel sighed inwardly. A £200 bill was really not what she needed now, given that she was paying Grace rent and had also spent so much money on presents and clothes. Talk about coming at the worst time possible. But she'd manage somehow; she always did. 'Okay. How did you want me to pay you?'

'What about bank transfer?' came his formal response.

'Yes I could do. I seem to have lost the fob though that allows me to transfer money online. I can go into my bank when I get a chance and see if they can...'

'Where do you work?' he interrupted brusquely.

Rachel hated the way he was talking to her. Fair enough, she'd stupidly driven into his car, but Nick was so rude he was making her feel angry. There was no need to be like this. She'd said sorry and she was going to pay, so what was his problem?

She cleared her throat. 'I work at Tidemans, in the make-up department. Pop Cosmetics.'

'Right, Tidemans,' he repeated. 'I'll come by this afternoon after two. Does that work for you?'

Rachel dreaded to think what he'd say if she said it didn't. He was so terse and uptight it was shocking. 'Yes that should be fine.'

'Right, I'll see you then,' he answered snappily.

Rachel opened her mouth to speak but he'd already hung up on her. She shook her head in disbelief, feeling affronted. She was dreading ever seeing that awful man again, and now he was coming to her work.

She waved at Amber as she made her way over to the counter. Grace had the day off, which was why Rachel was travelling into work alone.

'Hey,' Amber smiled. 'Good weekend?'

'It was okay,' Rachel replied. 'Grace and I went out Saturday night. Not a big one though and then we just chilled and watched films on Sunday. How was the market?' she asked, her eyes opening widely, wondering how Amber had got on being around Jack and Natalya.

Amber threw her eyes upwards. 'They'd had an argument,' she started, before explaining the whole day's events.

'So she's jealous?' Rachel questioned when Amber had finished. 'Well that's not going to be easy for Jack to handle,' she told her doubtfully. 'He'll soon get fed up if she's insecure.'

'Do you think?' Amber smiled. 'Sorry, I know I shouldn't feel happy about it, but I guess I can't help being slightly glad that Natalya isn't as perfect as I first thought. Imagine looking like her and still being worried that your fiancé was looking at other women. It's crazy. Especially seeing as Jack is such a loyal

114

person. I just hope he doesn't change the way he is because of her.'

'People do change,' Rachel replied sadly, images of Mark kissing Bianca in public flashing through her mind. 'Just look at Mark last week.'

Amber's mouth was a straight line as she remembered what Rachel had told her when she'd come back into work the following day after she'd seen them shopping together.

'Talking about that dreadful day last week, Nick called me,' Rachel said, raising her eyebrows morosely.

'Nick?'

'The guy whose car I smashed into, remember? He's just as rude and ill-tempered as I recall, and guess what? He's coming to the store this afternoon to get the money I owe him. £200! I really could be doing without this. I'm going to have to go out on my lunch break and get money out. He's like an ogre. A miserable, cold-hearted ogre.'

Amber pulled a face, 'Shit, £200 is a lot. That bloody Mark has a lot to answer for.'

'I'm not thinking or talking about him so would rather you didn't use his name,' Rachel said stoically.

Amber nodded and gazed at her sympathetically. 'Noted.' She sat deep in thought. 'Hey what does this Nick look like?'

'Quite attractive if he wasn't so arrogant and dismissive, but don't go getting any ideas, this isn't a Mills and Boon novel as much as it sounds like one.'

Amber laughed heartily. 'I'm allowed to wonder, aren't I? Is he really that bad?'

'Yes,' Rachel replied, her lips curving upwards. 'He pretty much just hung up on me,' she giggled, suddenly seeing the funny side.

It was around 4 p.m. that Nick arrived at Tidemans, just when Rachel was thinking he most likely wasn't going to show up. He marched over to her wearing a suit, looking self-important and attracting stares from the other women in the make-up department.

'Hi,' he said as he approached her. He didn't smile. He actually looked stressed out, as if the whole situation was one big irritation.

'Hi. I'll just get your money,' Rachel replied, being equally as standoffish and walking over to her bag. *Two can play that game, Mister.*

He stood there with his arms folded imperiously and Rachel couldn't wait for him to leave. Who did he think he was?

'Where's the menswear department?' he asked, looking around when Rachel came back.

'First floor,' she replied in her most professional voice. 'I'll count it for you, shall I?' Rachel suggested, holding up the money without waiting for a reply. She counted out ten twenty-pound notes. 'There you go. That's two hundred exactly.'

He stuffed the notes into the inside pocket of his suit. 'It's been quite a bit of hassle getting it fixed, I must say,' he added, about to walk away.

Rachel could see Amber watching on from the corner of her eye and she frowned in anger. 'I did say sorry. It's not like I drove into your car on purpose. I've paid for it, haven't I? There's really no need to be so impolite.' She put her hands on her hips. 'A thank you for the money wouldn't go amiss.'

Nick slightly raised his eyebrows, surprised by her outburst. He gazed at her for a while, as if trying to work her out and then his features seemed to soften as a faint smile appeared on his lips. It was as though the Mr-Bad-Man persona was all an act and he'd been caught out.

'You're right.' He looked towards the shop exit. 'You're completely right and I'm sorry if I've offended you,' he told her sincerely. 'It's no excuse but I'm going through some … thank you for the money,' he said, patting his jacket pocket. 'I'm not normally like this.' He looked a little embarrassed now.

Now it was Rachel's turn to apologize and she felt slightly guilty for her rant, despite still thinking there had been no need to be so ill-mannered.

'No, I'm sorry. I shouldn't have said that. You have every right to be mad at me after I bashed so carelessly into your car and caused you unnecessary bother.'

He half-smiled and his eyes seemed to light up making him so much more attractive. 'Like you said, it was an accident.'

Rachel smiled, unsure what else to say.

'I have to rush off now, but what about if I take you out sometime to apologize for my poor behaviour?' he asked confidently and appearing more like a gentleman with every second.

As Rachel looked at his handsome face she felt the doubts start to creep in. He was just being nice now, feeling he owed it to her to take her out for being such a dick. He was out of her league looks wise, and she felt all her insecurities rise to the service.

'You don't have to do that,' she told him, feeling flustered.

'I want to,' he replied seriously, in a crisp, precise voice.

'Sorry, but I can't,' Rachel said, shaking her head, her eyes downcast. 'Thanks for the offer but my answer is no.'

He looked disappointed, but smiled like he understood and walked away.

As Rachel swivelled round to face Amber, Amber looked shocked and quickly put her mobile away into her bag under the counter.

'There's no need to look like that,' Rachel said. 'He was mean to me at first and he's older and I don't know. I just couldn't have gone on a date with him the way I feel at the moment. I know you think I should get out there and date, and I will, in my own time. In fact, there's someone I've seen online who I like the look of. Maybe I'll go out with him.'

'It's not that,' Amber told her wanly, exhaling slowly. 'Rachel, I've just seen something on Facebook that you're not going to like. I think I should be the one to tell you before anyone else does.' She squinted her eyes as though she was regretting having seen it.

Rachel's heart plummeted. She could tell by the pitying look Amber was giving her that it was something big. She faced her with equanimity, ready for the news. 'What is it?'

Amber gave her a beady look as she said the words. 'Mark has just announced on Facebook that Bianca is having a baby. I hadn't got round to deleting him as a friend and it just came up on my timeline.'

Rachel felt the blood drain from her face. Her head was swimming. No matter how much she'd prepared herself, it was like someone had just slapped her in the face. Hard. A baby? Was this some sort of sick joke?

'Let me see,' she demanded, her voice scratchy, holding out her hand to see his post.

Amber handed over her mobile, her eyes burning with concern. 'Are you okay?'

Rachel couldn't reply as she gazed at the scan photo below Mark's name on Amber's timeline.

Christmas has come a little early for us! Myself and Bianca Kirk are expecting a baby. Due May 24th 2019 J We're over the moon!

Rachel stared at the phone, stupefied. Not only had they betrayed her in the worst possible way, but they'd also made a baby whilst doing it. She felt nauseous that she must have actually been with Mark, lying next to him in bed when he'd got her best friend pregnant. Was this why he'd left her? Was this the reason he'd finally had the guts to tell her it was over? Or would she stupidly still be with him while he had his cake and ate it if Bianca hadn't got pregnant? He was so callous and selfish. Rachel couldn't believe he was announcing their news proudly on social media. For all the world to see. *Look here everyone! I've cheated and lied and I'm having a baby! Rachel who?* He should be ashamed of what he'd done, not happily telling all their mutual friends and humiliating her even further. He was a horrible man and as for Bianca, she would never get over the shock of how disloyal she was when Rachel had always been such a good friend.

'Rachel, are you alright?' Amber asked again, looking worried.

Rachel handed her the phone back and took a deep breath. 'I will be,' she said, walking off and heading towards the escalators upstairs.

'Where are you going?' she heard Amber call after her, but she didn't stop or turn around. Rachel didn't want to change her mind. She just had to do it. She had to take a leap of faith and be brave. She'd been through so much the past few weeks and now there was nothing left to hurt her, was there? They were having a baby. There was nothing else they could do now. A baby would link them for life, no matter what happened. Their baby would always be there as a reminder of what they'd put her through.

Rachel strode across the shop floor as she reached the top of the escalator. She spotted him almost immediately, standing there looking through a rail of shirts. He looked up before she made her way over, as though he'd been expecting her.

'About that dinner,' she said boldly, gazing at him intently.

'Yes?' he said, his eyes sparkling in amusement.

'I've changed my mind.'

Chapter 14

Was it weird that Grace felt nervous? She felt silly for feeling this way, but she couldn't deny it was nerve wracking. Really terrifying stuff; even more so than her last date. She couldn't sit still so she checked her appearance for the hundredth time and re-applied her nude lipstick. Having a day off had been lovely, but she'd had too much time to think about that evening. Too much time to wonder whether she was doing the right thing. She usually just went with the flow and tried not to dwell on things. Grace had always thought she was different to other women; she wouldn't sit there for hours on end analysing a text message like Rachel would. She wouldn't be asking questions like, 'Did one kiss mean he wasn't as into her as two?' or, 'Did the fact he took so long to reply mean that he was seeing other women?' Grace had prided herself that she wasn't like that. She wasn't an over thinker. But today, she was starting to question whether she was, in fact, just like most other women. She'd done nothing but think back to when she and Simon had first met. She couldn't stop asking the question of whether somebody could *really* change. She knew she needed to give him a try though; she'd never forgive herself if she didn't. Simon deserved another chance. Just one more.

When she heard a key in the door Grace jumped, knowing

that Rachel was home from work. She had told Simon she would meet him at the theatre, despite his insistence that he pick her up. The truth was she didn't want to tell Rachel she was going out with him. She was supposed to be dating other men, not going back to Simon and she worried her friends wouldn't approve and would try to change her mind. She needed to follow her heart, and even though she hadn't been happy in their marriage, her heart still seemed to belong to Simon whether she liked it or not.

'Hi,' Rachel poked her head round the door into the lounge where Grace was sitting. 'How was your day off?' Her eyes flicked from Grace's heels to her make-up. 'You look nice. Where you off to?'

'Just to the theatre with my sister,' Grace lied, unable to keep eye contact. 'Nowhere special really. I didn't do much today. Just relaxed and then went to the supermarket for some food shopping. Still, it's nice to have a day off work.'

'Yeah, course it is,' Rachel said, sitting on the sofa opposite and kicking her shoes off. 'Did you see the news on Facebook?' she asked, looking desperate to talk about it.

Grace furrowed her brow. 'No, what news is that?'

'Bianca is pregnant. Mark posted it on Facebook today. Can you believe it? He went and got her pregnant when he was still with me.'

Grace's mouth formed a perfect 'o'. 'Oh my goodness, Rachel. Doesn't he have any shame? How are you taking it?'

Rachel shrugged, looking defeated. 'You know what, I kind of feel relieved that they can't do anything more to hurt me. That has to be the worst thing, right? Having a baby? I just need to stop thinking about it now, for good, and move on with my own life. I'm sure Mark won't be happy about getting her pregnant so soon; he was always adamant he wanted to be married first and I know his parents certainly won't approve.'

Grace nodded, feeling sad for her friend. It must be killing her right now knowing they were together and about to play happy families. She really hoped Rachel met someone else that made her happy when the time was right. For now, perhaps it was best for her to spend some time alone? Apart from the little setbacks from Mark, Rachel appeared to be really happy most days. She'd been through such a tough time, and Grace thought she was coping really well. She couldn't imagine the heartache she must have been through. Rachel didn't realize how strong she was.

'I wonder if they'll have a girl or a boy,' Rachel said, staring into space in another world. 'Mark has always wanted a boy. He was old-fashioned like that. He wanted someone to carry the family name. A little version of himself he could take to football and go fishing with.'

'The world certainly doesn't need another version of Mark,' Grace said tartly.

'No, I suppose you're right,' she replied, her face darkening. 'I hope it's a girl.'

'Who cares what it is?' Grace said, feeling exasperated on behalf of her friend. 'Let them get on with it. Having a baby isn't easy. It puts stresses and strains on the best of relationships. They haven't been together for two minutes. They'll soon realize having a baby is hard work; it's not all hearts and flowers.'

'I agreed to a date today,' Rachel told her, her mouth curving upwards slightly.

'With who?' Grace smiled widely, glad to be off the subject of Mark and Bianca.

'You know I told you about the guy whose car I bashed into?'

'The miserable man?' Grace questioned incredulous. 'You're going on a date with him?'

'Well, yes, I know I said he was rude and ignorant, but he's also … well…' Rachel searched for the words. 'He's quite hot, and he asked me on a date so I said yes,' she told Grace mulishly.

'Well, good for you,' Grace told her, genuinely meaning it. 'I say go for it. What have you got to lose?'

'Exactly. Thanks Grace.' Rachel smiled, stretching tiredly. 'I'm going to make myself a cup of tea. Do you have time for one?'

Grace looked at her watch, instantly feeling the nerves kick in again as she realized she needed to leave or she would be late. 'Thanks Rach, but I need to go to meet my sister now.'

Grace walked into the entrance of the theatre, her eyes roaming over the sea of faces in front of her for Simon. She felt someone tap her on the shoulder and swivelled round, unable to stop smiling when she saw Simon standing there with a dozen red roses and a huge grin. He'd done the same for their first ever date and straightaway, memories came flitting through her mind.

Grace had only had one serious relationship before Simon. She'd met Guy when she'd been a fresher at university. Guy had been the epitome of the student stereotype: lazy, unkempt and untidy, always looking like he needed a good wash. Grace had known she wasn't going to marry him. He had just been someone to pass a few years with. He had been fun, and she'd enjoyed having a boyfriend to talk to her friends about, but Guy had been the type of person to buy her a cheap box of chocolates and a faded, ancient card from the newsagent's down the road on her birthday. He'd been immature and inconsiderate, certainly not someone she would have wanted to spend the rest of her life with. So when Grace had met Simon and he'd bought her roses on their first date, she'd been taken aback.

'Oh wow,' she'd gushed gratefully, her face suffusing with colour. 'You really didn't have to.'

'Haven't you ever been bought flowers before?' Simon had asked her, looking bemused.

Grace hadn't. Guy wouldn't have dreamt of buying her flowers. Even on a special occasion. He had been a skint student of course, but even if he had money she just couldn't imagine it. It felt really strange being treated so nicely by someone she didn't know yet. Strange but amazing.

'You do know you're going to have to buy me flowers every time we go out now,' Grace had joked at the end of the date.

'Ah, so we're going out again, are we?' he'd asked, his face splitting into a smile. He seemed to be enjoying her discomfort that she'd assumed they would be seeing each other again.

'I'd like that,' Grace had replied. 'I'd really like that a lot.'

Now here was Simon in front of her, all these years later, making the same effort again. The flowers had stopped after they'd got married. Perhaps even after they'd got engaged? Grace couldn't remember exactly when it was. It seemed Simon had thought he didn't have to bother making the effort anymore. But these small things all mattered, Grace realized, as she thanked him and kissed him on the cheek. The small things were just as important as the big.

'I thought we could get a drink before it starts,' Simon suggested, leading the way to the bar where the cheerful barmen were all wearing Christmas hats. There were twinkly lights and tinsel everywhere, reminding her that Christmas was just around the corner. 'What would you like?'

'A white wine spritzer would be lovely, thanks,' Grace replied, surprised at how she was feeling inside. It really did feel new again, as though they'd just met and she didn't really know Simon. She had all the excitement of a first date, but was starting to feel relaxed in his company at the same time.

'How's your day been?' Simon asked, taking a sip of his drink as he handed her the glass over. 'What have you been up to?'

Again, it was weird that he was being so formal and interested when towards the end of their relationship he'd barely grunted when she'd walked through the door after a long day at work. He'd hardly ever kissed her hello in the end, something that had saddened Grace. Ever since she could remember her father had always kissed her mother hello and goodbye. It was the done thing, and her father had told her how important he thought it was in a marriage. A quick, simple act to show you loved the other person.

'I haven't done much really,' Grace confessed. 'Just a little bit of shopping and relaxing mainly as I had the day off work today.'

'Alright for some,' Simon gave a light laugh.

'How's your work going?' Grace asked him quizzically. She noticed this was the happiest she'd seen him look since they'd split up and she had to admit, it had hit him harder than she ever imagined. Grace honestly thought he just hadn't cared about her anymore. She was pleased to see she was wrong, and how being around her now seemed to be making him happy again.

'It's going well.' He nodded. 'Thanks for asking, but I won't bore you about it. What about you?'

'I've been doing more freelance jobs,' Grace told him. 'Weddings, that kind of thing. It's where the money is I guess. Everything is going good.'

'Glad to hear it,' he smiled. 'Is Rachel living in the house now?'

'Yes,' Grace replied, looking at the floor. 'It was too weird being alone there, you know? I'm glad to have company again – though it's strange sometimes, you not being there, spending ages in the bathroom and making a mess,' she said lightheartedly.

'I wasn't that bad,' Simon protested, laughing.

Grace adopted a serious expression. She was making light of the situation, but in fact, it hadn't been funny when she'd been living with him. Feeling unappreciated day in and day out had made her truly miserable.

'Okay, maybe I was that bad,' Simon told her ruefully. 'I've had time to think about where I went wrong and I know I wasn't the best husband. Especially where the house was concerned. Leaving everything to you was wrong. I can see that now.' He looked at his shoes regretfully. 'I know you deserved far much more attention too. You don't know what you've got until it's gone.'

'Let's just enjoy the evening, shall we?' Grace suggested, in an upbeat tone. They had plenty of time to talk about where it all went wrong and what needed to change. But now, she just wanted to enjoy being in his company. Being in Simon's presence once again had made Grace realize how much she'd actually missed him, and judging by the way Simon grabbed her hand and held it tightly as they made their way into the theatre, Grace could tell that he felt exactly the same.

The show had been brilliant and Grace felt on top of the world as they walked out of the theatre together into the bitter cold. The ground was still icy from the snow and Simon linked arms as they made their way to Grace's car. Grace didn't want to leave him. This was the Simon she'd fallen in love with; he was interested in her again. It was as though his vision had been blurred and he'd finally been given the correct prescription for his glasses.

Oh, here she is.

But say this was just a one-off? If she gave him another chance he'd probably go straight back to how he was before. She couldn't be fooled by his sudden change. Grace knew she needed much more than that.

'So,' Simon said, as they reached the car, 'I've had a lovely night. Thanks for coming with me.'

He looked nervous, like a teenage boy afraid of getting his heart broken.

'Thanks for the flowers,' Grace smiled. 'I've had a great night too.' She opened her car door.

'Can I see you again?' Simon asked hastily, afraid she was about to get in the car and speed off. 'I'd love to take you out again.' He was watching her intently. 'If that's okay with you, that is?'

'I'd like that,' Grace replied, flashing him a natural smile. She leaned forward and kissed him gently on the cheek. 'I'd really like that a lot.'

Chapter 15

'Diane, hi,' Amber said, hugging the petite woman in front of her. She'd known Jack's mother since she was a baby and Diane felt like a second mum in a way. She'd always told Diane everything happening in her life and felt completely comfortable with her.

'Amber, hello. How are you doing? I haven't seen you in a while,' she replied, her eyes shining brightly, looking pleased to see her. 'Gosh, it's freezing out there. Do come in.'

'Oh, you know me, nothing much new. Just working and going out with friends,' she told her, taking off her coat. 'Has Jack told you he's meeting me here? We're going to the new Italian restaurant that's just opened. Lovely Christmas tree by the way,' Amber admired, walking through to the front room. Jack's mother wasn't a mumsy mum who wore sexless floral smocks by any means. She'd always been elegant and stylish, and her beautiful gold and silver decorated living room was no different. It oozed class and Amber thought the room was beautiful, just like every year. She'd envied Jack growing up living in such a lovely, spacious five-bedroom house; she'd have swapped it for the two-bedroom flat she'd lived in with her mum when she was younger any day of the week and she loved spending Christmas there. But looking back, Amber realized material items and the size of your house didn't really matter; Amber had always felt loved by her mother, and that was what really counted. Her mother had given Amber everything she ever wanted, perhaps to make up for the fact her father had left, or maybe just because that's what mothers did. Either way, she knew was lucky.

Diane had always had good taste, especially when it came to buying her son's clothes when they were younger. Jack was often seen sporting the latest designer brands and the 'in' garments of the time, and as Amber had grown up, she'd often asked Diane to give her own mother a helping hand when buying her own Christmas gifts. Her own mother had been pretty much clueless and Amber had frequently found herself hunting through the receipts to sneakily take things back.

'No, I haven't heard from Jack, but it will be lovely to see him before he goes out. He's constantly busy nowadays with Natalya,' she said, clicking her tongue but smiling. 'Do you want a cup of tea?'

'Maybe just a quick one while I wait for Jack,' Amber responded, descending into the armchair.

A few moments later, Diane walked back into the room with two mugs of tea. 'So, what did you think of Natalya?' she asked inquisitively. 'Jack told me she joined you at the Christmas market.'

'She seems really nice,' Amber answered in a high-pitched voice, taking the mug from her, unable to say her true feelings. 'What about you? Jack tells me you all love her as much as he does.'

Diane nodded. 'She does seem like a nice girl, yes. Jack seems happy – that's the most important thing to us.'

'Yes, he does seem happy,' Amber agreed, not completely certain that was entirely true. Sure, he seemed really into Natalya, especially the first time she'd seen them together, but Amber was certain he would eventually get fed up if Natalya was as childish and needy as she'd recently seemed. There was just something about her that Amber wasn't sure of.

'Still, I'll always be secretly devastated that he's finally found a woman to take care of him,' Diane laughed. 'You know how Jack's a mummy's boy.' She smiled fondly.

'Oh, you know he'll still be like that,' Amber replied, trying to make her feel better. 'You two will always be close.'

Diane exhaled. 'I'm only joking of course. But I haven't seen as much of him since he met her. He's hardly ever here anymore and when he is, Natalya's with him. That's love for you, I guess. He had to fly the nest one day,' she smiled good-naturedly.

It stung to hear the word 'love'. Amber swallowed hard and tried to smile back.

'Me and your mum are secretly disappointed that the two of you didn't get married.' She gave a short bark of laughter, but looked genuinely disappointed. 'We always said how perfect it would have been when you were both little. We could have been grandmothers together. We'd have loved it. No rivalry.'

Amber was stunned by the comment. She knew Diane was half-joking, but she didn't realize how much she was wishing the very same thing, and she felt her cheeks flush a little.

'Don't be silly. We've always just been really good friends.'

'Oh, I know,' Diane grinned. 'I'd have loved you as my daughter-in-law though,' she said, looking crestfallen that this was now out of the question.

Amber wanted to scream that there was nothing that she'd love more than that too. She wanted to shout out that she loved Jack. Not just as a friend, but really, truly *loved* him. How she regretted that it had taken her all this time to realize. But she sat there, forcing a smile in silence.

Amber heard a key in the front door then and her heart leapt, knowing that Jack had arrived.

Diane's head turned towards the front door and she smiled widely. 'Oh hello.'

'You alright Mum?' Jack's voice came from around the corner.

Amber sat there, a smile frozen on her lips and as Jack walked through the door with Natalya following close behind him, her face fell instantly and she glanced at the pair on them in astonishment. Why on earth was Natalya there? Jack had told her it was just the two of them. If Amber had known he was bringing Natalya she would never have agreed to it in the first place. It was weird. Why would she want to go to dinner with another couple, only to feel like the spare part? Why had Jack not warned her? She was annoyed now. Really annoyed.

'Hi Diane,' Natalya shot her a sweet smile, her voice soft and honey like.

'Natalya, I didn't realize you were going to dinner as well,' Diane said, looking a little discomfited on Amber's behalf.

Jack's eyes flicked towards Amber's. He looked a little guilty and embarrassed. 'You don't mind, Ambs, do you? It's only Natalya had cancelled plans with her friends as she thought I was seeing her tonight. She got the day wrong. When I told her I was going out with you she asked if she could come too and I didn't think it would be a problem.'

Amber stood up, trying to hide her irritability. 'Look, why don't you two go alone? Three is a crowd and I don't want to cramp your style,' she said, feeling as though she was going to burst with frustration. What a coincidence Natalya had thought it was tonight she was seeing Jack. Amber would bet on it she didn't even have any plans to cancel in the first place. That was just to make Jack feel sorry for her. It was just to ruin their plans together. It had worked because Jack was too blind to see it. Or was he just choosing to ignore it? Jack always opted for an easy life.

'Oh, I feel terrible now if you're going to leave,' Natalya said in sulky tones, pouting. 'But if you'd feel uncomfortable and don't want to go…'

'Amber, you won't be cramping our style. I'm not going without you so please come,' Jack said firmly and seriously.

Amber looked at Natalya's mock guilty face and smiled tightly at her. 'If you really want me to come, Jack, then of course I will.'

'Good, that's all sorted then,' Jack said happily.

'I'm sure you'll all have a lovely time together,' Diane smiled sympathetically at her and Amber noticed a look of worry flash through her eyes. It was so obvious now that Natalya was anxious and trying to control Jack and who he spent time with. She couldn't let him do anything alone. If he did (like work drinks) she gave him a hard time about it. Had Diane noticed too? Was she beginning to see how manipulative Natalya was being? Or had Amber lost the plot? Was she imagining all these things because she now understood her true feelings for her oldest friend? Amber was unsure.

The restaurant was busy, understaffed and full, with several large tables of rowdy people clearly out for work Christmas dinners. As Amber sat there listening to Jack and Natalya laughing, she was beginning to regret agreeing to come. Natalya seemed to be purposely talking to Jack about things Amber couldn't join in with, and she was starting to feel well and truly fed up, no matter how hard Jack tried to include her. She couldn't help but feel a little betrayed by Jack. Why hadn't he put his foot down and told Natalya it was just going to be the two of them tonight and he could see her the following day or something? Did he really think this was okay, expecting her to tag along with another couple? Could he not see how ridiculous they looked?

'What's your mum doing for her birthday next week?' Jack asked, changing the subject from whatever it was Natalya was talking about.

'We have the concert remember? At the O2?' she reminded him, noticing Natalya's beady eyes watching her avidly as she spoke. She ignored her and spoke to Jack. 'It's us two and our mums. Mum has been looking forward to it for weeks.'

'What concert?' Natalya asked, looking slightly aggrieved, but attempting to hide it with an excited shrilly voice. 'You didn't tell me about this, Jack.'

Amber flapped her hand vacantly. 'Clearly he's forgotten about it, haven't you, Jack? Not a big deal.' Amber shrugged her shoulders nonchalantly. 'It's my mum's favourite, Rod Stewart. I can't imagine it would be of much interest to you, Natalya,' she told her breezily, knowing how much she was annoying her. 'We used to have to listen to his CDs all the time when we were younger. Our mums were obsessed. I think we know every word to all his songs.' She gave a hearty laugh.

'Yep, we certainly do.' Jack's mouth curves up in a reminiscent smile, his blue eyes crinkling in amusement.

'I wouldn't mind going.' Natalya smiled at Jack lovingly, ignoring Amber altogether. 'I'm surprisingly a Rod fan, you know.' She giggled coquettishly. 'I've always loved his music and I haven't been to a concert in ages.'

'We only have the four tickets I'm afraid,' Amber told her hastily, unable to believe she had the audacity to try and gatecrash their plans yet again. No way was she coming to this one. No way in the world would she manage to worm her way in again. Amber was onto her.

'I wonder if there's any chance of getting another ticket,' Jack said questioningly, looking over to Amber.

'It's a sellout,' Amber explained, attempting a disappointed expression. 'We were lucky to get the tickets we've got.'

'Pity,' Natalya replied, slightly narrowing her eyes, the light in them fading. She smiled at Amber. 'Never mind, can't be helped.'

'Perhaps I'll take you to another concert as part of your Christmas present,' Jack suggested kindly.

Didn't he see she just didn't want them to be alone together? What was wrong with him? The more time Amber was spending with Natalya, the more she was beginning to dislike her. She hated the fact that Jack was close to Amber. She didn't even want them to be together when their mothers were attending too! Just imagine how she'd feel if she knew Amber loved him as more than a friend; she'd be even more desperate to keep them apart. Another reason Amber needed to keep her feelings quiet.

She'd almost certainly lose Jack for good and she just couldn't risk that ever happening.

Chapter 16

'You look happy,' Rachel told Grace, frowning as she stared at her jolly expression in the kitchen as she made breakfast. 'Was it a good night at the theatre?' Rachel gazed at her friend in curiosity. There was definitely something different about her today; she looked lighter, merrier and as though she had received some good news. Even her hair seemed to be bouncing with happiness as she walked over to the breakfast table.

'It was great, thank you,' Grace smiled widely.

'How's your sister?' Rachel asked.

'She's really good. Same as always,' Grace replied, checking her mobile phone, her face splitting into a smile as she read a message.

Rachel put down her spoon which made a loud banging sound. 'Okay, okay, what's happened? What are you so happy for?' she asked her with a grin.

'What?' Grace looked taken aback. 'Oh no reason,' she said, shoving her phone into her bag a little suspiciously. 'Just in a good mood today that's all. It's nearly Christmas time after all. My favourite time of year.'

'Oh right,' Rachel sipped her tea. 'Who were you messaging?' she asked casually.

'My sister just said something funny,' Grace replied, looking out the window. 'What are you up to today?'

It was Saturday, the day she'd agreed to go out with Nick and Rachel was dreading it. She wasn't nervous or excited, she was simply worrying about how awkward it was going to be spending the day with such a rude and abrupt man. Had she been crazy accepting his offer? Now the day had arrived she was beginning to believe she was. It was Mark and Bianca's news that had led her to this. They really did have a lot to answer for.

'I'm meeting Nick, remember?' Rachel groaned.

'Where are you off to? Anywhere nice?' Grace asked her chirpily. 'What time are you leaving?'

'I have no idea. He said he would pick me up. I thought a daytime date would be a bit safer, you know. Lunch is more informal than dinner. I assume we're going for lunch anyway; he was curt and brief over the phone. No change there,' she said, rolling her eyes.

'Maybe he'll surprise you and be really nice,' Grace said optimistically.

'Mm, we'll see. What about you anyway? What are you doing today?' Rachel asked Grace.

'I may do a bit of Christmas shopping,' Grace told her distractedly. 'I'm unsure yet. Or maybe I'll just lay on the sofa and watch some Christmas films; it feels too cold to go out.'

'The heating is up full,' Rachel replied, 'and staying in watching films sounds like heaven. I'd swap that for this awful date I'm about to go on any day.'

Rachel didn't want to make a massive effort for daytime plans, so she wore jeans and a simple pale blue woolly jumper with a cream coat, hat, scarf and gloves. It had started to snow again and was so cold out that she hoped they were going for lunch in a cosy café or something; so long as it was warm she was happy.

Nick called thirty minutes later saying he was outside and

135

Rachel felt a deep sense of anxiety as she carefully walked on the icy ground outside to his car.

'Hi.' He shot her a friendly smile as she climbed in the passenger seat.

'Hey,' Rachel replied in a timid voice, unsure what to expect. 'How's things? I see you've had your car fixed.' She looked out to the wing mirror.

'Yes. I like to get things done,' he told her, his lips pressing into a serious line, looking ahead and putting his foot down on the accelerator.

He was wearing a smart navy coat and black jeans; he was actually quite gorgeous. Rachel just hoped he was in a good mood.

'What do you do for work?'

'I work in finance,' he told her. 'In London. It's all pretty boring and sensible. Not like being a make-up artist I'm sure.'

'It's not always fun in the shop,' Rachel replied, beginning to relax. 'Sometimes it's really quiet and there isn't much to do.' Nick didn't seem as uptight as before. It seemed without his suit he was a different character – much gentler and softer. Less impatient and rushed.

'How long have you worked there?' he enquired.

'About five years now,' Rachel replied. 'It's really convenient because of location and I've always wanted to do something I love.'

'Well, you're obviously very good at it,' Nick complimented, glancing at her quickly as they stopped at a red traffic light. 'You look beautiful today.'

It was so unexpected to hear Nick say something nice that Rachel felt herself blush and was thankful when Nick shifted his gaze back to the road when the light turned green.

'Thanks,' she replied shyly. 'Where are we going anyway?'

His lips turned upwards. 'I thought I'd take you somewhere different. Somewhere fun. I used to love going here when I was younger.'

'Which is where?' Rachel asked feeling puzzled.

'To the zoo.'

'The zoo?' Rachel repeated, her voice squeaky. 'But it's freezing outside!'

'Oh, come on, where's your sense of adventure?' he asked, amused by her response. 'You've wrapped up warmly. You'll be fine.'

Rachel couldn't believe it. She'd had Nick down as someone that would prefer fine dining in a top restaurant to traipsing round the zoo looking at animals. What else was he going to surprise her about? It wasn't exactly ideal in this weather, but he was right, she had her hat and gloves on and she didn't want to complain. She was going to try to enjoy herself whatever happened. She had never done anything like this before with Mark; he was Captain Sensible and wouldn't have dreamed of going to the zoo in the cold. In fact, she couldn't remember the last time she did anything fun or different with Mark at all. Mark knew what he liked and was scared of change; so much so that they'd been going to the same local Indian, ordering the same dishes ever since they moved in together two years ago. When it came to booking holidays, Mark always wanted to go back to Barcelona and stay in the same hotel. Once, Rachel remembered, she had turned her nose up and challenged his decision.

'Mark, do you honestly want to go back to the very same hotel, *again?*' she questioned. 'There are countless other places we could try instead. Don't you think it's getting a bit boring? We know everything about the place. Why don't we travel somewhere new, like Italy or Cape Verde? Or Amber has been to Croatia recently; what about trying there? She loved it apparently. I'm happy to research and plan it all. I'll find somewhere great for a reasonable price with a bit of hunting on the internet. What do you think?'

'I like it in Barcelona,' he'd defended himself firmly. 'It's great value and we know what we're getting. No disappointments. The staff are nice, the food is great and the place is clean. What more do you want?' he'd asked her as though she was strange and difficult to suggest going somewhere different for once.

So, Rachel had just gone along with it because that was what Mark wanted. He liked to know what he was getting. It was funny that he hadn't felt that way about his girlfriend, Rachel thought sourly. No worries about change there.

'I feel like a child,' she giggled, brought back to the present as Nick paid for their tickets at the entrance. 'I can't remember the last time I went to the zoo.'

'Exactly. It's different,' Nick said, looking pleased with his decision. 'Going for something to eat or to the cinema is so predictable. I wanted to surprise you.'

'Well, you certainly have,' she smiled, as they made their way to the lions. 'I never had you down for the type of guy to come here for the day.'

He eyed her interestedly, cocking his head slightly to the side. 'And what type of guy did you think I was exactly?'

Rachel cleared her throat, unsure how to word it. 'You weren't exactly nice to me the day I went into your car. Every time I've seen or spoken to you, you've come across so serious and snappy, like you're annoyed about something, and not just the car. Like you're annoyed about everything. I was quite nervous to come today,' she admitted in a small voice.

His brow furrowed as he glared at her intently. 'Yes, I guess you could say I've been fairly irritated and snappy.'

'Fairly?' Rachel snorted. 'Any snappier and they'd have to put you in there!' She pointed at the crocodile enclosure.

Nick stared at her blankly. 'I have my reasons,' he told her gravely, looking away after a long pause. 'I apologize for my behaviour though. There's no excuse and the last thing I'd want you to feel is nervous. I'm really sorry,' he said, looking as though he meant it.

'What are your reasons?' she ventured, worried she'd overstepped the mark if there was an explanation for his previous behaviour.

Nick looked awkward. 'Let's move on, shall we? Do you want to feed the reindeer?'

'Reindeer?' Rachel squeaked. 'Very funny.'

Nick looked both confused and amused. 'What do you mean by that?'

'There's no such thing,' Rachel laughed. Her forehead crinkled. 'Is there?' Suddenly she felt silly, unsure as to whether there really were such animals or whether they were just mythical creatures in Christmas stories.

Nick laughed then. A real belly laugh, before stroking her head fondly. 'That's cheered me up,' he told her. 'Of course they're real. Come on, let's go feed them.'

Rachel grinned as she kept catching Nick's eyes, making him laugh gaily all over again about the fact she hadn't known that reindeers truly existed. 'Okay, okay,' she giggled, 'I'm not normally that stupid. I just can't remember ever having seen them before. Not in real life.'

'I don't think you're stupid for a second.' He smiled warmly, linking arms with her as they made their way to the restaurant for a coffee.

Rachel realized she was actually really enjoying herself as she watched Nick walk over to the table she was sitting at. She liked Nick. Really liked him. He was a lot easier to get on with than she'd imagined. He was handsome, fun and had a good sense of humour; gone was the rude man she'd met that awful day.

'That day I met you,' Nick said seriously, sitting opposite, 'you were upset about something. You don't have to tell me if you don't want to, but I just wondered if it was all sorted now?' he asked delicately.

He looked concerned about her and it made Rachel like him even more.

Rachel took a deep breath, determined not to talk about Mark and Bianca for more than a minute. She was done with thinking and talking about them for a lifetime. 'It was just to do with my ex,' she explained.

He nodded understandingly.

'And my best friend,' Rachel added reluctantly. 'We kind of overlapped,' she indulged. 'Now she's pregnant with his baby.'

He eyes widened. 'Oh wow. I'm so sorry.'

'Don't be,' Rachel told him, realising if those things hadn't happened then she would never have met him. 'I'm sure if it wasn't her it would have been someone else. Everything happens for a reason, right? I feel fine about it now. I'd just seen them together, before I crashed into your car. But let's not talk about that for a second longer.'

He nodded thoughtfully and Rachel wondered whether he thought she wasn't ready to be dating if she was still crying over her ex. She wanted to tell him she was. She hadn't felt like this for a long time. She hardly knew Nick, but she could already tell there was something between them. On her part anyway; he was making her feel excited and happy, and she wanted to know everything about him.

'I've had a nice day with you,' he said, reaching across the table and squeezing her hand.

Rachel's stomach flipped over with nerves and she shot him a smile. 'Me too. I'm pleasantly surprised by you,' she confessed. Just like Grace had said she might be.

Nick's phone beeped then and his expression changed suddenly. He looked worried and intense and quickly put his coat on. 'I'd best get going,' he told her in a clipped voice, his gentle personality seeming to do a complete U-turn. 'I'll drop you home.'

'Is everything okay?' Rachel enquired in bafflement.

'Yes, fine,' he replied stonily, his face closing down. 'I just need to leave,' he said, marching ahead.

Rachel couldn't help but feel confused and disheartened. Just as she thought she was really starting to like Nick, he was back to being standoffish and cold; what was going on with him? She followed along behind him, trying to keep up. The date had gone great, but it had been ruined by the text message he'd received. Why wouldn't he say what was up? Rachel had been open about Mark and her life, so why was Nick being such a closed book?

The car journey back was tense and Rachel attempted to talk to him, but she could tell Nick's mind was elsewhere.

'Are you sure you're okay?' she tried asking again as he pulled up outside. She was also wondering whether she was going to see him again but didn't want to be the one to ask.

He gave a weary sigh. 'Yes, don't worry. Everything is fine,' he said looking distracted, giving her the impression he really needed her to leave.

Rachel bit her lip, unable to hide her disappointment. 'Well, thanks for a lovely day,' she managed.

'You too,' he replied hurriedly, looking at his watch.

Rachel kissed his cheek quickly before opening the car door and getting out, waving as he sped off. She was baffled; everything had been fine. He'd been enjoying himself, she could tell. Then everything had changed; *he* had changed as soon as he'd looked at his phone. Until he could find the words to explain it to her Rachel had made up her mind. She wouldn't be going out with Nick Cunningham again.

Chapter 17

Grace giggled as Simon nibbled her earlobe and unhooked her bra. When she knew that Rachel was going out on a date with Nick, the plan had been to have Simon over for lunch and watch a film, but no sooner had they sat on the sofa together, they began kissing like two lovesick teenagers. It felt amazing. Natural, yet electrifying at the same time. Grace couldn't believe that just from some time apart Simon was being this passionate. Somehow, everything seemed new and fresh again. Simon felt like a stranger.

'Shall we go upstairs?' he'd asked breathlessly with a suggestive glint in his eye after a short while.

'Yes,' Grace had laughed, wanting nothing more.

'You're sure this is what you want?' he asked considerately.

Grace had smiled, rolled her eyes and pulled him off the sofa with urgency. 'I'm certain.'

Now they were lying in their warm cosy bed. It was hard to believe that only months ago Simon had been sleeping here snoring, Grace awake next to him worrying about their relationship.

Grace snuggled up to Simon's warm body, feeling his soft kisses all over her neck. How she'd missed this. How she missed being intimate with her husband and feeling wanted by him. She certainly hadn't felt wanted at the end, both of them knowing they were only having sex in the hope that Grace would get pregnant. It hadn't been enjoyable, and Grace had found herself thinking about things such as the washing that needed to be put on and emails she had to respond to.

'That feels good,' Grace groaned.

The sound of the front door banging downstairs made the pair of them freeze.

'Hello! Grace?' came Rachel's voice from downstairs.

'Shit,' Grace muttered under her breath. 'I didn't think she'd be home this soon.'

'Why does it matter?' Simon whispered, continuing to kiss her collarbone.

Grace gave a heavy sigh. 'I don't want them to know about us just yet, that's why. I'm just not ready,' she said quietly.

'Grace? I'm coming up,' Rachel called out.

'You're going to have to hide,' Grace hissed to Simon.

He looked horrified. 'What? Hide? I'm your husband, for Christ's sake!'

'Please,' Grace pleaded in hushed tones. 'Things are going well between us. I don't want anything to ruin it.'

'Okay,' Simon jumped up at lighting speed, slipping under the bed, just before Rachel knocked on the door.

'Grace?'

'Yes,' Grace replied, sitting up in the bed. 'You can come in.' She almost laughed out loud at the thought of Simon under the bed in only his boxers. Just imagine if Rachel spotted him!

'Oh, you're in bed?' Rachel looked surprised as she opened the door. 'Are you ill?'

Grace stretched her arms. 'Just had a little nap, that's all. I wasn't feeling too well, no, but I feel much better now.' She forced a yawn. 'How did the date go? You're back earlier than expected.'

Rachel looked unsure. 'It was weird. It was good and bad. I began to really like him, but then he went all peculiar at the end

143

when he got a message on his phone. He wouldn't tell me about it either. I'm not sure what to think.'

'Why don't we go out and you tell me all about it?' Grace suggested, thinking it was a good idea to get out of the house so that Simon could leave unnoticed afterwards. 'What about to Vic's bar? I'll just quickly throw some clothes on.'

'Okay, good idea,' Rachel replied.

'Give me five minutes and I'll be downstairs.'

As soon as Rachel had closed the door, Grace pulled on a jumper and peered under the bed, laughing. 'Sorry about that, I tried to get her out as quickly as possible. I'll get dressed and you can go after we've left.'

Simon stood up, pulling Grace towards him, kissing her hungrily. 'Couldn't you have made it fifteen minutes?' he panted desperately.

'Not now, Simon,' Grace said in regretful tones. 'We can't. Perhaps it wasn't the best idea in the first place. We're supposed to be taking things slow, aren't we?'

Simon pouted looking like a child who'd just had his favourite toy snatched away and Grace kissed his cheek softly. 'I'm sorry.'

'No, you're probably right,' Simon told her. 'We should be taking things slow. I want it to work and if that means waiting, then wait we shall. It's not going to be easy though.' He looked serious. 'I've missed you, Grace. I've missed this. The thought that I'd lost you makes me realize how lucky I was to have you in the first place.'

'Text me, okay?' Grace said, kissing him once more before going downstairs to Rachel who was ready and waiting by the front door.

'Ready?' she asked.

Grace nodded, 'Yep, ready. Right, I want to hear all about this date.'

Thirty minutes later they were sitting in Vic's bar sipping two cocktails.

'I think you should just ask him outright what's wrong. You should demand to know why his mood changed so much,' Grace advised, perusing the food menu on their table.

'I did! He just changed the subject. He clearly wasn't up for talking about it. Honestly, he turned from hot to cold in a few seconds. I feel like giving up on men altogether,' Rachel exhaled, tapping her nails on the table in front of her. 'We need to be single for the Christmas ball anyway, don't we? We made a pact. So perhaps I should just wait until the New Year to start dating again. Maybe I should just accept that this year isn't my year to be lucky in love. And you know what? I'm fine with that. I actually feel different about settling down since Mark and I split. There's no rush. You can't force it. So long as I'm happy in my life, who cares if I'm single?'

'Exactly, though you shouldn't give up on Nick just yet. He deserves a chance, at least, if you do like him. I'm sure you'll find out what's up soon.'

'Maybe I don't want to know,' Rachel fretted. 'Maybe he's married or something and his wife keeps calling him? Maybe he's in debt and owes lots of money? Or maybe someone in his family is ill? It could be anything, couldn't it? It's obviously something he doesn't want me to know about.'

'I guess,' Grace said, her mind elsewhere. She wondered what Simon was doing with the rest of his day. He'd already sent her a message saying how he couldn't wait to see her again. They were going to go to the cinema one evening in the week to watch the new Christmas film that was out and Grace was already looking forward to it. It was even more thrilling that she was seeing him in secret too.

'Anyway, I shouldn't moan and complain about being unlucky I guess. You're in the same boat as me, most likely about to go through a divorce and you never complain, do you? I need to be more relaxed like you. You never panic about your age and the fact that you thought you'd have kids by now. Sometimes I can't believe I'm still dating, but then I've come to learn it's really not the be-all and end-all.' She raised her eyebrows.

Grace was taken aback slightly, unsure how to answer; the truth was, she wasn't in the same boat as Rachel at all. She was seeing Simon again and they were already married. She didn't know for certain that things were going to work out and wouldn't just go back to how they were before, but she did know that right now she felt happy and content. They were back on the right track. 'Exactly.' She cleared her throat and studied her nails, unable to look Rachel in the eye. 'And you will meet someone, Rach, one day. I just know you will.'

Rachel narrowed her eyes at Grace suspiciously. 'What about you?'

'I'm happy being single.' Grace gave a nervous laugh, her eyes flicking back to the menu.

Rachel's eyes were thin as slits as she observed Grace's every move. 'You're seeing someone, aren't you? I knew you seemed happy this morning. There's no way that smile was from something your sister said so don't deny it,' she stated boldly, looking certain she was right.

Grace opened her mouth to protest but decided against it. What was the point in lying? 'You're right.' She smiled widely.

'I knew it!' Rachel laughed. 'Oh my God, Grace, I can't believe it. You've really taken this dating game like a bull by the horns, haven't you? You've surprised me. I need to take a leaf out of your book. I didn't even realize you'd been going out with people. Who is it? That Steve guy from the wedding?' Rachel didn't wait for an answer. 'Good for you. I admire you for not only leaving a relationship that clearly wasn't working, but being brave enough to seek happiness elsewhere. You've always believed in happy endings, haven't you? Maybe it's about time I did too.'

Grace couldn't speak. The words were on the tip of her tongue that it was Simon she was seeing again. The man she'd been unhappy with. But looking at Rachel's respectful gaze the words just wouldn't leave her mouth. She remained silent and questioned why that was. Was she embarrassed that she'd run straight back to the comfort and familiarity of her husband? Or were things going so well that she didn't want to jinx it and hear any negativity about the situation?

'So, are you seeing him again soon?' Rachel asked curiously.

'This week,' Grace answered, feeling relief that at least this part wasn't a lie. She was usually so honest and lying really didn't come naturally to her. 'We're going to see a Christmas film at the cinema.'

'Oh lovely.' Rachel shot her a friendly smile. 'So do you think things could become serious between the two of you? What's Steve like?'

Grace took a deep breath, trying to work out what to say. 'I think they could become serious, yes. I wasn't sure at first; I wasn't certain he could make me happy, but he's beginning to change my mind.'

Rachel beamed. 'I'm so happy for you, Grace. It's lovely to see you looking so full of life again. It just goes to show, doesn't it? You wasted all those years being married to the wrong guy, and now, here you are, smiling from ear to ear about someone new. You give me hope,' she told her excitedly.

Rachel's phone vibrated then, and her face lit up as she read a message. 'It's Nick,' she said brightly. 'He's apologising for his behaviour and asked to meet up again.'

Grace tucked her hair behind her ears and tried to push aside the feelings of guilt because she hadn't been entirely truthful to her friend. She flashed her a hopeful smile. 'Perhaps you're about to start believing in happy endings much sooner than you think?'

Chapter 18

'So I told Gill she needs to start saying no to babysitting all her grandkids. She had Ollie's children every day of the week while Suzy went to work and then Caroline's three stayed over Monday and Tuesday night. The poor woman doesn't get a break; she looks tired all the time. I told her it's time to start saying no.'

'Most definitely,' Diane agreed, looking slightly outraged. 'People don't seem to be looking after their own children these days. They're always relying on their parents or putting them into nurseries all day.'

Amber drummed her fingers on the table in the bar they were sitting in as she listened to the mundane conversation between her mother and Diane. Where was Jack? She'd called him earlier that day to confirm where they were meeting at the O2 and he'd seemed to be really looking forward to it. She glanced at her watch again noticing that he was now twenty-five minutes late.

'He's probably caught up with work,' Amber's mother stated, reading Amber's mind.

'Yes, he does tend to work long hours,' Diane said in agreement, checking her phone. 'He hasn't called me so I assume he's just running a little behind. Why don't you call him, Amber?' she suggested.

Amber tried calling Jack for the second time, frustrated when it went straight through to voicemail again. Still, perhaps that meant he was on the tube unable to get signal. They were right; Jack was most likely working later than planned, unable to get out of the office. She wished he'd hurry up though; it certainly wasn't the same without him.

'Did you hear that Rosie Connolly's daughter is pregnant with twins? Identical girls apparently,' Amber's mother said, changing the subject and turning back to Diane who gasped in shock.

Amber heaved a heavy sigh. It wasn't like Jack to be late. She wasn't worried about him coming though; he'd never let them all down, but she couldn't help but wonder what the hold up was. Maybe there was a signal failure and he was stuck on the tube? He still had plenty of time before the concert started.

'Another wine?' Amber's mother offered. 'Shall we get Jack a beer for when he arrives?'

Amber's mobile rang then and she smiled when she spotted Jack's name flashing on the screen. 'I'll just ask him; that's him calling now,' she said happily.

'Hello, Ambs?' Jack's voice came down the phone.

'Yes, where are you? We're waiting in the bar and just wondered what drink to order you. Beer?'

There was a pause. 'Listen, tell your mum, and mine for that matter, that I'm really sorry I can't make it,' he said.

Amber's heart sank and she frowned deeply. 'Why? What's happened?' she questioned wanting to scream in disappointment.

'It's Natalya; she's really unwell, the poor thing. Her parents are away and she lives alone. She needs someone with her,' he said.

Amber was fuming and struggled to hide the anger in her voice. 'Hasn't she got any friends to sit with her? We've all been really looking forward to this. Surely she has someone else?'

'Apparently not,' he replied, sounding just as upset for letting them all down. 'Most of her friends live quite far away from her.'

'Right,' Amber said in disbelief, biting her lip furiously. There was no way that Natalya was ill and there was even less chance that she didn't have someone else to look after her. This was about control and power. It was about the fact she hadn't been invited to the concert. It was about showing Amber who was boss. How could Jack be so oblivious? Couldn't he see what Natalya was doing?

'She feels really bad and wanted to say sorry to all of you,' Jack added.

'I'm sure she does.' Amber couldn't help but laugh sarcastically.

'What do you mean by that?' Jack asked, his voice becoming sharp and unfamiliar. 'She's not going to make up being ill, Amber,' he said, sounding unable to believe that she was hinting at such a thing.

'I know, I know,' Amber said hastily, cursing herself. 'Forget I said that. Wish her well from me and we'll speak soon,' she said sadly. Jack was making it very clear that he wouldn't tolerate Amber saying anything bad about his precious Natalya. It saddened Amber; they had been so close once, but now she just felt he was slipping away. She loved Jack and would love nothing more to be with him, but right now, she would be lucky if she even got to be his friend. It felt like he was being torn from her into the arms of a psychotic bitch. Slowly but surely, Jack was being manipulated and was exactly where Natalya wanted him.

'What's happened?' Diane asked, when Amber put the phone down. 'Why is he not coming?'

'Natalya,' Amber replied, still seething inside. 'She's really ill and needs Jack to look after her. Her parents are away and her friends don't live close enough.' She knew she sounded as though she didn't believe it, but she didn't care. It was a lie. Amber could feel it in her heart.

'Oh, what a shame,' Diane replied crestfallen. 'I was looking forward to seeing him.'

'Ah but there's not much he can do if his girlfriend's ill, is there?' Amber's mother said, clicking her tongue. 'Such a nice boy going to look after her. Perhaps she has the flu; I can't believe how many people I've heard that have gone down with it. Still, I guess it's the cold bringing people down, isn't it? My sister is always ill at Christmas. Every single year, I swear it.'

Amber's nose felt tingly and her eyes burnt, threatening tears. 'Yes Mum, I'm sure it's probably the flu,' she pretended to agree, attempting breezier tones. She cleared her throat. She was going to have to swallow it down and accept that Jack was always going to be on Natalya's side. He wasn't going to notice all the little ways she was trying to control him. Natalya was going to be the winner so Amber was going to have to be careful. She was going to have to do her best to ignore it, or she could lose Jack for good. She scraped her chair backwards and stood up. 'Now shall I get that wine?'

Amber decided not to call Jack the following day. She was too upset with the situation and, anyhow, meeting up with him alone was almost impossible now. As soon as Natalya caught wind of it, she'd be joining them with some excuse or another. Amber was just going to leave it to him to contact her.

She lay in bed feeling miserable, knowing what she had to do. She clicked onto Facebook and then through to Natalya's page. She remembered seeing her tagged into something with her mother and sister a few weeks back. Amber clicked through to Natalya's mother's page, noticing that she had her place of work stated. Natalya's mother, Lorraine, worked at a hair salon and Amber found herself clicking on the hair salon's Facebook page, her finger hovering over their telephone number. Should she call and check to see if Natalya's mother was away like she said? If she was away on holiday then Amber could relax a bit more and accept that maybe she was obviously a bit paranoid. Hopefully this was the case and then she would make sure she would relax where Natayla was concerned. It would mean Natalya was telling the truth and that Amber needed to give her a break. Was there a chance it was all in Amber's head because she wanted Jack for herself? Maybe Natalya was perfectly innocent?

Amber's heart began to beat faster as she clicked on the number and it started to ring.

'Hello, Sophie Louise hair salon,' said a young-sounding lady on the phone. Amber could picture her now; a teenager earning minimum wage with some kind of trendy hairstyle, bored out of her brains while she answered phones, swept the floors and if she was lucky, got to wash some hair.

Amber could hear the sound of hairdryers in the background as she opened her mouth to talk. 'Oh, hi there. I was just wondered if I could get a haircut today,' she spoke slowly.

'A haircut? What time did you want?'

'I don't mind,' Amber responded, feeling bad for wasting the poor girl's time. 'I was hoping that Lorraine could do it?'

'Lorraine?' The girl answered.

Amber's mouth was dry. This was the moment she was waiting for. 'Yes please. She cut it before, a while back. I was really rather impressed.'

'She can fit you in at one o'clock. Or she has three o'clock, but she's fully booked for the rest of the day apart from that.'

Amber exhaled slowly, relief flooding through her that she wasn't going insane. She *knew* Natalya was lying. 'Was Lorraine in yesterday?' she questioned, just in case Natalya's parents had only arrived back late the night before or something.

'Errr … yes,' she said sounding puzzled. 'Lorraine was in all day yesterday. Did you want to book in today?'

'I'll just see if I can rearrange a few things and call back,' Amber told her, keen to get off the phone.

'Okay. no problem.'

Amber hung up and stretched out in bed. She had been right, just as she feared. She needed to get up for work; she was going in later today after booking the morning off a while back. She'd

152

assumed she'd be a little hungover after drinking with Jack at the concert, but after being stuck alone with just their mums, she felt as right as rain. She'd only had a couple of glasses of wine in the end.

An hour later, just as Amber had parked her car and was about to walk into work, her mobile rang. She was surprised, yet happy to see it was Jack calling. Maybe he'd worked out that Natalya was lying and had called to tell her? Maybe he could finally see her for what she truly was?

'Morning,' she answered, unable to help but smile.

'More like afternoon. You on your lunch break?' he asked.

'I took the morning off,' Amber explained, putting her car keys in her bag as she walked to Tidemans.

'How was last night?' he asked.

'Rod was good, sang loads of Christmas songs you would have loved, but it wasn't the same without my singing buddy,' she admitted despondently. 'How is Natalya?' she forced herself to ask. *The lying little cow.*

'She's feeling a lot better today thankfully,' he replied. 'She's gone to work.'

Amber rolled her eyes. 'That's good. Lucky it wasn't something serious,' she said, trying to sound genuine when she was really being caustic.

'Yes, she's feeling fine now, which is good. I feel so bad not going last night though. I still have your mum's card and present to give her. I just spoke to my mum and I've arranged to make you all dinner to say sorry on Friday night at my place.'

Amber's spirits lifted a little, but her thoughts immediately turned to Natalya. 'Who will be going?' she questioned, assuming that she was worming her way in somehow.

'Just our mums and us,' he said. 'I owe it to you all for bailing out.'

'It wasn't your fault,' Amber told him, feeling immensely pleased that Natalya wasn't invited.

'I know, but still, it's going to be 7.30 p.m. on Friday at mine, okay?'

'Perfect,' Amber smiled widely.

She opened the door to Tidemans feeling a little better about everything. But there was still a niggling fear that she couldn't shift. A fear that Natalya was going to ruin this night in some way too and eventually take Jack away for good.

Chapter 19

Rachel couldn't help but notice that Amber looked distracted as she waltzed into work. Her mind was very clearly elsewhere.

'Everything okay? How was the concert?' she asked.

Amber pulled a face. 'It was great, thanks, but Jack didn't end up going. Natalya was ill.' She threw her eyes upwards. 'Such a liar. She would have said anything to stop him going.'

'What? Do you think she made it up so he wouldn't go?' Rachel was stunned someone would actually do that. 'I'm sure she wouldn't. Maybe she really was ill?'

'Of course she did!' Amber replied, looking thunderous and throwing her scarf and gloves off onto the counter as though it were their fault. 'Apparently there was no one around to look after her. She told Jack her parents were away. I wanted to check if I was going crazy being so suspicious and imagining things, so I called her mum's hair salon and found out it was just a big fat lie. Her mum is in work today and she was yesterday too. She made it all up. She's trying to control him. She wants Jack all to herself.'

'You actually called up the salon?' Grace asked in shock, appearing out of nowhere.

'Yes, I did. I know it may seem a bit stalkerish—' she held out

155

her hands '—but I had to know that I wasn't just being an over-protective friend.'

Rachel was astonished. Natalya had seemed really nice in person the day she came in to get her make-up done, and if she was honest, she'd just assumed everything bad Amber had said about her was because Amber was jealous that she was with Jack. But maybe she was wrong? 'What did Jack say?' she asked inquisitively.

'I haven't told him obviously,' Amber looked at Rachel as though she had two heads. 'I'm scared to say anything bad about her. He sticks up for her right away. Honestly, I feel like I'm treading on eggshells when we speak about her. He just can't see how manipulative she's being.'

'Maybe he knows but doesn't want to admit it to himself?' Grace offered. 'Or maybe he really doesn't see it. He obviously loves her; sometimes it's hard to see the faults in the ones we love.'

'Nonsense. You could see the faults in Simon, couldn't you?' Amber asked rhetorically. 'You weren't crazy enough to stay with him.'

Grace looked away looking slightly uneasy and Rachel assumed she was embarrassed she'd put up with it for so long.

Rachel didn't know what to say; she really felt for her friend. Amber was head over heels in love with Jack and Rachel couldn't believe she'd never seen it before. It was so obvious now Amber had finally admitted it. To watch him fall in love with another person was hard enough as it was, but for it to be someone deceitful and conniving was a different matter altogether. It was a very tricky situation and she understood that Amber didn't feel she could voice her opinions in fear of losing him.

'Changing the subject, has Grace told you she's in love?' Rachel grinned.

'I am not,' Grace gave a light laugh and turned her back on

them, looking a little self-conscious as she looked through the foundation drawer.

'Why have I not heard about this?' Amber asked interestedly. 'In love with who? Where did you meet him? Tell me everything.'

Grace stood up looking flushed. 'There's nothing to tell,' she said shyly.

'She's been seeing that Steve in secret. You know, the guy she met at the wedding she did make-up for a few weeks ago?' Rachel revealed, wondering why Grace was being so shady about it. The three of them usually told each other everything.

'Have you?' Amber looked impressed. 'Are things going well?'

'Yes,' Grace replied bashfully. 'Things are going well for us at the moment. I feel happy. Hopefully it stays this way.'

'I want to meet him,' Rachel said, keen to find out what he was like.

'Well, you can't bring him to the Christmas ball, remember? We made a pact. No dates. We go together,' Amber said in a mock-stern voice. Then she looked thoughtful. 'I bet you're going to end up going with Steve and you'll be with that moody Nick guy. I'm going to be single on my own, aren't I? Not that I care, you know me. I've always preferred to be single, but it's not like I could ask Jack – Natalya would never let him go with me. Can you imagine what story or excuse she'd come up with?'

'Stop worrying, there's really no need,' Grace tutted. 'We promised to go together, didn't we? So let's just stick with that plan.'

'Yes and I don't even know where I stand with Nick,' Rachel stated. 'He's on and off with me every time we meet.'

They'd planned to meet up again the following evening and Rachel was looking forward to it, but hoped he wouldn't be moody again. Why couldn't life ever be simple? Why couldn't Rachel just meet a straightforward man she liked? She knew she hadn't dated many people since Mark, and she certainly wasn't sure if she wanted to jump straight into another relationship, but she had really liked Nick. There had been something different about him. She couldn't deny that she liked the security of having a boyfriend. She loved feeling relaxed with the familiarity of the same person. She knew she wasn't cut out for being single all the time like Amber was. Being alone for a little while was fine and she was happy at the moment, but try as she might, Rachel couldn't help but worry that she was getting older. There wasn't as much time. She didn't want to be in her forties when she finally met the love of her life, only to discover that by then, it was too late and she'd missed the boat to have children. She craved a family. She thought back to when she was in primary school and their teacher at the time, Mrs Patterson, had asked them all to draw what they wanted to be when they were older. Thomas Murray had drawn a fireman and she recalled her friend, Lily Humphries, had drawn a nurse – a picture of her attending to someone in their hospital bed. Mrs Patterson had been impressed and funnily enough, the last Rachel had heard, Lily Humphries had gone on to be a doctor, so she'd been pretty accurate at seven years old about her future career. When Mrs Patterson had walked over to have a look at Rachel's drawing, she stood above her in bafflement.

'Rachel, what have you drawn?' she asked her.

'A mother,' Rachel had looked up and explained. 'I want to be a mother.'

She hadn't understood Mrs Patterson's face crinkling in amusement back then.

Rachel was brought back from her memory as she turned around on the make-up counter and spotted Bianca standing there staring at her. Rachel's jaw dropped open and her face grew hot. It took a few moments to digest what she was seeing. How on earth did Bianca have the nerve to turn up at her workplace unannounced? Rachel had been caught off guard and it was a horrible, vulnerable feeling. Like one of those dreams when you looked down and realized you were naked in public.

'Hello, Rachel,' Bianca said in a tiny voice. She looked nervous. 'I was wondering if you could spare a few moments to talk?'

Rachel was pleased to see how ill at ease Bianca looked; she knew it must have taken a lot of courage to come and she guessed it showed she actually did care. She was due her lunch break now that Amber had arrived but wasn't entirely sure she wanted to listen to anything Bianca had to say. She hated her. Her so-called friend had messed up her life, hadn't she? She took a deep breath trying to compose herself. She refused to feel intimidated or unnerved; Rachel wasn't the one who had done anything wrong.

'What is it you have to say?' she demanded, folding her arms across her chest imperiously.

'Can we go somewhere?' Bianca looked around, 'Somewhere private?'

Rachel sighed. 'I'll meet you in the café on the third floor in five minutes,' she replied reluctantly. She knew Bianca didn't deserve the time of day, but Rachel couldn't help but feel curious as to what she had come to say.

'Wow, she's brave,' Amber muttered in lowered tones, as Bianca walked away.

'Do you think you'll forgive her?' Grace wondered.

'I have no idea what she's going to say, but I've agreed to meet her now.'

'Well, good luck,' Amber said sweetly, squeezing her hand before Rachel walked to the escalators.

She noticed Bianca sitting at a table in the middle of the busy café straightaway. She had two mugs on the table. *It'll take more than a cup of coffee to make it up to me after what you did.*

As Rachel made her way over she inhaled slowly. She couldn't look at Bianca the same way; she just wasn't the person she'd thought she was.

'Thanks for seeing me,' Bianca started in a wobbly voice, her mouth twitching with anxiety.

Bianca was usually so confident and loud; it was so strange seeing her sitting there looking sorry for once.

Christmas music was playing softly in the background and there were people sitting on other tables looking cheerful, chilling out after a long day Christmas shopping. Rachel felt anything but chilled out.

'Well, I haven't got long,' Rachel replied, glancing at her watch.

'I didn't know if you wanted something to eat; I would have bought you lunch. That turkey soup looks delicious,' she said, glancing over to another table as they ate.

'Thanks, but I'll eat afterwards,' Rachel said coldly. Lunch wasn't going to fix the fact she'd betrayed her in the worst way possible. 'I heard congratulations are in order,' she said, jutting her chin upwards.

Bianca looked discomfited, as she studied her nails. 'It wasn't planned, obviously,' she said weakly.

'I can't imagine it was, no. Mark was still with me when you got pregnant, wasn't he? I certainly can't envisage Mark purposely trying to knock up his girlfriend's best mate before he had the decency to leave her, can you?' she said hotly.

Bianca looked ashamed. 'I don't know what to say. I didn't come here to fight with you. I know what we did was terrible and we've apologized. Both of us have. I just miss you so much; you're my best friend.'

As Rachel gazed at Bianca she couldn't believe the way she now felt about her. It was like she was a different person. She used to think Bianca had her back; she'd been the fun and cool one, and Rachel had believed she'd have been there through anything. She knew that Bianca had depended on her more though, that was the way their friendship had always been. When Bianca wanted to complain about the way some man had treated her, it would be Rachel listening to her. If Bianca had needed a lift somewhere, it was Rachel she would call. Rachel was always lending her money that Bianca conveniently forgot about. Lending her clothes that she would stain and hand back unwashed. Looking back, it was clear to see that Rachel had been taken advantage of. What had Bianca ever actually done for her? Rachel couldn't think of a single thing. Now, as she looked at her stooped shoulders and guilty expression, Rachel couldn't help but feel sorry for her. Bianca was the one who had lost a true mate. It was Bianca who was missing her loyal, trustworthy friend. Rachel actually hadn't missed Bianca much at all. Cutting her out of her life had been a lot more painless than Rachel had ever imagined. She didn't *need* Bianca at all. She'd never needed her and looking back, she couldn't believe she'd let Bianca treat her the way she had. Bianca was just a user.

'I don't know, it's probably my hormones, but I just feel really down at the moment. I'm sad about what's happened. Not about the getting pregnant part, but the fact I've pushed you away. It's not been easy for me, Rach. None of this has.'

'What about me?' Rachel snapped back curtly. 'It's still about poor little you, Bianca, isn't it? No thought for anyone else. You've always been like that; I've just been too much of a pushover to ever notice it. Everything you've done has been brought on yourself.'

Bianca nodded solemnly, slowly breathing outwards. 'I know that. I didn't mean for it to sound as though it was all about me. I know you're the victim in this. I just want to be friends again; I know it's a lot to ask. But I really need you. I can't stop being sick,' Bianca laughed, clearly hoping she would smile back, but Rachel remained expressionless. 'I can't believe they call it morning sickness when I'm literally feeling sick all day.'

'My heart bleeds for you,' Rachel shot sarcastically.

'Can you find it in your heart to ever forgive me?' Bianca's eyes were wide, watery and full of fear.

Rachel breathed out slowly. 'Probably. One day,' she replied. 'But I could never be friends with you again, Bianca. I could never trust you again, not like before.'

'I understand that. I really do,' Bianca said hopefully. 'But perhaps in time we can be friends again. You'll feel different about it all, I'm sure you will. I can't imagine you not being in my baby's life, Rach…'

'I won't be,' Rachel interjected, truly disturbed by the thought. 'I'm sorry Bianca. I'll eventually forgive you, but I'll never forget. I can never be friends with you again. Not now and not ever. Do you understand? You've always treated me poorly. It's just taken me a really long time to see it. I've been the better friend, despite all of this, and you know it. Did you honestly think you could lie to me and steal my boyfriend and everything would be okay again? Good old Rachel, forgiving you again like she has before. I know I've always given you another chance for some awful things you've done to me in the past, but not this. *Never* for this.'

'I can't believe you're saying these things to me. When have I ever been a bad friend to you?'

'When have you ever been a good friend?' Rachel challenged defiantly.

Bianca looked stuck for words.

'Exactly,' Rachel said sadly. 'That's exactly my point. Now if you don't mind, I'm hungry, and I want to go and eat. Alone.'

With that, Rachel pulled back her chair, stood up and marched away, without looking back.

Chapter 20

'Where are we going?' Grace asked in enthusiastic tones.

'Now that would be telling,' Simon grinned in amusement. 'It's somewhere you'll like. It'll be fun.'

Grace nodded, flashing Simon a smile. She loved surprises. This reminded her of when she'd first met Simon and he used to whisk her away to unusual places without telling her. Their relationship had always been so special and exciting at the start. She couldn't remember when it had changed, but eventually it had, and even a trip to the local cinema had become a thing of the past.

They were on a train going into London and Grace linked arms with Simon and snuggled up a bit closer as she tried to keep warm.

'I've missed you the last few days,' Simon told her affectionately.

Grace couldn't help but beam. 'I've missed you too.' She had such a warm and happy feeling inside, she never wanted it to end. She was delighted that Simon was making such an effort to change, clearly wanting to do anything and everything he could to save their marriage. The truth was, she'd have been heartbroken if he hadn't. She realized that now.

As they got off the train and walked along the street together,

Grace frowned. 'Are we going over there?' she asked him, pointing to an ice rink in the distance.

'I don't know what you're talking about,' Simon replied, half-smiling.

'That's definitely where we're going,' Grace said again, knowingly. 'I know you, Simon. You're great at skating too; I think you're going to have fun showing me up,' she laughed good-naturedly.

'Don't worry,' Simon laughed back, 'I'll help you up when you fall down.'

Grace shoved him playfully. 'You never know, it might be the other way round.' She giggled, excited to go skating. She hadn't been in years.

'Mulled wine?' Simon offered, looking over to a man selling it next to the ice rink.

'I see your plan, Simon Chapman,' she said in mock serious tones, narrowing her eyes. 'You're trying to get me drunk so I'm not as good as you are on the rink.'

'Suit yourself,' Simon smiled widely.

'I'll have one after,' Grace told him, never able to turn down mulled wine. 'I'm going to need my wits about me.'

Skating was fun and Grace tried her best to stay upright, but laughed good-humouredly when she slipped over several times, taking Simon's strong arm to pull her back up again. As he pulled her up the last time, he took her into his arms and kissed her softly on the lips. 'Why don't we do things like this anymore?' he questioned sadly.

'I've been thinking the exact same thing, Simon. We used to always go out doing different things. One day it just seemed to change.'

He kissed her again then. 'Well, I want it to change back. I've missed this. I've missed *us*.'

Grace took his hand and pulled him off the rink. 'I think it's time for my mulled wine now,' she told him cheekily. 'A nice walk and a mulled wine sounds perfect.'

As they walked along the busy streets they stopped and listened to a group singing Christmas carols.

'I don't want to leave you tonight,' Simon told her. 'Stay with me,' he said longingly.

Grace bit her lip, feeling exactly the same. Now they were back spending time together, fixing the problems in their relationship, she wanted to be with Simon all the time. It was killing her that she wasn't waking up next to him every day. Or was that all part of the excitement? Seeing him in secret and creeping around together was thrilling, there was no denying that. 'But where though? I'm not staying at yours. No offense, but I remember how untidy your cousin Paul's place was.' She pulled a face. 'You can't come to mine either. Rachel is there and, as I said, I don't want to tell people about us just yet.'

'Then we'll get a hotel,' he said gazing into her eyes with desire. 'We're surrounded by them, after all. I don't care how much it costs; I just want to be with you for the night. The whole night.' He looked around. 'We can get the train to work early in the morning.'

Simon began to kiss Grace's neck gently and she could feel any reservations she had slowly starting to weaken. She wanted Simon and he was her husband. It would be silly to wait any longer before they spent the night together. It felt different somehow too; as though they'd been apart for years and desperately needed each other.

'Okay,' she whispered breathlessly.

Simon grinned. 'Let's go find a hotel. The very best one around.'

There was something enthralling about booking a hotel for the night and Grace couldn't wait until they were alone. She hadn't been certain that the spark she was now feeling was ever going to come back. She'd resigned herself to the fact that everyone's relationships eventually turned a bit sour, mundane and routine. Now she was feeling delirious with passion again, and it was a fantastic feeling. She'd forgotten what it felt like.

The hotel room was nothing special – just an average double bedroom with basic amenities, even though it had cost Simon a small fortune, but Grace couldn't have cared less where they were. Being together again was all that mattered.

'I should tell Rachel I'm not coming home. She'll be worried otherwise. She's actually going on a date herself tonight.'

'Where did you tell her you were going?' Simon wondered, cocking his head to one side as he sat down on the bed and lay back.

Grace pressed her lips together. 'She made the assumption that I'm seeing this guy,' she told him, feeling uncomfortable and not wanting to divulge further.

'Was there another guy?' Simon ventured, his eyes full of fear.

'No!' Grace told him quickly. 'It was nothing. It was just one date and I only did it so they would stop going on at me to start enjoying being single. I wasn't ready. It was weird going out with someone else. It was strange that it wasn't you,' she explained sincerely.

Simon closed his eyes momentarily. 'You don't have to feel bad, you know. So, you went on a date? It's no big deal. Let's just not talk about it again though, okay? It scares me that I could have lost you for good. Now come here,' he said suggestively, patting the bed next to him.

'Not just yet,' Grace said with a smirk. 'I'm just going to get a little more comfortable. It's quite hot in here, don't you think?' She asked seductively, raising an eyebrow as she peeled off her cardigan and blouse.

Simon was gawping at her, as though Christmas had come early and Grace had to prevent herself from laughing at how transfixed he was as she pulled off her clothes to reveal some new sexy red underwear. She was so glad she'd worn it now, though she honestly hadn't planned for this to happen. She'd seen the neglected underwear at the back of her drawer when she was getting ready and she could hardly remember wearing it before or buying it. The doubts about rushing too fast into getting back together seemed to have gone out the window and Grace simply couldn't help herself. This wasn't a cheap and tacky one night stand. This wasn't a fling. She was with her husband; Grace just needed to take a leap of faith and trust that the change in him wasn't temporary.

Simon's mouth was open as she made her way over to him, and Grace pushed it shut before starting to unbutton his shirt.

The next morning Simon's alarm went off early at 6 a.m., and Grace's face creased into a smile as he cuddled up close to her and kissed her cheek.

'Morning,' he said in a sleepy voice.

'Morning,' she replied, closing her eyes again. The bed was so lovely and warm that she didn't ever want to leave it.

'God, it's so nice to be waking up to you again,' he replied, snuggling up to her, his head resting on her shoulder. 'I'd love to just call in sick, but I can't.'

'Me either. I couldn't leave the girls short staffed and they'd think I'd decided to spend the day with my mystery man. They'd be demanding to meet him then; they already keep telling me how keen they are to be introduced.'

Simon looked at his watch and heaved himself out of bed. 'I need to get ready otherwise I'll be late. Shall we quickly grab a coffee and some breakfast downstairs before we leave?'

Forty minutes later they were at the train station. Simon wasn't going home before work, seeing as they were already in London, but accompanied Grace on the walk.

Grace scrunched her nose up. 'Aren't work going to notice you're in the same clothes today?'

Simon laughed. 'I work in media; half of them wear the same clothes all week. Anyway, I have a spare jumper I'm going to change into when I get in.'

She hugged him in the entrance to the station. 'Thank you for yesterday and last night. I really had a good time.'

He kissed her softly. 'Me too. I'll send you a message about where I'm taking you next. Then maybe next time I'll just stay at the house rather than us keep booking hotel rooms.'

Grace was looking forward to it already, but felt awkward about Simon coming back home, even if just for one night. Rachel would be there. She wasn't sure why, but because things were going so well she didn't want anyone else to know about them. She liked Simon being a secret. She didn't need to listen to everyone else's concerns and opinions. She could make her own mind up and if she wanted to believe that Simon was serious about changing, and if she wanted to give him another chance, then that was her choice. She didn't want to be influenced by anybody else. She worried that Amber and Rachel would just think she was scared of being single so she'd run straight back to him for convenience. 'I don't know if that's a good idea. I'm not really ready to start telling everyone about us.'

Simon's forehead creased with lines. 'Really? But why, Grace? We're not doing anything wrong. What are you so afraid of? Why do you care what people think? We're married for Christ's sake.' He shook his head in puzzlement and disbelief.

Grace bit her lip and wrapped her scarf around her neck tighter. 'I can't explain it, Simon. I've told them all about how unhappy I've been. I can't admit I've just run straight back to you so soon. They'll tell me I'm crazy giving you another chance, I just know it. I've promised to be single; we even made a pact to all be single at our work Christmas ball...'

'So I'm not invited to that?' Simon looked hurt. 'I mean, it's not the fact I'm not going to the ball, it's the fact that you'd rather go without me. Alone, or single as you've just put it. I've always been with you every year.'

Grace frowned. 'Yes, you have Simon. But things haven't been good between us for a long time. It's going great at the minute

168

and I'm really happy. I don't want to rush straight back into our relationship for all the problems to still be there. I can't and won't do that. I'm terrified of that happening. You need to let me get there in my own time, okay? I don't want to feel pressured,' she told him worriedly. They'd had the most wonderful night together and she really didn't want it to be ruined. Couldn't Simon see that he couldn't just jump straight back into her life immediately?

'Okay, I get it,' he said understandably, taking her hand. 'Whatever you want to do, I'm down with, okay? I understand you don't want me to move back in right now or anything drastic like that, and I can see why you would be afraid. But things will be different from now on between us, I promise you, Grace. If it takes you a long time to see that then I'll just have to wait. I don't understand why you can't tell your friends, but that's your choice.'

'Just give me time, okay?' Grace asked, looking into his grey eyes. She was relieved he was accepting her decision to keep quiet about the fact they were rekindling their relationship. She was glad he was considering her feelings and willing to do whatever she wanted. But picturing the Christmas ball without him by her side made her feel sad inside. She desperately wanted Simon to be there; it wouldn't be the same without him. But she could never let her friends down by bringing him along, could she?

Chapter 21

'Cheers,' Amber's mother said in merry tones, as they clinked their champagne glasses together.

'Cheers,' they all joined in.

Amber smiled widely. She loved nothing more than when it was the four of them together and she couldn't believe the effort that Jack had gone to. The table was laid out delightfully. Red napkins with ornate gold napkin holders had been displayed beautifully by their large gold plates. Large white and red candles had been lit and the food Jack had just brought to the table looked delicious. He even had Rod Stewart's Christmas album gently playing in the background.

'It's very nice and festive,' Diane chuckled in approval. 'Honestly, Jack, I didn't know you had it in you to make such a beautiful dinner. All those years I used to cook for you and you were hiding these amazing culinary skills.'

Jack laughed. 'You haven't tried it yet,' he said, passing the dauphinoise potatoes. 'Thanks though; I thought I'd get into the Christmas theme with the red table decorations. I can't believe it's only in a few weeks to be honest. I haven't even done much shopping.'

'Typical man leaving it until the last minute,' Amber's mother giggled happily. 'What will you be buying your fiancée? Oh, it feels weird saying that,' she said, her lips turning upwards. 'Feels like only yesterday that you two were small being mischievous together. Do you remember that Christmas, Diane, when they managed to sneak a bottle of brandy up to Jack's bedroom? Only just seventeen you were I think. Jack ended up handing it back because they didn't like the taste.'

Diane laughed heartily and Amber couldn't help but smile herself when she caught Jack's eye.

'I'm not sure what I'm buying Natalya just yet,' Jack revealed, cutting up the chicken on his plate. 'I guess I'll need Amber's expertise in that department.'

Amber swallowed hard, unable to bear the thought of shopping for Natalya. She forced a smile. 'Of course. Whenever you like. You know I'll always help you buy presents.'

'So, Amber,' Diane began in between a mouthful of food, 'how's your love life? Have you met anyone nice enough to sweep you off your feet yet?'

Amber's mother snorted. 'That'll be the day; she's too fussy.'

Amber tutted. 'I am not. I'm just…' She searched for the word. 'Selective. I don't jump into relationships easily. They're usually complicated and I find it easier being alone.'

, 'You've never met anyone good enough for you, I've always said that,' Jack said in agreement. Amber stared at him and smiled thanks. *He* was good enough for her. If only he would see it.

'Where is Natalya tonight?' Diane asked inquisitively, and Amber wondered if she was thinking the same thing: how come she's allowed this to happen without intervening?

As Jack opened his mouth to answer, there was a sound at the front door and Amber's heart plummeted when Natalya waltzed through the door holding a cake in her arms.

Jack looked shocked to see her there. 'Hi.' He stood up and kissed her, 'I wasn't expecting you to come round?'

'Hi everyone.' She quickly glanced in their direction. 'I'm so sorry to intrude on your evening.' Then she turned to Jack in a hushed voice, but obviously aware that everyone could hear her. 'I'm just bringing you the other dessert I said I'd make. Not everyone will like fruitcake. Did you take the potatoes out of the oven when I said?'

'Oh, that's nice, you've brought a dessert over,' Amber's mother grinned. 'She must be a keeper Jack. Will you not join us, Natalya? Seems silly to have all this food and only four of us.'

Amber rolled her eyes, not caring if anybody saw her. She could feel the anger coming off her in waves and had to refrain from telling her mother to be quiet. Her mother had absolutely no idea that this was obviously all planned on purpose. Amber had been a fool to think they were really going to spend the evening just the four of them. Of course Natalya was going to spoil it. Obviously she wouldn't have been able to miss out.

'Oh no, don't be silly,' Natalya replied, her voice shrill, flicking her hair. 'I couldn't possibly impose. I was just bringing over this chocolate cake I made. Jack was going to buy one, but I told him that homemade is so much nicer. I thought not everyone would like the fruitcake he's got.'

'I do,' Amber said sharply, folding her arms across her chest. 'I love fruitcake.'

'Well, you may as well join us now you're here,' Jack offered, going to the kitchen to get another plate.

'Don't be silly,' Natalya protested without conviction. She was already taking her coat off.

'Take a seat, Natalya,' Diane told her kindly. 'You're here now and how lovely that you've made us a chocolate cake.'

'Well, if you all insist,' Natalya replied gratefully.

Amber was fuming, so much so that she couldn't even talk. She'd completely lost her appetite. This was weird; was she the only one to see that? Was everyone completely blind as to how Natalya was controlling the situation? It was getting ridiculous now. Just as Amber had thought and feared, she'd managed to gatecrash their evening. Just another strange thing to add to the list. She wondered what Jack thought about it. Why hadn't she given him the chocolate cake earlier? She was so transparent and it was driving Amber stir crazy.

'Sorry sweetie,' Jack said, handing Natalya the plate. 'I thought you were out tonight with Gemma. That's why I didn't ask you.'

'She cancelled,' Natalya responded, attempting to look disappointed. 'Besides, I know how you four have a special bond together.' She smiled. 'The last thing I'd ever want to do was get in the way. Jack has told me so much about you,' she said, her eyes flicking to Amber's mother. 'I'm Natalya, so nice to meet you.'

'She's beautiful, Jack,' Amber's mother complimented her. 'You're going to make a stunning bride, Natalya. Pleasure to meet you.'

Amber was screaming inside. She couldn't look up from her plate. What was the point in joining in any conversation with Natalya? She wanted nothing to do with her. It was getting to the point where she just felt like admitting defeat. If Natalya wanted to steal her best friend and he was ignoring the fact she was some kind of sick psychopath, then so be it. Amber wasn't sure she had the strength left to fight for him. She wasn't going to win; not against *her*. Jack was in love with Natalya, and Amber was just a family friend. Even though their friendship had always been tight, it was hardly going to last that way with Natalya around. She was pulling them apart, and Amber was no longer certain she could stop it. Natalya had the wool pulled over all their eyes, Amber thought, as she watched them all chatting politely round the table. Perhaps even Diane was now a fan; she certainly looked it as she admired her cashmere jumper and told her how much she loved her blonde highlights.

Amber knew that Natalya was beautiful, a real head-turner. But she was gutted that Jack had chosen to marry someone so downright fake.

'You okay, Amber?' Jack questioned. 'You seem a bit quiet?' He looked over at her with a concerned expression.

'Not feeling too well,' she lied. 'I hope none of you mind, but I think I may call it a night.' She pushed her plate away, aware of the puzzled glances they were shooting each other.

'But you've barely touched your food,' her mother pointed out.

'I'm not hungry,' Amber told them. That part wasn't a lie.

'Oh, what a shame,' Natalya said, probably sounding sweet and caring to the others, but nothing but sarcastic to Amber. 'But if you're not feeling well, perhaps it's best to get an early night. Make sure you cut yourself a slice of chocolate cake on your way out, won't you? It really is delicious.'

Amber blanked her, refusing to react like she knew Natalya probably wanted her to. She was most likely getting immense pleasure from the fact that Amber was leaving. Natalya's plan had worked perfectly.

'Well, if you're sure,' Jack said, standing up and walking her to the front door. 'It's a shame though.'

Amber let Jack help her put on her coat at the front door. 'Thanks for the dinner and everything. Sorry I'm leaving early.'

Lines appeared on Jack's forehead. 'Are you really okay? I feel like something is up with you. What is it? You know you can tell me anything,' he offered affectionately.

Amber stared at her handsome best friend and her heart ached for him. He was slipping away from her, when all she really wanted to do was confess her true feelings for him. Tell him that, in fact, she was in love with him and that despite all of this, he shouldn't be with someone like Natalya. But she would never do that. She couldn't watch him turn away from her. Losing him for good would hurt too much. She took a deep breath and gazed into his eyes.

'Are you happy, Jack?'

He looked confused, like it was a trick question.

'Yes,' he replied slowly. 'What does this have to do with me though?'

'Nothing,' Amber answered sadly. 'Nothing at all.' She kissed him goodbye and walked out into the street.

Fifteen minutes later she pulled up outside the block of apartments where she lived. It was freezing out, but it hadn't snowed in a while and Amber wondered if it would again and whether they would be lucky enough to have a white Christmas; she couldn't remember if that had ever happened before. Amber had lived in the same block all her life. She had grown up in number three and lived there with her mother until they heard number nine upstairs was available to rent when she was twenty-six. Finally deciding it was time to move out, Amber went for it, laughing with her mother that she was still in the same building. Still, it was good for when she got lonely and she would often find herself popping into her mother's apartment or vice versa. It was nice living so close if she ever needed her for anything, though eventually, Amber planned to buy her own place. A small house was the dream and Amber made sure she saved money every month when she could. There was a man standing outside her apartment block, peering through the door and for some reason, it made the back of the hairs stand up on her neck. He was ringing someone's number, but obviously wasn't being buzzed into the building. It was dark out, and Amber felt a little vulnerable as she walked over. She couldn't just let him in, could she? But she could hardly go in herself and slam the door in his face. Perhaps he was locked out? Though from behind she didn't recognize him as one of her neighbours.

She coughed to make him aware she was approaching and he quickly glanced behind, before ringing the doorbell again. It was at this point that Amber noticed he was ringing number three, her mother's apartment.

'Are you looking for someone?' Amber ventured nervously.

As the man turned to face her, Amber froze on the spot, recognising him instantly.

'As a matter of fact, I am,' he replied, shooting a friendly smile. 'I'm looking for Camilla Houghton? I'm not sure if she still lives here.'

Amber gulped, her whole world spinning around, making her feel dizzy. 'Dad?' she croaked. 'Dad, is that you?'

Chapter 22

Everything felt different. The sun seemed to be shining brighter, her skin seemed softer, more plump and glowy, and even her orange juice tasted fresher than usual. It was as though everything had a filter on it, making Rachel feel uplifted and joyous. Rachel knew she had never felt this way with Mark, not even once. Yet, she'd only been out with Nick three times so far and she couldn't stop thinking about him. He gave her hope that everything was going to be okay. A little laugh almost escaped her lips; perhaps everything really *did* happen for a reason? The fact she'd found him made her feel better about the whole Mark and Bianca situation. Maybe Nick was her true soulmate? What if everything was meant to happen so he could rescue her from the situation? Show her what a real, fun relationship was supposed to be like? She knew she was thinking too far ahead, but she couldn't help that. She'd never been able to help that. She didn't have time to waste with men at her age; if she didn't see them as a potential husband and father of her future children then she wouldn't bother. But with Nick, she could see him as both of those things. The thought made her smile again for the millionth time that morning.

Their date two nights ago had gone well. Amazingly well. Nick had taken her out to a stunning restaurant and they'd got on like a house on fire. There had been no moody, cold Nick this time and Rachel was hoping that was the last she'd seen of that side of him. He'd been cool, laidback and funny. He'd been *perfect*. When Grace had messaged Rachel saying she wasn't coming back, Rachel had invited Nick back to the house for a nightcap. After a few drinks, she knew he'd be over the limit if he drove home, so she suggested that he stay the night.

He'd raised an eyebrow, his eyes sparkling mischievously. 'Where will I be sleeping? Is this just a ploy to get me into bed?'

Rachel had grinned, about to tell him he was being ridiculous and he would be staying in the spare room or on the sofa. Rachel would never sleep with somebody so soon. She had rules; she'd never been the type of girl to have sex with someone so suddenly. They had to wait. She had to check they were in it for the long run. Everybody knew you would give the man the wrong idea if you just jumped into bed with them. They'd never call you afterwards, would they? But as she'd stared at his broad shoulders and muscles through his fitted navy shirt, she'd found herself wondering what it would be like to run her fingers across his tanned skin. Suddenly, the idea didn't seem like a ridiculous one at all. Rachel was always sensible and self-controlled. She was never as relaxed about life as Grace and she'd never been as crazy and carefree as Amber; maybe it was her turn to just do what the hell she liked without worrying about the consequences? This time perhaps she shouldn't fret about her future plans? Grace clearly wasn't, if she was staying out for the night with Steve.

'Do you want to sleep in my bed?' she'd asked Nick boldly. The glasses of wine she'd drunk at dinner had given her a new-found confidence.

Nick had laughed and then his brow furrowed. 'You're being serious?'

She'd shrugged then and stood up from the sofa, tucking her hair behind her ears. 'I'm going up to bed. You're more than welcome to join me, but if you'd rather sleep here…' She smirked as she walked slowly up the stairs, hearing his footsteps behind her.

As soon as Nick was in her bedroom they were kissing, grabbing each other and pulling at clothes. It had been amazing. Passionate and lustful, the complete opposite of how it had been with Mark. The word to describe her sex life with Mark had been ordinary. Like the flavour vanilla.

'You're sure?' Nick had whispered before they dived under the covers.

'Yes,' she whispered.

Rachel hadn't even felt awkward the following day like she thought she would. Nick hadn't ditched her and left at 5 a.m. before she woke like she'd panicked he might. He was still there, smiling at her and playing with her hair. She was relieved he still wanted to know her, even though she'd slept with him so soon. There had been nothing to worry about at all. It had been difficult to get out of bed that morning and tear herself away from Nick's warm body, but they'd both had to get to work.

Nick had texted her all day at work, and Rachel felt like she was floating. She was giddy with happiness and excitement. When Grace had arrived at work, she'd seemed happy too and Rachel couldn't believe how both their luck in love was changing so soon. As much as Rachel liked being in a relationship, after Mark, she expected to be single for a while. She really hadn't planned to meet someone else she liked so soon. But didn't people always say you found love when you least expected it?

Rachel was brought back to the present as she heard Grace's footsteps coming down the stairs.

'Morning.' She smiled brightly.

'Cup of tea?' Rachel offered, jumping up to make her one.

'I'd love one,' Grace smiled, sitting down at the kitchen table and looking outside. 'The sun is shining; I was hoping it was going to snow again,' she commented.

'It's going to again according to the weather forecast,' Rachel replied happily. She loved the snow. Rachel adored Christmas, especially when she felt as happy as she did right now.

'What are you up to today?' Grace asked.

'I'm seeing Nick this evening,' Rachel couldn't hide the enormous grin. 'Are you seeing your lover boy today?'

'This evening, yes,' Grace answered, studying her nails. 'But I've agreed to watch my niece in her nativity play this morning.'

'Ahhh cute,' Rachel replied, picturing Grace's niece, Poppy, dressed as an angel. She had a curly mop of blonde hair if she remembered rightly so she would certainly look the part.

'You don't fancy coming along, do you?' Grace invited, looking hopeful. 'Please don't leave me alone with my sister and her mum friends. The mum friends' chat is so dull and somehow they always involve me in their conversation as though I'm interested in talks of potty training and chicken pox. I've promised I'll go now so there's no getting out of it.'

'Well…' Rachel didn't have any plans, but couldn't say the thought of a nativity play was the most appealing thing in the world. She'd much rather be lying around relaxing, daydreaming of Nick all day.

'I'll cover the next late shift at Tidemans,' Grace said hurriedly, now looking desperate that she was going to be left to attend alone with her sister.

Rachel laughed. 'I was going to say yes anyway, but you've offered now. The next late shift is all yours.'

'It's worth it. As soon as the play is over, I can use you as an excuse as to why we have to leave. We'll just say you have some make-up clients, something along those lines,' she planned, looking satisfied.

Rachel smiled. She didn't mind going to the play, not really. She was looking forward to the day she had her own children. If everything had all gone to plan with Mark she would have been pregnant by the end of the following year, straight after the wedding. Not that he'd proposed or had any intention of proposing. He'd always made it clear that children should come after marriage. It was laughable when she thought that he was about to become a dad with Bianca now. She pushed the thought far from her mind and concentrated on the weekend and the future instead. 'I was thinking we should have a few nights out in the run up to Christmas,' she said to Grace. 'Let's plan some dates with Amber.'

Two hours later and they were sitting in an assembly hall at Grace's niece's primary school.

'I remember primary school as being big,' Rachel said, glancing round at the miniature chairs stacked up in the corner of the hall. 'It's actually really rather tiny though, isn't it?'

'Yes,' Grace agreed. 'I guess we were smaller so everything seemed bigger back then. Makes sense.'

Grace's sister, Amanda, was sitting next to Grace chatting to a petite woman next to her with pointy features. She could hear them saying something about the latest homework and another woman in front was now turning round and joining in with the conversation interestedly. It was easy to see why Grace had wanted Rachel to go along as well. Rachel had never seen three women talking about something so mundane as homework with such enthusiasm and vigour; watching them was like looking at the definition of a mothers' meeting. It was as though they were fighting to speak, desperate to get their words out.

A teacher appeared on the stage to welcome everyone and Rachel's thoughts turned to Nick and what they should do that night. As much as she'd love him to, he wouldn't be able to stay at Grace's house again if Grace was going to be there; it would be disrespectful to bring him back when it wasn't her house. Rachel wondered if she would be invited to his place and what it would be like. She hoped he was clean and tidy; there were just so many things she didn't know about him, and again, she felt the feeling of fear creep up on her that she'd slept with him so soon. He was practically a stranger, and if he never contacted her again or answered her calls, she wouldn't even know how to reach him.

Some little boys came on the stage dressed as shepherds and one of them tripped over his gown, falling straight over into a little heap on the floor. As a teacher reached to help him up, his chin started to wobble and he looked out into the audience to his parents.

'Oh, bless him,' Grace said compassionately.

'Poor little thing,' Rachel replied, narrowing her eyes in sympathy as she watched him run over to his parents in the crowd. She couldn't quite see them.

'His mother won't be pleased about that,' Amanda pointed out in hushed tones. 'She's like Little Miss Perfect. The poor child is probably so anxious to be the best that he's tripped over. The dad is kind of hot though,' she whispered, her eyes twinkling.

It was at that point several people sat back further in their seats and Rachel could see the parents of the little boy that Grace was talking about. Rachel gasped, instantly bringing her hand up to her open mouth. There, sitting alongside a tall, blonde, immaculate woman was Nick. What on earth was he doing here? Rachel's heart thudded violently as she watched the little shepherd boy run straight into Nick's arms, Nick hugging him tightly and kissing him tenderly on the forehead.

'Oh my goodness. Am I going crazy, or isn't that Nick?' Grace questioned looking perplexed. 'You only showed me that photo from his LinkedIn profile, but he looks identical, doesn't he?' Her eyes darted to Rachel and her face dropped. 'Oh Rach, it is him isn't it? Are you okay? You've gone all pale.'

'What's that?' Amanda asked in puzzlement as she gazed at Rachel. 'What's happened?'

Rachel felt her face becoming hot. 'That man over there. It's Nick Cunningham, isn't it?'

Amanda was frowning as she nodded, looking intrigued. 'Yes, Claire and her husband, Nick Cunningham. They're Noah's parents; he's in the same class as Poppy. Why? Do you know him or something?'

Rachel felt like she had been kicked in the stomach. 'Oh my God. This isn't happening.' She put her head in her hands feeling hurt and betrayed. He was married. He had a child. Of course he did; why had she not questioned why a man of thirty-five was still single with no baggage? She hadn't ever asked him. She'd been *such* a fool.

'She's been out with him on a few dates,' Grace explained quietly to Amanda. 'He never told her he was married.'

'Oh my God,' Amanda looked astounded by the news, her eyes as wide as saucers. 'He failed to mention he was married?'

Rachel nodded, feeling humiliated.

'Just keep it quiet,' Grace said sternly before turning to Rachel who was still in a state of shock. 'Shall we leave, Rachel? Perhaps it's best we just go.'

'Yes,' Rachel replied, putting her coat on. 'I can't stay here. He lied to me. How can I just sit there when he is playing happy families with his wife and son just a few feet away? I feel like such an idiot.' Her eyes were burning with tears.

'You're not,' Grace said putting wrapping her scarf round her neck. 'Don't say that, Rach. Don't let him upset you; he's not worth it.'

'Sorry Amanda. I'll see you soon,' Rachel said, turning to leave.

'Yes, sorry,' Grace added. 'Make sure you video it and send it to me.'

'You don't have to leave,' Rachel pointed out to Grace, feeling guilty.

Grace eyed her with a look that said, '*Shut up, I want to leave*'. 'No, I won't leave you on your own. Let's go.'

Rachel swallowed the lump in her throat and stood up, hunching down as much as she could, not wanting to cause a scene as she made her way to the exit at the back. She was mortified, stunned to the core. She couldn't believe he was married! How glad she was that she'd found out sooner rather than later. How would she ever trust a man again? Were they all just lying cheats? It certainly seemed that way. Why did she seem to pick the wrong ones all the time? She was trembling in shock.

'I don't know what to say,' Grace said softly when they were outside in the car park. 'I'm just so sorry.'

'I just can't believe it. He acted single. I didn't feel the need to ask him! He told me how much he liked me and I believed him. *Stupidly*, I trusted his every word. I slept with him on the third date,' she said regretfully, shaking her head in disgust. 'He must have been laughing at me the whole time. I hate men. I seriously want to remain single forever!' she declared dramatically. 'I wasn't even looking to like someone else so soon after Mark. I *wanted* to date people, go out with you girls and enjoy myself. How have I ended up feeling like this again so quickly?'

'I don't know, but you'll be okay,' Grace said supportively. 'What are you going to say to him? Aren't you supposed to be seeing him later?'

Rachel's heart plummeted as she thought about how excited she'd felt earlier. She felt both nauseous and sad. How could Nick have done that to her? Especially after she'd told him the story about Bianca and Mark. She didn't know if she was more disappointed with him or herself for falling for him. She didn't even know him and somehow she'd managed to get feelings already! She was being hurt by someone who was practically a stranger. She felt pathetic. So worthless. Had he been feeding her a load of lies, amusing himself that she was so gullible? Did he not think she'd had her fair share of heartache for one year? What kind of monster was he? She breathed slowly to calm herself down. 'I don't know. I don't want to see him but I want him to know that I know. I can't speak to him tonight though; I'm far too angry and upset.'

'Do you want me to stay in with you? I'll happily do so,' Grace offered kindly. 'We can get a takeaway and some wine. Spend the night slagging men off.'

Rachel smiled, despite the way she was feeling. 'Thanks Grace, that's really nice of you, but no. You go out with Steve. Just because I'm down in the dumps doesn't mean I should be dragging you down with me.'

'You're sure?' Grace checked.

'I'm certain. I'll just be drinking myself into a drunken stupor and eating ice cream anyway.'

'Well, if you change your mind,' Grace said softly.

Rachel shot her a grateful smile as she put her seatbelt on. She was angry and decided there and then to never let a man treat her this way again. She had her guard up and knew it would take someone extremely special to ever break it down. She was going to be looking out for herself now and felt as though maybe Amber had it right all along; there were tons of reasons why it was better to remain single. She wasn't sure what would happen in her future and she was really okay with that. If there was one thing she was certain of, she wanted nothing more to do with Nick Cunningham. She never wanted to see that man again.

Chapter 23

Amber sat on the park bench watching a group of teenagers waltzing by smoking. She remembered the first time she'd tried a cigarette. She and her school friend, Lindsey, had met up with Jack and a few of his friends after school one day in the summer. They'd only been about fourteen, and when Jack's friend had offered her one, Amber had felt silly saying no, so she took it. Jack had tried to stop her; he'd hated smoking and had never been one to cave into peer pressure. He'd always looked out for her, even back then. Of course she'd brushed him off, terrified of not looking cool.

'It's only a cigarette, what's the big deal?' Amber had asked casually, inhaling the nicotine and trying not to cough. She'd passed it over to Lindsey in the hope that she'd smoke the majority of it. She wasn't about to admit she hated it. Jack had shrugged helplessly but Amber had secretly loved that he cared about what she did. When her father had left Amber had thought there wouldn't be a male figure to look out for her again, but Jack had always been protective over her, giving her his opinions and guidance. It had felt so comforting that she could ask him for some male advice and he would be honest and open with her. She knew he had sympathized with the fact that her father had left, especially seeing as he was so close to his own, but he'd said things to make her feel better.

'It's his loss,' she remembered him saying once. 'He's the one losing out, Amber. He's lucky to be your father; anyone would be proud to have you.'

He'd understood that she hated talking about her dad and when one of Amber's friends once asked why she hadn't searched for her father, he'd replied for her. 'Why should she? If anyone should be searching it should be him.'

As Amber sat on the park bench she felt a chill run down her spine. It was still freezing outside, despite the ray of sunshine. The threat of snow remained and she wished she'd wrapped up a little warmer. Seeing her father waiting outside their block of apartments had been the biggest shock in the world. She'd recognized him almost straightaway; he hadn't changed apart from his hair now being grey instead of black and a few more wrinkles, as though someone had taken a pencil and drawn lines around his eyes. But other than that, he was still the same man in the photographs from when she was younger. He was still the same faded memory.

He had looked gobsmacked when he realized who Amber was.

'Amber?' he'd half-laughed, half-gasped. 'It can't be you, can it?' He'd looked her up in down in awe. 'Wow, you look so grown up. So beautiful.'

Amber had felt unsettled and angry suddenly. Her father was standing opposite her, but he was a complete stranger. What was he there for? What did he want after all this time? She was annoyed that he hadn't announced he was coming. What right did he have to suddenly turn up on their doorstep without letting them knowing he was coming after all these years? Who did this man think he was?

'Yes, I grew up,' she stated harshly. 'Who were you expecting to see? The five-year-old girl you abandoned?'

He looked ashamed, shifting on the spot awkwardly. 'I know

you must be angry, sweetheart. I know there's absolutely no excuse for what I did all those years ago—'

'And to my mum too,' she interjected in steely tones. 'Why are you here after all these years?'

He looked tormented. 'I've been meaning to come back for years, darling. It's complicated; there's so much more to it than your mother has probably told you. You were just a child, Amber. Times were hard back then. I don't want to cause you or your mother any stress or upset by showing up. I came here to tell your mother that my cousin, Michael, recently passed away. I know she hasn't seen him for years, but they were close back then and I'm aware they sometimes call each other for a chat. She'd want to know. I thought by coming here I might be able to see you too. I've thought about you every day.'

Amber had frowned furiously. 'All this time you knew where I lived. You've never once called. You've never even wished me a happy Christmas or birthday; why on earth would I ever want to talk to you? You deserted me, Dad, and you've never looked back.'

'That's not true. Like I said, it's complicated.' He looked humiliated and clearly he was finding the situation terribly difficult, his eyes darting from the floor to her face as he spoke. 'I want to see you. I've always wanted to see you but the longer it went on, the harder it was. I know there's nothing I can do to ever make it up to you, but I'd like to get to know you again, Amber.'

Amber didn't know what to say so remained silent, unable to believe that her father was really standing in front of her. Over the years she'd dreamt of this moment; hoping that one day he would realize he was an idiot who wanted her back in his life. She'd always had a feeling of rejection, and no matter how many people told her it was his loss, she couldn't help but feel unwanted and disregarded.

'Listen, I know this is all probably a huge surprise to you,' he'd told her, putting his hand in his pocket. 'But please give this note to your mother. Is there any way I can take your mobile number?' he asked hopefully.

Amber bit her bottom lip thoughtfully. She could be really stubborn and tell him no. He wasn't wanted. He'd missed out on years of her life and he could never be forgiven. He would never get those years back. How could any man leave their child at five years old and not come back without an explanation? But the other part of her wanted to hear what he had to say. Whether she liked it or not, this man was her *father*. He was responsible for her existence and she was curious as to what he could possibly say. But did he really have anything worth listening to? Her mother had told her they'd had an argument one evening about money. Her father had a gambling problem and she'd had enough. After cross words, her father had stormed out and never come back again. No call, no letter, nothing. Even her grandparents on her father's side had ditched Amber and her mother. Her mother told Amber when she'd called them to ask where her father was they'd said she should have been more supportive of him and that they had no idea of his whereabouts. By all accounts her father hadn't been close to his parents, who had lived in Devon, and Amber wasn't even sure if they were alive anymore. Like her father, she'd never known them. They hadn't cared.

Her father had held out his mobile with a desperate look in his eyes. 'Please, Amber,' he'd begged.

So she'd found herself punching her mobile number into his phone, unsure what to say to her mum when she spoke to her. She felt like she was betraying her and vowed that she would make sure her mother was okay with it before she answered her father's calls. Then she had that awful thought that he may not call her. How pathetic would she feel if her dad changed his mind and didn't contact her? What if he was disappointed in how she'd turned out? It pained her that she craved his acceptance. If he now ignored her she would feel even more worthless than he'd already managed to make her feel for most her life.

Amber was brought back to the present by someone shouting out to their friend walking through the park. She hadn't slept much the previous night and she still hadn't given the letter to her mother. She did plan to that evening, but first, she wanted to meet up with Jack. She needed to tell him all about it and wanted his opinion. Jack would know exactly what to do. He was the only one who would know how much this really meant to her. The only one she trusted to guide her in the right direction. She didn't care about the whole Natalya issue at that moment in time; she had far more important things to worry about. After she'd texted Jack saying she needed to see him alone urgently, he'd replied back straightaway saying where and what time. She knew she could count on him when she really needed to. He was always there when she most needed it.

She spotted Jack walking towards her, a navy scarf draped round his neck matching the beanie hat on his head. He looked so handsome without even realising it. He was just perfect. Especially without Natalya by his side.

'Hey,' he said, leaning in for a kiss. 'What's up? Your messages sounded serious. Everything okay?' He sat down next to her.

'You're not going to believe what's happened,' Amber began, still in disbelief. 'When I left yours last night, there was a man standing outside our apartments. When I got closer I noticed he was buzzing my mum's door and obviously getting no response.'

Jack's brow furrowed. 'Right…'

'It was my dad,' Amber announced. 'After all this time, he's come back. Wants to get to know me apparently. Though the main reason he's come back is to tell my mum that his cousin died. He said they were once close and she'd want to know.'

'Oh my God, Amber. I can't believe it. How can he show his face after all these years? What kind of man walks out on his wife and daughter and then tries to swan back into their lives after what … twenty-four, twenty-five years? He makes my blood boil.'

'I didn't know what to say. I was just standing there in shock. Shaking. He gave me a note to give to my mum. I gave him my mobile number.' She squinted her eyes, embarrassed that she hadn't just told him where to go. Would Jack think she was an idiot? Most likely.

'Do you want to meet him? Do you want to hear his side?' Jack questioned gently, his eyes full of concern. There was a vibrating sound from Jack's coat pocket, which he ignored.

'A part of me does. I'm stupid, aren't I?' she said honestly, biting her nails. 'After everything he's done. Or should I say not done.'

Jack exhaled heavily. 'No. Yes. I don't know. The thing is, it's easy for me to say that you should slam the door in his face, but he's your father, not mine. Maybe I'd be the same in your position?' He shrugged in wonderment. 'Who knows? But I certainly wouldn't trust him. Not for a very long time.'

Again, his phone vibrated, making a continuous irritating buzzing sound. Whoever it was that wanted to speak to him wasn't going to give up and Amber had a strong feeling she knew who that person was. Jack looked out onto the grass, acting as though it wasn't happening.

'I wouldn't trust him,' she replied finally. 'I'm just intrigued about him, I guess. I've wondered what he's like for all these years. I hate him for leaving us and I'll never, ever forgive him for what he put my mum through. She's never got over it; why else would she have been single for all these years? I just want to know what he's like, that's all. It feels weird that I actually have a father. I think in the end I just told myself he didn't exist; that way it stopped hurting that he'd abandoned me.'

'I just can't believe he's suddenly shown up,' Jack said, shaking his head in disbelief, 'I'm so shocked, so I dread to think what you feel like.' He paused for a moment. 'Perhaps you're right. Maybe the best thing to do is meet the guy and see what he has to say?'

'I'll see what my mum thinks about it first. If she doesn't like the idea of me seeing him, then I won't. My loyalties will always lie with her.'

'Yes, agreed,' Jack responded, looking distracted when his phone started buzzing again.

'I think you should answer your phone,' Amber said, trying to remain patient as she pointed at his coat pocket. 'It sounds as though it's something really urgent.'

Jack pulled his phone out his pocket and frowned as he viewed who was calling him. He stood up and walked away as he spoke. 'Hi Natalya.'

Amber shook her head furiously. He couldn't even meet her in the park for a chat about something important without bloody Natalya getting jealous; it was getting disturbing.

'I'm just with Josh and the lads,' she heard Jack say in the distance.

He'd walked away to a big tree and was leaning against it. He was speaking in a lowered voice and Amber guessed she thought he couldn't hear what he was saying.

'No, I won't be too long.' He paused. 'Yes, I'll pick you up a bit later on.' Another pause. 'I swear to you, yes. We'll do something nice, how about that? Dinner and drinks or cinema, whatever you fancy. Okay see you soon. Yes, love you too.'

Amber couldn't help but wrinkle her forehead as he walked back to her. She was dumbfounded. Jack was lying to Natalya about who he was with? Were things really that bad? Surely he knew that wasn't healthy? It would never work. Jack never lied either; he was such an honest man, and Amber couldn't believe what she'd just overheard.

'Why did you say you were with Josh and the lads?' she questioned, not really caring anymore about offending him about his peculiar relationship. It was weird that he was lying to his fiancée. He wasn't doing anything wrong and there was really no need to lie.

'What?' Jack looked a little agitated that she'd overheard. 'Oh, that. Never mind,' he said, trying to brush it under the carpet. He cleared his throat.

'Well, actually I do mind,' Amber said sternly. 'Why do you feel the need to lie about seeing me? Are you not allowed? Is that it? Has Natalya forbidden us to meet up or something?'

'No, it's not that,' Jack replied hastily, looking really uncomfortable at the subject of conversation. 'It's just that … oh, I don't know … she said something about the fact that she thinks you've got a problem with her. She thinks you don't like her because she's my girlfriend and something about her not being good enough for me. I can't remember the exact words. I told her she was crazy and that you're really not like that…' He tailed off, clearly not wanting to go into further detail.

Amber was fuming. What had Amber actually ever done apart from want to spend time with Jack? She'd never done a thing to Natalya; she'd only ever been polite and friendly. Natalya was just trying to make her look jealous, as though *she* was the one in the wrong. 'I cannot believe she said that,' Amber snapped defensively. 'I've never done or said anything horrible to her before, so what on earth is she talking about?'

'I know. Just forget I said anything. I told her you like her. You have no reason not to,' Jack replied, sounding fed up with the whole thing before it had even started. 'Please. Don't say anything. Just be, I don't know … perhaps just make more of an effort with her?' he pleaded.

Amber wanted to scream with rage. She *had* made an effort, but Natalya was doing everything in her power to stop her being friends with Jack, so why would she want to be friends with her? At the start, Amber had been really friendly and polite. How did he seriously not see this? Amber knew it was only a matter of time before she told Jack what she really thought of Natalya. The funny thing was, Natalya didn't know the extent of Amber's true feelings and she was still acting like a psychopath. 'Jack, I've been nothing but nice to her. Please, explain to me what I've ever done wrong?' she begged.

'I'm not saying you have done anything wrong,' Jack responded sounding distressed, sighing heavily. 'It's just she says she gets a vibe from you that you don't like her much. I don't know; I guess leaving early last night when she turned up for example, things like that. You were dead silent when she arrived. The whole atmosphere seemed to change,' he said, looking confused. 'I know I shouldn't be lying to her about seeing you, but sometimes it's just easier, you know?'

'No, I don't know,' Amber said sulkily. 'If you feel the need to lie about seeing me, then perhaps you shouldn't?' She knew she was being ridiculous, but she felt gutted that he thought she wasn't making an effort with his fiancée. She was frustrated that he couldn't see what Natalya was doing here. Natalya was right, of course. Amber did have a problem with her now she'd got to know her better; but Natalya *knew* deep down why this was. If she'd been a lovely, innocuous girl all along, Amber would have been just as friendly back. She wasn't purposely going out of her way to not like her.

'Don't be silly...'

'No really, Jack. I don't want to get in the way of you two, and you're right, perhaps I don't like Natalya. I don't think she's good for you,' she blurted out. She knew she couldn't take it back now she'd told him the truth and she was scared how he was going to react. 'I think she's conniving and domineering. I think she tries to control everything you do. She doesn't want you having a life outside of being with her; she wants you all to herself. How can you really not see that?'

Jack looked flabbergasted with what Amber was telling him. He turned to face her with a wounded expression. 'What? Amber you're taking this a bit far now. I mean, I know she likes seeing me a lot, but there's nothing strange about someone wanting to spend time with their fiancé.'

'Oh really? It's funny how she just happened to turn up last night unannounced with the cake, isn't it? Or when she was ill so you couldn't come out to the Rod Stewart concert. Do you really think that's a coincidence?'

'I'm not sure what you're trying to suggest here,' Jack retorted indignantly.

'I think you know perfectly well what I'm trying to suggest, Jack,' she riposted. 'I think deep down you know exactly what I mean. There's no way you can't have noticed. You can't seriously marry this girl,' she said, her voice raising an octave. She knew it wasn't her place to say it. She knew she should just shut up, keep quiet and walk away, but she couldn't. There was no way she could sit back and let her best friend marry Natalya, whether she was in love with him or not. Natalya wasn't the one for him.

'I really don't think who I marry has anything to do with you,' he said, a flinty edge to his voice. 'Geez Amber, I can't believe you're saying these things to me. You're supposed to be my friend. You're supposed to support me in my decisions and that includes who I want to marry. I've always done the same for you; even when you were dating that complete idiot who cheated on you and you gave him another chance. What was his name? Charles. You took him back and despite the fact I thought it was the wrong decision and that you were making a huge mistake, I just accepted it was your choice. I was friendly to the guy. You don't even know Natalya.'

'I know enough,' she said robustly, her mouth dry. There was no backtracking now.

'You've just made things so hard for me,' he said, his nostrils flaring as he ran his hands over the stubble on his chin. 'Natalya is having a Christmas get together and she wanted me to invite you along, but I don't see how I can now you've made it clear how you feel about her,' he said looking both incredulous and crestfallen, shaking his head.

'Of course she does,' Amber couldn't help herself. 'She wants to look like the good guy. She knows I would never go to her Christmas get together. Especially now I know she's trying to stir things between us.'

'Don't you think you're being rather childish?' Jack reprimanded her.

'Me the childish one? It's *her* that's being weird and childish. I just want to spend time with my friend sometimes. Alone. I'm hardly committing a crime, but she's doing everything in her power to prevent it happening. She always has to be there; she always has to tag along.'

He frowned deeply, looking stunned at the words coming out of her mouth. 'She just wants to get to know you because she knows how important you are to me, that's all. She wants to feel included and involved.'

'Well, she's certainly been involved and included, hasn't she?' Amber shot pointedly with a harsh laugh.

'I'm not listening to this anymore,' Jack said, standing up and looking agitated. 'The whole thing is just ridiculous. You're sitting there, insulting my fiancée. Insulting the woman I *love* and I won't stand for it.'

As always, the words that he loved her were like a dagger to the heart, but Amber felt infuriated too. She was livid that Natalya was getting her own way and winning, because there was no way she was going to make an effort to see Jack again. If it was too much of an issue seeing her, if he actually had to lie about it, then Amber would make it easy for him and disappear from his life. She'd avoid him; it was just too painful to sit back and watch the power and influence Natalya had over him.

'I'm just being honest with you about what I think; haven't you always been the same with me? I can't lie to you and pretend I like her,' she said matter-of-factly, pursing her lips stubbornly. 'I don't think you should feel the need to lie to the person you'll be spending the rest of your life with.'

'I've had enough of this,' Jack said in a grim, foreboding voice, shaking his head profusely. 'I'm going before you offend me any more than you already have. It's a shame things have ended on this note,' he added, thrusting his hands into his coat pocket before walking away. 'Good luck with your father.'

'Thanks,' Amber responded moodily, looking at her gloves. She hated things being like this between them. It was strange; she couldn't remember the last time she'd had a cross word with Jack. It simply never happened. They weren't the kind of friends that argued. They usually had each other's back.

Amber's chin wobbled and tears threatened her eyes. This wasn't how she'd intended their conversation going and it certainly wasn't the outcome she'd planned. But however bad she felt for saying those awful things about Natalya, she also felt something else – relief that she was actually telling the truth. She didn't have to hold in her feelings anymore.

She just hoped that one day soon Jack agreed with everything she'd said.

Chapter 24

Grace sipped the delicious glass of red wine distractedly. She was aware that Simon was talking, but her mind kept wandering elsewhere.

'Grace?' Simon half-laughed. 'What's up with you tonight? You seem a million miles away.'

She'd told him all about what had happened to Rachel earlier when they'd met up. They were sitting in a beautiful cosy pub, in big comfy armchairs by a crackling fireplace. 'Sorry, I was just wondering if Rachel is okay. I just felt so sorry for her earlier; she's been through such a rough time lately.'

'Sounds like it,' Simon nodded. 'Maybe send her a text, check that she's alright? I'm certain she's fine though. She's best off out of it,' he expressed, shooting her a reassuring smile.

'Yes, perhaps I will text her,' Grace said, fishing for her phone in her bag.

'Another wine?' Simon offered, standing up to go to the bar.

'Please,' Grace flashed him a wide smile. She watched him walk over to the bar and felt lucky that he wasn't a liar or a cheat. He may have been lazy and taken her for granted towards the end, but she trusted Simon wholeheartedly. She genuinely didn't think it was in his nature to be deceitful. Not only was he not a ladies' man, but Simon had always been honest, sometimes too honest, she remembered fondly. It was after Christmas a few years back that she'd asked him if she'd put on weight, expecting his immediate answer to be 'no'. She'd completely over-indulged during the festive season as usual, and she knew her jeans were tight, the folds of skin bulging over her jeans, but wanted his opinion. She could just recall him lying in bed, cocking his head to the side as his eyes roamed all over her body, before responding, 'Yes, you've definitely put weight on.' Then he went back to reading his paper before adding without even looking up again, 'Suits you though.'

That had certainly been enough to start the diet! She knew his intention hadn't been to offend her, he was just telling her the truth, even if it had hurt a little.

She was brought back to the present as she saw Simon walking back with their drinks. If things just stayed like this between them, it would be perfect and Grace had never felt happier; it was really just like the beginning of their relationship. But if Grace allowed Simon to move back in, would things go back to how they were? She was worried to take the chance. The thought of Simon treating her how he had just before she'd left her filled her with dread and panic. *This* Simon in front of her was the one she loved. He looked at her like she was special, precious even. She could tell he loved her again. Appreciated being with her. How had he changed so much so soon? Clearly the thought of losing her for good had been what he needed and Grace was pleased. Things were all surprisingly working out.

After a few more drinks, Simon stood up. 'Where shall we go now?'

This was the part where Grace just wished things were back to normal. She'd love nothing more than to go home and open a bottle of wine to drink watching a nice Christmas film. Instead they'd have to part ways, and the more Grace was seeing Simon again, the more she was hating their goodbyes. As much as she loved Rachel, perhaps she'd been a bit hasty in moving her into her house? If she lived alone still, then Simon could come back, and no one would be any the wiser that she was seeing him again.

'I don't know. I don't really want to go for another drink anywhere and it's too late to go to the cinema or anything like that.'

'Yes, you're right,' Simon said thoughtfully, 'I'm not sure where to suggest either.' Then his eyes lit up. 'I have an idea,' he said, his voice rising. He grabbed her hand and pulled her towards the exit.

'What? Where are we going?' Grace asked, laughing lightly, confused by his eagerness to get her out into the cold.

'Carol singing,' he laughed, pulling her along.

Grace couldn't hide how horrified she felt at the suggestion. 'Oh no you don't,' she said, pulling her arm back. 'You know I can't sing. And it's too cold; I don't even have a hat or gloves. I can't walk in these heels.'

'Excuses, excuses Mrs Chapman,' he smiled amusedly. 'You told me the fun had gone out of our relationship, but who's the party pooper now?'

Grace smirked. She was a little tipsy and Simon was right. She wanted him to be spontaneous like before, so how could she now be the boring, dull one? 'Okay Mr Chapman,' she said more confidently than she felt. 'You're on.' She took his hand and they walked to the first door. The lights were on and Grace knew it was just her luck that they were going to answer.

A middle-aged lady opened the door with a look of surprise when she saw the two of them standing there.

'Can I help you?' she enquired, her eyes as thin as slits as she looked at them with suspicion.

'No, but I think we can help you,' Grace giggled and Simon joined in. 'We wish you a merry Christmas after three. One, two, three…'

They burst into song and Grace had to stop herself from

exploding into fits of laughter several times, especially as she sang her off-key notes so loud and proud. The lady stood in front of them with a face like thunder as they sang, her arms folded across her chest. Then, as Simon switched songs to *Holy Night* and Grace sang completely out of tune, she really did begin to laugh and in a matter of seconds it was uncontrollable, a real belly laugh with tears streaming down her face. Simon suddenly bent over, unable to stand up through his laughter. No sooner had they stopped laughing and caught each other's eye, they started again, Grace even snorting, which made her laugh more.

'Well, was that it?' the lady questioned, her hands now on her hips. 'I do hope you're not expecting any money for that nonsense?'

'No,' Grace replied breathlessly in between laughing, 'but we do wish you a Merry Christmas.'

The lady raised an eyebrow as though they'd both gone insane. 'Right. And to you too,' she said, before closing the door.

'I cannot believe we just did that,' Grace said, her voice croaky from so much laughter as she wiped her eyes.

'Oh my God, that was hilarious. Your voice, Grace,' Simon laughed again wholeheartedly, 'I'd forgotten how bad it was.'

They walked hand in hand, not needing to say they were heading back to Simon's car. They didn't need to ruin and disturb someone else's night with their hideous singing voices.

'I don't want to leave you,' Simon said yet again, sounding despondent suddenly. 'Why don't I just come back to the house for a bit? I won't stay the night if you don't want me to.'

Grace gulped, not wanting to disappoint him. This was becoming a routine every time they met; he would ask to stay and she would say no. She hated repeating her issues with the idea of him coming back. Rachel had just had the most terrible day and Grace knew it was important to go home alone tonight and at least sit with her for a while to talk about it. Besides, she wasn't ready to tell her friends about Simon yet, and she knew it was starting to upset him. She could see it in his eyes and hear it in his voice that he wasn't enjoying being a secret.

'Simon, I can't,' she sniffed as they reached his car. 'Rachel is there. She's really upset and I told you before…'

'She doesn't know about us,' Simon cut in rather abruptly, as though he was bored of hearing the same old story.

'Well yes. I don't want to announce to the world we're seeing each other just yet. I'm sorry,' she blinked several times wishing he would understand where she was coming from.

He gave a gusty sigh. 'I just don't see when though, Grace. When can we start just living normal lives again? It won't be the same as it was before, I swear to you. I would never, ever risk losing you again; you mean the absolute world to me. I'm nothing without you. I just want to live together again and get on with our lives. I hate it like this. I don't like the sneaking around and having to park up the road just in case Rachel sees me outside. I hate not having you in my bed every evening. I really don't care what your friends think. I only care about you. I need to know if you're willing to let me back and give me another chance. I can't live like this anymore.'

Grace's brow knitted. She didn't like feeling under pressure. She guessed Simon wasn't used to her saying 'no' to things. She was usually so laidback and easygoing that she let him make decisions about everything. He could usually persuade her to do something in a heartbeat. But not this. Of course, she understood everything that Simon was saying, but it was up to her whether she wanted him back for good or not. She was going to make the decision when she was ready. What on earth was she supposed to say to Rachel anyhow? She'd only just moved in for Christ's sake and Grace was going to feel incredibly guilty. 'I don't know why you can't just be happy with how things are at the moment, Simon. I'm giving you a chance, aren't I? Why can't you be happy with that? I wanted to take things slow. You told me we would and now there just seems to be a huge rush about moving back in and going back to normal.'

Simon closed his eyes momentarily as they stopped at some traffic lights. 'Of course I'm happy to have another chance, Grace. I'm over the moon I haven't lost you like I thought I had, but you can't blame me for getting frustrated that I can't even come to your Christmas ball. I just worry, that's all. I want people to know we're back together. I want them to know you have a husband who adores you; I don't like the thought of people thinking you're single. Sorry if that comes across as jealous, but perhaps I am a little? I just want to be included in your life again, that's all. All parts of it.'

Grace looked up at him in adoration and put her hand on his knee and squeezed it. 'Soon, Simon. I promise you I'll tell everyone soon. Just give me a bit more time.'

He nodded, looking satisfied.

'So obviously you can't come back to the house and I don't want to go to your cousin's either,' she stated, 'but that doesn't stop us having a little bit of fun in here, does it? There's loads of quiet roads at this time of night,' she said seductively, her head swivelling round. 'And plenty of room in the back.'

Simon raised both eyebrows and put his foot down on the accelerator. 'I know just the place.'

Chapter 25

Rachel ignored Nick's phone call as she watched his name flashing across her mobile for the fourth time that night. *Go away*, she thought furiously, *go back to your wife and child.* She still couldn't get the sight of the three of them out of her mind. It was all she could think of. That, and how stupid she'd been to trust another man so quickly. She had been destined to get hurt sleeping with him so soon. This was the reason why she didn't do things like that. You usually only ever got hurt. No good ever came out of it. She had to admit it was tempting to just answer the phone and hurl abuse at him, and her finger hovered over the answer button as she imagined all the things she would say. But it was much more satisfying to leave him in the lurch and make him wonder what it was that he had done wrong. He clearly wanted to have this affair with her quite badly, having called four times and sent two text messages. He must have liked her in some way, a small comfort in the grand scheme of things. She slurped her white wine noisily, relieved when she heard the front door opening meaning Grace was finally home.

'Hey,' Grace beamed walking through the door. 'It's nice to get in from the cold. It's freezing outside.'

'How was it? Did you have a lovely night? You look really

happy,' Rachel pointed out, noticing her rosy cheeks and twinkling eyes and really glad that one of them was.

'Oh, you know. It was nice. We went for dinner first and then to a pub for some drinks. I had a good night,' she replied, the smile not leaving her face.

'I'm so pleased for you, Grace. I think this one is *the one*, you know. I haven't seen you this in love in years. When do we get to meet him? I'm dying to know what he's like.'

'Soon I guess,' Grace said in non-committal tones.

'Well, make sure we do. We need to check he's good enough for you and not just like Simon,' Rachel told her caringly. 'Wine?'

Grace sat on the sofa and kicked her shoes off. 'You know what, I've actually had enough for one night. I'm tired,' she yawned, stretching out on the sofa. 'Has he called you?'

'Four missed calls and two text messages,' Rachel replied pursing her lips. 'I haven't answered him,' she said feeling proud of herself.

Grace's brow knitted. 'No, you're doing the right thing. Don't even give him the satisfaction of knowing that you care. I wonder where he goes to make his calls to you? He must have to go into another room or leave the house in case his wife or son overhears. Seriously, some people really don't deserve a family; it's amazing what extent they go to, to cheat and lie, isn't it?'

'Maybe I just attract cheats?' Rachel wondered hopelessly staring into space. The wine was definitely making her a bit lightheaded and when she went to pour herself another glass she realized she'd actually drunk the whole bottle. 'Maybe I'm just always going to have this problem?'

'Don't be so ridiculous,' Grace tutted. 'You'll meet the right person when the time is right.'

'I know, I know. Maybe after my last two situations, I won't want to meet anybody else? I think for now I should spend some time alone. Maybe I should go away next year and do a bit of travelling. Really find myself. I'm sure Amber will be jetting away somewhere; I'll go with her.'

'Sounds like a good idea,' Grace smiled widely. 'Sometimes you just can't plan what life throws at you and you've just had some bad luck. Take it easy on yourself,' Grace said, adopting a sympathetic smile.

Rachel sighed. 'I'm trying to be more relaxed like you. I thought I liked Nick, but I promise I'll pick myself up again and just forget about him.' She licked her lips tasting the wine, looking down to notice an empty glass. 'I may just open another bottle. I won't drink the whole thing, but I fancy another glass,' she felt the need to explain.

'Hey, you go for it,' Grace gave a tiny giggle, 'I would normally be joining you if I didn't feel so tired. Do you mind if I call it a night? Are you certain you're okay?'

Rachel flapped her hand in Grace's direction. 'Of course, you go. I probably won't be up for much longer and yes, I'm fine. It's not like I've been seeing Nick for long; I'll just have to put it all down to a bad experience,' she said nonchalantly, standing up to get a bottle of wine from the kitchen.

Rachel poured herself a large glass, unable to prevent herself going over the last date with Nick. He'd been so charming and funny and since that night, Rachel had somehow allowed herself to imagine a future with him. She knew it was soon, but it wasn't completely unheard of to know someone was important so quickly, was it? Nick was handsome and successful and most of all, he'd made it very clear he was interested in *her*.

She recalled the moment after they'd finished dinner and she'd placed her purse on the table about to offer to pay half the bill. He'd looked at her as though he'd wanted to laugh.

'You're not paying Rachel, so please put your purse away, as lovely as it is,' he'd said, gazing at her in amusement, his mouth twitching.

She'd chortled then. It was an old purse and the zip was broken.

The black leather had started to fade in places making it appear ancient, which Rachel guessed it probably was. 'Thanks. You're sure?' she checked gratefully. She and Mark had always gone fifty-fifty with everything. She wasn't even sure he'd paid for her the first time they'd gone on a date. It made a nice change and Rachel appreciated it.

He'd stared at her with unwavering, intense eyes. 'I'm certain. I like you Rachel,' he'd told her in a soft voice as he handed the bill and money to the waiter. 'I like you a lot. There's something about you,' he said, as if he was trying to work out what it was.

'I like you too,' Rachel had replied bashfully, her eyes aglow with delight.

Now here she was in the lounge, jumping as she almost nodded off, her wine swaying back and forth in the glass she was holding. She looked at the time, surprised to see it was now nearly one in the morning. She'd been sitting there longer than she realized and had drunk half the bottle of white wine. She groaned, knowing she was going to pay for it in the morning. She looked at her phone and read Nick's last text message again.

Hey, what's going on? Are you okay? Are we still meeting tonight? I've tried calling you several times but no answer. Let me know when you get this.
Nick x

Perhaps Nick needed a piece of her mind. Maybe she'd been wrong to just ignore him. He deserved to be pulled up on the appalling way he'd not only treated her, but his family too. Who did Nick think he was, she wondered heatedly, feeling a sudden urge to shout at him and tell him how enraged she was. She dialled his number, her vision slightly blurring as she stared at the coffee table in the centre of the lounge and waited. The phone clicked through to voicemail and she waited for the beep.

'Hi Nick, if that's even your name,' she slurred her words as she spoke. 'God knows what other lies you've told me. It's Rachel, the girl you said you liked. The one you've called four times this evening, just in case you have multiple women on the go.' She stood up as she spoke, but felt a little dizzy so sat back down on the sofa again. 'The reason I'm calling is just to tell you why I didn't want to meet tonight. The thing is, *Nick,* I know all about your wife and son. I saw the three of you together at the school play. I think you failed to mention you were married, didn't you?' she said curtly. 'Just a slight problem there, because I don't date married men. I will not be a home wrecker!' she burst out, breaking off and breathing hard. 'So stop calling me and leave me the hell alone. I'm not interested and I won't be lied to anymore by arseholes like you. I was right about you the first time we met; you really are a dick. So just go back to your wife and your son, who by the way is really cute.' She breathed in deeply. 'It's Rachel by the way in case you don't know what girl is calling.' She hung up the phone, feeling she may have just repeated herself a lot, but unsure due to her fuzzy wine brain. She cringed, despite being well and truly drunk, hobbled up the stairs and got into bed, dreading how she was going to feel in the morning.

By Monday, Rachel had started to feel a little better about the situation. Nick had called several more times the day before, and each time he rang and Rachel ignored it again, it made her feel a little stronger. She felt embarrassed when she recalled leaving the voicemail on Saturday night when she'd got drunk and was almost thankful she couldn't remember what she'd said. It didn't matter anymore, did it? The fact was that Nick was married with a child and she had no choice but to move on and forget about him. She planned to go out as much as possible and make plans for the New Year focusing on herself. She'd been browsing bootcamps in Portugal for next May and was even looking at ways to further her career in make-up and beauty by taking some new night courses.

She walked through to the Pop Cosmetics department with Grace, noticing that Amber was already there. She looked just as morose as Rachel had been feeling on Saturday and Rachel instantly knew that something was up.

'Hey, how was your weekend?' Grace asked, shooting Rachel a concerned expression.

Amber sighed. 'You won't believe what happened,' she said in a small, pained voice as though someone was squeezing her throat. 'Not only did Natalya show up at dinner on Friday, ruining yet another night…'

'You're joking?' Rachel interrupted, incredulous.

'I wish I was,' Amber answered miserably. 'She just turned up with a cake and of course the others then felt the need to invite her in. I left as soon as she turned up. Anyway, Natalya is the least of my worries,' she said, her voice breaking slightly.

'Go on. What else happened?' Grace gently pressed.

Rachel thought Amber looked thin and pale as she spoke.

'My father showed up,' Amber told them in disbelief, a look of puzzlement on her face, her eyes darkening. 'He was there on Friday evening when I arrived home, looking for my mum. After all these years, he was just standing there, like he'd never been away. I couldn't believe my eyes. I still can't believe it.'

'Oh my goodness, Amber,' Rachel gasped, her jaw dropping.

'Then to make things even worse I met up with Jack to tell him about it. We ended up having a huge fight and I told him what I really thought of Natalya; it all just came tumbling out of my mouth. I've ruined our friendship just like I feared I would.'

Grace bit her lip. 'Oh, I'm sure things will smooth over between the pair of you. You're so close. I'm sure this won't change that.'

'Yes,' Amber replied wanly. 'We *were* close. But not now. Not now that he's met her and she's trying to dominate him. He's on her side. He seemed so surprised by the things I was saying, as though I'd lost the plot.'

'What did your mum say about your dad showing up?' Rachel

wondered curiously. It seemed weird that Amber was talking about her father. It had always just been Amber and her mum since Rachel had known her. Amber's father had never been in the picture and she never spoke about him.

'I'm seeing her this evening,' Amber said worriedly. 'I have no idea what she's going to say. I had planned to see her the day I met up with Jack but I was too upset. I had too much on my mind. Then yesterday she was out with friends and she sounded so happy when I spoke to her on the phone that I didn't want to ruin her mood. I'm really dreading telling her.'

'Maybe it won't be as bad as you think,' Grace said, lines appearing on her forehead as she squeezed Amber's hand.

'Anyway,' said Amber in slightly brighter tones, 'how were both your weekends? What did you get up to? I'm thinking tomorrow night we need to go out for Christmas drinks. I need cheering up.'

'I was going to suggest going out too,' Rachel replied, before telling Amber all about the play and seeing Nick and his family. Amber looked dumbfounded as the story unfolded.

'Wow Rach, you seem to be having such a hard time,' she said empathetically. 'Looks like you definitely need drinks tomorrow as much as I do.'

The rest of the day seemed to fly by; Tidemans was manically busy with people rushing around, busy ticking presents off their Christmas lists. Rachel didn't even notice the hours going past as she was kept occupied recommending make-up products to customers as well as applying make-up when they wanted it. She didn't hear him approach her from behind and she didn't hear him when he called her name. The Christmas music was blasting out making it difficult to hear much at all. But Rachel did see Amber gesticulate that she needed to turn around and Rachel almost gasped when she saw Nick standing there in front of her.

'I can't talk,' she said, irritated that he'd actually turned up at her workplace and feeling flustered in front of the customer she was serving. 'I'm busy.'

'I understand that,' Nick replied in placatory tones. 'The store closes in fifteen minutes so I'll wait. I really need to speak to you.'

'What is there to say?' Rachel snapped, ignoring the stares from the customers that were overhearing.

'Rachel, please,' he pleaded patiently. 'I'll be waiting for you outside. I'm not going anywhere until I've spoken to you.'

'Ah, give him a chance love, he sounds like he's sorry,' said a grey-haired lady who had been browsing face creams, flashing her a smile.

'Sorry?' Rachel challenged. 'He lied to me. I was seeing him and then found out that he's married with a child!'

'Oh dear, what an awful thing to do,' said the grey-haired lady pushing her glasses further up her nose, staring at Nick with daggers in her eyes.

Nick held his hands up. 'She hasn't even given me a chance to talk to her. I need to explain a few things...'

'Are you or are you not married with a child?' Rachel demanded to know, noticing that more customers were now standing around listening to what was going on.

'Yes, be honest with the girl,' another tall lady commanded in an angry voice.

'Okay, okay,' Nick responded, sounding beaten, looking round at the crowd of furious faces gazing in his direction. 'Yes, I'm married and I do have a child...'

'Then that's all I need to know. Now leave me alone,' Rachel barked icily, before swivelling round and getting back to her customer.

She swallowed hard. That really was all she needed to know.

Chapter 26

Amber felt nervous as she knocked on her mum's door, holding the letter from her father. This was it. There was no turning back now and no excuses; she needed to tell her mum that her father was back. She just hoped it wouldn't upset her too much.

'Hello, how was work?' her mum said as she opened the door. 'Your make-up looks lovely. I have a little work Christmas do I'm going to on Friday and was wondering if you could do my make-up? I've taken the day off so will pop into the store to see you.'

'Yes of course,' Amber smiled, sitting down in the kitchen. 'Perhaps come around two o'clock when we've all been on our lunch breaks. I'll put you in the diary.'

It was clean and tidy as usual, the surfaces sparkling and the grey tiled floor gleaming having just been cleaned. The little Christmas tree in the corner of the room was immaculate; red and gold decorations scattered perfectly covering the whole tree as though she'd measured the space between each ornament. Amber always wondered why she hadn't inherited her mother's need for everything to be spotless; she had a much more relaxed approach when it came to house cleaning and decorating.

'I've made us spaghetti Bolognese,' she said, stirring the mince-meat on the stove.

'Perfect. Thanks,' Amber replied, her heart beating a little faster as she held onto the letter, her hands starting to become clammy. 'Mum, I need to tell you something.'

Her mother turned round to face her, a look of confusion on her face. 'What's up?'

Amber took a deep breath and swallowed hard. 'On Friday night when I came back home after Jack's dinner, Dad was here. He was looking for you and I recognized him. He wanted to tell you his cousin, Michael, has recently passed away.' She cleared her throat. 'Anyway, he's left you this letter.'

'Well, I never,' her mother finally said in amazement as she took the letter. 'Talk about blast from the past.' Her mouth fell open as she read the letter in silence.

'Are you okay?' Amber panicked when her mother put the letter on the kitchen surface and stared out of the window vacantly.

'Mm?' Her mother span around looking a million miles away, her eyes filled with tears. 'Yes, it's just come as a bit of a shock, that's all. I haven't seen your father, Phillip, in years and Michael, well, I haven't spoken to him in a long while either. Though he did always keep in touch. What else did he say?'

'He said he was sorry and that he wanted to see me.' Amber blinked a few times, adding hastily, 'He doesn't deserve it though of course, and I'd never speak to him again if I knew it would upset you. I know he's a waste of space who ditched us, and you're the one who has been there for me.'

Amber's mother gulped and looked distracted. 'There's a bit more to the story than I told you, Amber.' She sat down opposite Amber and held her hand, looking a little guilty.

'What?' Amber ventured.

Her mother inhaled deeply. 'Perhaps it wasn't *all* your father's fault for what happened.'

Amber frowned intensely. 'What do you mean, Mum? Don't go making excuses for him. He had a gambling problem. He left

213

us. He's never tried to contact me all these years. There's nothing you can say to excuse that.'

'Yes, he did have a gambling problem.' Her mother nodded, looking deep in thought. 'He had been lying to me. So many lies,' she said, looking as if she still couldn't take it in all these years later. 'He was in lots of debt and it became his whole life; the obsession of trying to make the money back was his main priority. He lived in a dream world, his own little bubble. I hardly ever saw him and when I did, he was quiet and tired, his mind on how to make his next bit of money. How to win back what he'd just lost. He believed he would be up in the end. That's the problem – gamblers can't see when to quit and they really do think they can win more, until it's too late. He was depressed, but I didn't realize at the time. His cousin, Michael, was there for me. He was the one I confided in when your father didn't come home after losing loads of money or spending all his nights in casinos, and I'm ashamed to say that our relationship grew to become more than just friends. I was fond of Michael, he was a lovely man, but I never loved him like I did your dad. I just relished having someone there to comfort me.'

Amber was astounded. 'You had an affair?'

Her mother bit her lip and nodded, looking ashamed, her eyes downcast. 'Yes. I'm certainly not proud of it, but you can't imagine what it was like to live with your father, Amber. He became a stranger to me and the constant lies and deceit just got too much for me to handle. When he found out, he was devastated and left. That was the last time I ever saw him. I was so angry that he hadn't stuck around to even attempt to make our marriage work; he wouldn't take responsibility for anything. He was devastated and so hung up on the fact he'd been betrayed that I don't think he took enough time to consider that he was leaving you. He blamed the failure of our marriage on me,' she said defensively, looking sad. 'He did write to me about six months later asking whether he could see you, but I was so irate and angry that I ignored him. I didn't see Michael after that either, though he's always called me throughout the years just to catch up. I couldn't be with Michael though; it wouldn't have been fair to him. I would have been using him because I was lonely. My whole life had been turned upside down but I vowed to get through it all on my own. When your father left I told myself I was better off alone than ever depending on a man again.'

Amber couldn't believe it; her mother had had an affair and she'd never been told. She was furious that her mother had never told her the whole story, but it still didn't make it acceptable that her father had just left them. One little letter asking to see her six months later didn't make much difference, did it? He'd hardly made a massive effort. But at least now she could understand her father's reasons for having to go. For just getting up and departing. It made much more sense and the thought was easier to bear now she knew he'd had his heart broken.

'Please say something, Amber. I feel really bad for never telling you the truth, but I was just terrified you'd blame me for your father's absence. I've felt guilty for years, wondering what would have happened if I hadn't had the affair. We could have seen a counsellor. I should have got your father more help, perhaps, I don't know. He wasn't a good husband when he became an addict, but then I wasn't a great wife in the end either.' She sniffed and wiped under her eyes.

'I don't blame you, Mum. I don't know what to think, but I do understand there's a lot more to the story now than I ever realized. I just wish you'd been truthful; for all these years I genuinely just thought my dad left me for no reason at all.'

'And for that I'm really sorry. I just didn't want you to hate me,' her mother said, a tear rolling down her cheek. 'The truth is, I really loved your father. I truly loved that man and a part of me always has. His gambling was an illness; it didn't mean it was okay for him to lie, but he needed help. I should have tried to get help for him rather than turn my back on him and cheat myself. I've always wished that things had turned out differently. The truth is, I've blamed myself for all these years, though I've never agreed with the way he just run away either. If I have any advice, it's that when you find love Amber, never let it go. Do everything in your power to keep it and make it work, because true love doesn't come around very often,' she told her seriously, gazing into her eyes. 'Do you understand what I'm saying, Amber? If you find love, grab it with both hands and never let it go. Do everything you can to keep it.'

Amber nodded. 'I'll bear that in mind for future.'

Her mother looked at her knowingly. 'Darling, you need to tell Jack how you really feel about him. I know you too well. Don't be stubborn and proud like I am. Tell him how you feel before it's too late. You'll never forgive yourself otherwise,' she told her sagely.

Amber was about to deny it and tell her mother she'd got it all wrong, but realized at that point that it didn't matter what she said, her mother knew the truth. Obviously to her mother, it was clear to see how she really felt about Jack. 'I'm scared, Mum. We argued on Saturday about Natalya. If I tell him how I really feel, I'm petrified I'll lose him forever.'

Her mother nodded in understanding. 'Just tell him, Amber. At least then you won't live with regret. There's nothing worse than that. He can't hate you for loving him, can he? Follow your heart.'

Amber looked into the distance, unsure what to do. Jack wasn't even talking to her at the moment. It definitely wasn't the right time to come clean. Would there ever be a right time? Was her mum right? Would it be worse to live with the regret if she never told him how she really felt? 'What shall I do about Dad?' she wondered. 'I had a missed call from an unknown mobile number last night that I'm assuming was him, but I wanted to talk to you first.'

'Amber, please don't worry about what I think. If you want to see your father then I won't ever blame you. You only get one, after all. He may not have been the best dad in the world running off for years and only ever sending one letter, but I do feel partly to blame for that. I broke his heart. Maybe just hear him out? Then if you decide you never want to speak to him again, at least you know you did try.'

Amber nodded slowly digesting what her mother was saying. She was right. Perhaps her father deserved a chance, even if it was just one.

She couldn't deny that meeting her father again was going to be scary, but it was nothing compared to telling Jack how she really felt. Amber took a deep breath making the decision to call her father back as soon as she went home.

She didn't know exactly when she would tell Jack she loved him as they'd left things on such bad terms, but she knew it would be soon. She just prayed to God that he felt the same way or she was going to be spending Christmas with an extremely broken heart.

Chapter 27

Grace giggled as Simon quickly zipped up his jeans and did the buttons on his shirt up.

'Quick,' she hissed. 'I think I heard someone go into another cubicle.'

They were late night shopping as Grace needed a new dress to wear to her work Christmas ball. No sooner had Simon caught a glimpse of her stripping down to her underwear through the curtains he'd pounced on her, and, as much as Grace had found it a turn-on doing it in such a risky place, she also hoped that no one would actually catch them; she would be mortified. She cringed as she imagined a sales assistant flinging back the curtains and catching them during the act. The thought made her more flustered than she already was. What had got into her lately? This kind of thing only happened to couples in a new relationship during the honeymoon period, didn't it? As she ushered Simon back to the seating area outside the changing room, she smiled, unable to believe what they'd just been up to. Their relationship hadn't been half as exciting before she'd left Simon, and it was remarkable what a change there was in him. It gave her hope for their future together.

Grace buttoned up the long sleek, black dress which was a

blend of cashmere and silk and felt completely effortless. It was perfect for the party and the look on Simon's face as she waltzed out of the cubicle and span around confirmed this.

'Wow, you look incredible,' he said genuinely, his eyes lighting up.

'Do you think?' Grace said, turning round to view herself in all angles. 'You're sure it doesn't make my thighs look big?'

He shot her a look as though she was crazy. 'Grace, you look stunning. I swear to you. That's the dress, trust me.'

Grace couldn't help but smile. 'Thanks,' she said, walking back into the changing room to get dressed back into her clothes.

'Are you taking it?' Simon asked as he stood up moments later when she walked out, ready to go.

'Yes.'

'Let me buy it for you,' he offered kindly, taking her hand as they walked to the cash register.

'No, don't be silly,' Grace replied, not used to Simon being so generous. He'd never been one to splash his cash on clothes and usually hated shopping. He'd been giving and thoughtful at the start of their relationship, often buying her flowers and little gifts, but all that had soon faded away the longer they were together.

'I want to buy it for you, Grace,' he said earnestly. 'Please let me get it. It can be part of your Christmas present. I've already bought you a few things but I'd like to pay for this dress too; you look beautiful in it.'

Grace smiled widely and kissed him on the lips. 'Thank you, I really appreciate it.'

As they shopped for the rest of the evening, Simon seemed quiet and withdrawn.

'Shall we stop quickly and get a coffee?' Grace suggested, wondering if he was tired with shopping. It certainly wasn't normally something they would do together and she guessed Simon was most likely getting bored.

She watched him as he walked over with two steaming mugs.

'What's up?' she asked. 'You've suddenly gone all silent – you're in a world of your own. Do you want to go home? I think I'm pretty much done now anyway.'

'Okay.' Simon nodded, looking at a spot on the table, something clearly on his mind.

'Come on, Simon. Is something the matter? Please say,' Grace begged, racking her brains for a reason as to why he'd suddenly turned miserable.

Simon took a deep breath. 'I was just thinking, that's all. I watched you come out of that dressing room looking like a million dollars, and I just thought, I should be there. I should be going with you to that ball. All the single men that work in your store will be all over you and you know it. How do you think that makes me feel? I'd never do this to you. I'm your husband and things have been going great between us. We had a blip in the road like tons of couples do, but we'll make it work. I just can't see why you're so ashamed to admit to your friends and family that you've given me another chance. It's not like I've had an affair or anything,' he huffed grouchily.

Grace narrowed her eyes. 'You were awful to me, Simon. I really don't think you realize how unhappy I was at the very end. I used to dread you coming home...' She tailed off remembering the bad memories. 'I used to cry myself to sleep for Christ's sake. You'd changed. You didn't seem to care about anything. I felt invisible and insignificant. It was unbearable being married to you. I hated being around you.' The words flew out of her mouth and Simon flinched, looking really hurt.

He tapped his foot under the table irritably as he spoke. 'Wow. Thanks, Grace,' he said, looking really put out by her words. 'I've been trying so hard. I just want to come home. I want to go to your ball and spend Christmas with you. I don't care about whether it's with your family or whether you want to spend the entire day freezing cold in a park somewhere; I just want to be with you. You either forgive me and give me another chance or you don't. I just can't be kept on a piece of string, hoping that today is the day you let me back for good. I can't sit back and watch you live your life as though you're single one minute and back in a relationship the next. It's not fair on me.' He pushed his chair back and stood up.

'Simon, don't you think you're overreacting? You know I don't want to be with anyone else, especially any of the men from Tidemans.' Grace clicked her tongue, surprised by his outburst. 'Come on, just sit back down. Please. I will be ready soon. I'm just scared, I told you before.'

'Of what, Grace? That I'll turn straight back into the person I was at the end? Really? Can't you see I've learnt my lesson? Do you honestly think I'd just risk it all again?'

Grace bit her thumbnail. 'I don't know.'

'Well, let me know when you do know,' Simon said, at the end of his tether, before spinning round and walking away. 'I can't wait around forever.'

Grace sipped her coffee, a tear sliding down her cheek. What was wrong with her? Why couldn't she just go back to normal with Simon? Did she really just think he'd go back to the old Simon again? She wasn't sure anymore, but she knew she would feel guilty taking him to the Christmas ball after their pact. However silly that may be. But how would she feel if the roles were reversed? Grace had always been carefree and easygoing, but she had to admit she could see where Simon was coming from. Perhaps he thought she was having her cake and eating it? Even though she wasn't seeing anyone else. The only person she loved was Simon. He was the only man she had any interest in. Thinking about it now he'd left, she *did* want him by her side at the Christmas ball. It simply wouldn't be the same without him. He seemed pretty angry though, and Grace just hoped she wasn't too late.

Chapter 28

Rachel had been to her parents' house for dinner and as she walked up the path towards Grace's house to go home, she heard a car door open behind her.

'Finally,' she heard a voice say loudly, and she knew instinctively it was Nick. She spun round to see him standing there, his bright blues eyes piercing through her.

'You scared me,' she gasped. 'Didn't your mother ever teach you not to jump out at young women alone in the dark?' She couldn't believe he was waiting for her. It made her feel better though she couldn't help feeling sorry for his wife. What on earth was he playing at?

'Sorry, but can I please talk to you?' Nick pleaded.

Rachel fumbled in her bag for her house keys, 'Honestly, what on earth can you possibly say? How long have you been sitting there?'

'A couple of hours maybe.' Nick shrugged casually, as though it wasn't a big deal. As though she was worth it.

'I'm tired. You should be at home with your wife,' Rachel told him stonily.

'Just hear me out for five minutes, how about that? If you still want to never talk to me again, then I'll accept it and never bother you again,' he said, opening his car door and gesticulating for her to get in the passenger seat.

'How do I know you won't kidnap me?' Rachel asked suspiciously, raising an eyebrow.

'Damn, my grand plan to kidnap you has been uncovered,' he replied, deadpan.

Rachel sighed. 'Very well. Five minutes only.' She made her way into the passenger seat of his car, inhaling his lovely aftershave scent. 'I just don't know what you can possibly say to me though. Not when you've admitted you're married.'

'Will you ever just let me speak?' he asked impatiently with a frown.

Rachel paused for a moment. 'Go on then. Speak.'

Nick looked out of the front window as he spoke. 'I met Claire at college.' He glanced at her quickly and then added, 'that's my wife.'

'I gathered that,' Rachel replied touchily.

'We were young and after a few years together, we split up. Not for any particular reason, but I guess things started to get serious and we both got cold feet. It was only for a month, but during that time I had fun with friends. I was forever going out and getting drunk, meeting new people. Just a typical bloke in his early twenties I guess. I just wanted to forget about it all, you know? Anyhow, Claire wanted to get back together and when we did she found out that I'd slept with someone she knew during our break. She went crazy and looking back, I think she never trusted me again after that point, even though I hadn't done anything wrong. We should never have got back together.' He shook his head. 'It's easy to see that now. Claire had this need to be the perfect couple and after I'd been with this other girl, she felt that everyone thought our relationship was a joke. As though it had become tarnished. She's always cared too much about what others think.'

'I don't see what this has to do with anything,' Rachel stated, feeling perplexed.

'Claire was a bit possessive with me after the break. She'd make up excuses as to why I needed to be home if she knew I had a night out, or she'd swear that I fancied a waitress in a restaurant when I hadn't even noticed anybody else around me. She became very unsure of herself, relying on me and wanting me by her side, and I wanted to make things work. Despite it all, I guess I still loved her. I proposed to her when I was twenty-seven and we got married when we were twenty-nine. Eventually she started to be the old Claire again and I thought everything was great. She fell pregnant with Noah shortly after the wedding though, and that's when things started to fall apart.' He sighed, clenching his jaw. 'It was as if all the old insecurities and paranoia issues came back as soon as he was born. She's always been a bit of a control freak, you see, and she hated how having a baby changed her life and her body. She became so difficult to live with and it was as though there was nothing I could ever do that was right. She went to a doctor and got help, but our relationship just wasn't the same. I don't think it can ever be the same again. We've been separated for nearly a year now, but Claire has always been one to keep up appearances and has begged me not to tell anyone at Noah's school. Noah doesn't really understand what it means that I don't live there anymore as we just tell him I'm working and Claire wants it to stay that way until he's a little older and we can explain. Her parents divorced when she was younger and she's been really worried about the effect it will have on Noah. Obviously our family and close friends know we're no longer together, it's just people at Noah's school who don't. I know all the mums think Claire's perfect, but it couldn't be further from the truth. I couldn't care less who knows, but Claire does; it's just the way she is.'

Rachel nodded, feeling relieved that Nick was actually single and she hadn't been part of a sordid affair. 'The phone calls. Were they from her? Was it Claire who was making you angry all those times?'

'Yes it was,' he admitted. 'It was my decision to separate and Claire likes to still try to be in charge of me, even though we're no longer a couple. She's started to use Noah as a weapon if I don't do what she wants. She makes my life hell at times, if I'm honest. I think it's partly my fault for allowing her to get away with it for so long. I've always respected her as the mother of my child, but lately I've been thinking that enough is enough. I've had enough of dancing to her tune. If I can't make time to collect Noah when she wants, she threatens that I won't ever see him again. But then the following weekend she'll be going out with friends and suddenly I wake up with a text message that she's dropping him over for the weekend, slating me because I don't see him enough. When she's had a bad day, she'll send me abusive messages. I can only ever see Noah when it suits her. I don't want any kind of relationship with her ever again; I just want to be a good father to my son. I'm going to take her to court and get parental rights. I don't want to have to ask her if it's okay to see my son anymore and let her call all the shots. I've had enough.'

'Things can't be that bad if you were with her the other day at the Christmas play though, surely?' Rachel questioned, unable to help still being a little suspicious. She'd really believed that Nick had been married and it was hard adjusting to the new picture, though she was thrilled with the news.

'She told me if I didn't go with her that I wouldn't be able to see him the week after,' he explained, a vein pulsing in his neck. 'I wanted to go of course, but I just think it's about time we told Noah we're no longer together. I don't want to have to pretend to be a couple. Personally, I think we're just confusing him.'

'But she can't stop you from seeing your son if you don't do what she tells you?' Rachel was horrified.

'This is why I know I must take her to court. I've been so worried she has the power to stop me seeing Noah as much as I'd like to, and I stupidly thought if I did the little things she wants, she'd let me have a good relationship with him. Now I know I just need to find out my rights. I'll see him as much as I can,' he said looking tired with the situation. 'After you stopped talking to me because you thought I was married, I realized this all has to stop, like I said. I've had enough of being manipulated and controlled by Claire. We're over and I need a clean slate.'

Rachel had to admit she felt overjoyed with the news. She was relieved. Could she handle being with a man with so much drama in his life? She wasn't so sure. Mark had always been so straight-forward; she didn't think he even had an ex-girlfriend, but look how that had turned out in the end. He'd certainly never had a deranged ex-wife who tried to pretend to be perfect and rule over her ex-husband with their son. Would Claire make their lives difficult? As she gazed at Nick's mesmerising blue eyes, she knew she had to give things a go with him. She would deal with any difficulties they faced when it happened. 'Does Claire still love you?' she wondered.

'Honestly?' Nick stared outside again. 'I just think being with me is a habit. I think she doesn't quite know how to be without me. She likes to think she has me at her beck and call if she needs it, but I told you, not anymore. Meeting you has probably been the wakeup call I needed to realize that the way she treats me is unacceptable. The truth is, I haven't been happy in ages; not until that day you drove into my car.'

'Perhaps it's lucky I'm a bit of a careless driver then?' Rachel smirked. Her stomach turned over when he reached over and took her hand in his.

'I'm sorry that I didn't tell you I was married. I was meaning to. I just didn't know how to begin to even explain what Claire was like. I was worried if I told you I wasn't yet divorced and had a child, you'd run a mile. Especially because I like you so much, Rachel,' he said seriously.

'I like you too. Why do you think I was so upset that you were married? I just really wish you'd been honest with me from the start.'

He sighed heavily. 'I know I should have been. Please forgive me? I promise I'll be honest about everything from now on. I was just scared, that's all. I found it hard to believe that you'd be interested when I come along with baggage.'

'It's not surprising to meet a man in his thirties whose been married and has a child,' Rachel told him. 'Besides, I like children. I wouldn't have minded. I'd rather just be told the truth no matter what.'

'Noted and I'm so sorry,' he repeated.

'Okay, I forgive you.' Rachel gave him a warm smile.

'Good. That's that then. Let me take you for dinner on Saturday night? I want to make it up to you. I promise you won't regret giving me another chance.'

Rachel smiled; it was like music to her ears. She'd felt so down in the dumps again after being told Nick was married and had been trying to brush herself off, hold her head high and get involved in the cheeriness of the Christmas spirit. But now she felt content again, she couldn't wait for celebrating and doing all the things she usually loved. She was about to reply that she'd love nothing more than to go to dinner when she remembered it was the Tidemans Christmas ball. She felt disappointed immediately, knowing that she couldn't see him Sunday due to plans with her family, and Christmas was only a few days after that. Life would be manic. He could tell by her face she wasn't free.

'Do you have plans Saturday?'

'It's my work Christmas ball,' she told him ruefully.

'Ah, I understand; my work doesn't allow us to bring anyone else along either.'

'No, it's not that,' Rachel replied. 'We're actually allowed to bring partners along if we wish...' She stopped speaking, feeling silly for the reason he couldn't go. She'd have loved nothing more than to take Nick along with her. She wanted to spend time with him and get to know him. Every little thing about him. Now she'd discovered he was separated she really wanted her friends to meet him and see what a nice guy he actually was. 'My friends and I made some silly pact, that's all.'

'A pact?' Nick looked like he was about to laugh. 'Sounds like something teenagers would do in a film or something.'

'Yes I know, but we did. When me and Mark split up and Grace broke up with Simon, we decided that we would be single at Christmas and promised we'd go to the Christmas ball just me, Grace and Amber. You know, so we wouldn't feel alone. No dates allowed.' She attempted a smile, but couldn't help but think about what would happen if she changed her mind and invited Nick.

'Okay,' Nick said understandingly, brushing the hair away from her face. 'I'm sure I can see you another time,' he said before turning her head towards his and kissing her mouth.

Rachel felt like she was melting and drifting away to another world as they kissed. She couldn't see Nick before Christmas or even afterwards. In fact, she was worried she wouldn't be able to see him again until after the New Year. She had so many people in her family to see and her grandparents would be staying over. She doubted there would be much free time to go out and meet him, there never usually was. Christmas was always such a busy period and she was working back at Tidemans the day after Boxing Day. 'The thing is,' she admitted, chewing the flesh inside her lower lip, 'I want to see you on Saturday. It will be so busy afterwards and I'm certain you'll also be busy seeing family and friends over Christmas.'

'Well, yes,' he agreed.

'Come to the ball with me?' Rachel asked before she had a chance to think about it. She felt guilty the moment the words passed her lips; she'd promised the others she'd be single for the ball and she knew they weren't taking dates. Surely they would understand her situation though? Finding out that Nick was single again was the best news she'd had in ages and she knew her friends wanted her to be happy. They wouldn't be too annoyed with her, would they? She was hardly committing a crime bringing a date along. Maybe she would convince Grace to bring her new man, but then what about Amber? She certainly couldn't allow Amber to be the only single one and things with Jack were pretty fragile at the moment.

'Are you sure? What about the pact?'

Rachel grit her teeth together. 'I can't believe I'm saying this, but I'm so pleased you're not still with your wife, that I don't care. Everyone is allowed to be selfish sometimes, aren't they? I want you there with me and I'm sure my friends will get over it. They'll be glad for me, I'm sure. Maybe I can just say that you turned up as a surprise?' She thought, blinking hard as the idea came to her.

His lips twitched into a half-smile. 'They won't believe you.'

'Well, it's worth a try,' Rachel responded, feeling excited that Nick was going to go with her. 'I want you there,' she said in a honey-like voice, touching his arm gently.

Nick shot her a devastating smile. 'Then I'll come.'

As he kissed her, Rachel pushed the thoughts of breaking the pact to the back of her mind. She just hoped her friends weren't taking it as seriously as she envisaged.

Chapter 29

It didn't matter how many times Amber told herself that her father was back in her life, it still felt alien to be sitting across a table from him. Here he was finally; the man she had tried to picture countless times in her head. She could see she had the same dark grey eyes and olive skin. Finally, she could see where she'd inherited her straight, slim nose from; her mother's was a completely different shape. She'd wondered for years what her father was really like, and now he wanted a relationship with her after all this time. Just like she'd always secretly longed for. It still didn't stop her feeling angry that he hadn't tried harder to have a relationship with her over the years, but Amber was attempting to give him a chance. After all, he was the only father she'd ever get and he'd missed out on enough of her life.

'So your mother told you what happened?' he said, taking a sip of hot chocolate.

They were sitting in a local coffee shop.

'She did. I didn't know about the affair. Mum never told me about that part,' she explained.

'I won't go into it now she's told you. The truth is, your mother broke my heart, but I know I had a problem back then and I was too stubborn to admit it, even to myself, and I wouldn't let her help me. I was depressed, but it was years and years before I realized it. It's no excuse for not being present in your life though, Amber. I will forever be sorry for that. I should never have stopped trying to see you.' His voice broke off and he swallowed hard. 'I know I haven't been a father to you, but if there's any way we can ever have any kind of relationship then it would make me the happiest man alive. There isn't a day gone by that I hadn't thought about you and regretted my decision.'

Amber felt a flash of embarrassment that her father was wearing his heart on his sleeve. She moved about in her chair feeling discomfited. 'Okay,' she said finally. 'I'd like to give it a try,' she offered, shooting her father a friendly smile. 'I'm not sure how I feel about you disappearing for good after Mum's affair, but I'm willing to look past it for the time being. I can't promise anything, but I'll try to give our relationship a go.'

Her father breathed a sigh of relief. 'That's all I wanted to hear,' he said joyfully, his face transforming into a huge grin.

'We have lots to catch up on,' Amber said, a faint smile on her lips.

'Tell me about yourself. Are you still close with Diane and her family? Is your mother still friends with her?'

'Yes,' Amber replied, unable to stop her first thoughts being of Jack. 'We see them all the time. Jack is one of my best friends.'

'That's lovely,' he beamed. 'How is Jack? A lovely boy, that one. You were always close back then, even as young children.'

Amber forced a smile. 'He's great. He's actually getting married,' she told him as brightly as possible, though it pained her to say it.

'Oh wow,' her father responded, his gaze falling on her hands. 'And you? Any sign of a husband on the horizon?'

Amber shook her head firmly. 'No, not yet. I'm not sure I want to be married,' she told him robustly. But something felt different when she said it out loud this time. Amber hadn't ever been interested in marriage growing up, that much was true, she had never needed a man in her life to feel happy. But now she'd actually admitted that she was in love with Jack she questioned whether this changed things. Would she like to marry Jack? The thought of him being her husband didn't scare her at all. In fact, when she thought of Jack marrying Natalya instead of her, it made her want to scream out loud and she wasn't sure that just being Jack's girlfriend would be enough for her. She wanted him forever and she wanted everyone to know that he was hers. Her heart ached that she'd never acknowledged her feelings before. It was hurtful to think of him with somebody else. Especially Natalya of all people.

Her father changed the subject and they spoke about what they'd both been up to through the years. Amber was pleased that it wasn't too awkward between them; despite not seeing each other for so long and being virtual strangers, it certainly didn't feel that way. Her father was easy to talk to and genuinely interested in everything she had to say.

'I have a gift for you,' he said, after a short while. 'It's an early Christmas present. Only something small,' he told her, handing her a navy-blue box with a red ribbon on.

Amber felt a slight colour coming to her cheeks. A gift from her father was most unexpected and she stared at the box blankly.

'Open it,' her father encouraged her.

'Thanks,' she said, as her fingers untied the silky bow. 'You really didn't need to get me a gift.'

'I have a lot of catching up to do,' her father told her ashamedly. 'I wanted to get it. I'm pretty sure I owe you years' worth of gifts.'

Amber opened the box, a small gasp escaping her lips. It was a beautiful silver locket and as she opened it, there was tiny photo of her as a child, around four years old she guessed, with her father. She was smiling manically at the camera, oblivious that this man who she clearly loved beside her was going to be gone one day from her life. As she looked up, her father's eyes were watery.

'Like I said, it's not much, but all I've ever had are photos of you and this one was my favourite,' he said, sounding choked.

'Thanks,' Amber said holding the locket tightly. It was a thoughtful gift and she'd treasure it. She looked up at that point, startled when she spotted Jack walking into the coffee shop. 'Jack!' she called out.

Her father spun round too and Amber watched as Jack approached them with a concerned expression lining his face.

'Amber, hi,' he said, before glancing at her father curiously.

'This is my dad,' Amber said. Would the words always sound so strange when she said them out loud?

Jack held out his hand. 'Nice to meet you.'

Amber frowned at Jack, wondering what on earth he was doing there as her father spoke. 'Well, you've certainly grown since the last time I met you. Lovely to see you again, Jack. I was friends with your father when I was married to Amber's mother. How is he?'

'He's well, thank you. I'll tell him you said hello,' Jack replied politely.

'Do you want to join us?' Amber was bewildered as to what he was doing there. Was something wrong?

'Amber I need to go anyway,' her father said, glancing at his watch. 'Why don't I buy you both a drink before I leave?' he suggested kindly.

'Thanks,' Amber smiled. 'I'll come with you to get them.'

The barista took their order and Amber turned to her father. 'Thanks again for the locket. It was really kind of you and I didn't expect it.'

He hugged her. 'Don't be so silly. It was nothing. I was hoping to see you around Christmas time if you have any free days. Of course, I understand if you're busy…'

'I'd like that,' Amber replied with a natural smile. 'I'm certain there will be some days I have free before going back to work.'

'Merry Christmas,' he said cheerily, looking happy that she

233

would meet him again. 'I know this will be the best one I've had in years.'

Amber kissed her father goodbye, delighted that it didn't feel uncomfortable between them as she'd feared it would. She had taken to him surprisingly well, despite the fact she resented him. She wondered if that feeling would ever leave her. She took the gingerbread lattes from the barista and walked over to where Jack was sitting, feeling slightly nervous about talking to him after their argument.

'How come you're here?' she asked him, placing the mug in front of him. 'Is it just a coincidence?' she questioned.

'My mum spoke to yours and told me you were meeting your dad here,' he said looking grave. 'I don't know why I came. I guess I just wanted to check you were okay. I thought he might have gone by now and I don't know, I was just a little worried I guess. I know how much of a big deal this must be to you.'

Amber fiddled with the sleeve of her jumper and twisted her fingers feeling unsettled that things were tense between them. 'I thought you hated me after what happened,' she confessed. 'The things I said about Natalya. I know I upset you. I wasn't sure you'd even care how I was.'

'Don't be so ridiculous,' Jack scolded her sharply. 'I'll always care about you and you know that. I've known you forever; I knew how much it meant to you to have a father figure in your life and I just wondered if things had gone okay, that's all. I didn't want to encroach or anything.'

'Okay, calm down,' Amber's eyes widened. Jack was definitely not over their row; he was never usually snappy with her. 'Things actually went really well with my dad,' she stated happily. 'I didn't expect it to, but there's a lot more to the story I never knew about, and my dad wants to get to know me. I know he hasn't been around all these years, but it's kind of difficult to say no. I feel like I've missed out and I owe it to myself to give him a chance.'

'He's the one that's missed out,' Jack reminded her protectively.

'But I'm glad to see everything went well. I was concerned I was going to come here to see you in floods of tears or something.'

'No, luckily not,' Amber smiled at him fondly. He still had her back despite their cross words the other day. But did he just care so much because he saw her as a sister-type figure in his life? How would she know if there was more to it unless she finally came clean? 'I'm sorry for what I said about Natalya.'

'Good,' Jack replied, his tone softening. 'You were pretty harsh about her.'

Amber took a deep breath trying to build up courage. Her palms were sweaty and her heart was beating loudly in her ears. 'It's because I care about you, Jack, that's all.' She had no idea how to tell him. Where to start?

'I care about you too, Amber, you know that; I just wasn't expecting you to start telling me I'm marrying the wrong woman.'

'You are though,' Amber told him with certainty.

'Let's not go into all this again,' Jack said, looking away, attempting to brush off the comment.

'I have to,' Amber told him in slow, heavy tones. 'I'd never forgive myself if I didn't say it.'

'Say what, Amber?' Jack questioned irritably. 'I told you, let's just leave it.'

Amber paused for a moment as Jack gave her a beady stare. 'Why did you really come here today, Jack? Why would you bother putting yourself out and taking time out of your day to check that I was okay?'

His face creased in puzzlement. 'You're my friend. I wanted to check you on you. Why are you asking me that?'

'Is that really it?' Amber tried to sound calm, but her voice began to wobble a little. 'Am I really just a friend?'

Jack looked stupefied again as he gazed at Amber with swivelling, inquisitive eyes. 'I don't understand what you're saying…'

'I'm telling you that I'm in love with you, Jack,' Amber blurted out in shrilly tones, a wall of panic hitting her as she considered the consequences. She could see the light slowly dawning on his face as it changed to one of astonishment. 'Don't marry Natalya. And I'm not just saying that because I'm in love with you, but because she isn't the right girl for you, but there, now you know. I love you, Jack. I probably always have.' She giggled nervously. 'I just haven't been able to really see it until now.'

Jack's face turned pale. 'You love me?' he repeated in shock.

'Yes,' Amber told him boldly. She looked away from him at the floor.

'But all those years ago when I tried to kiss you, you pushed me away,' he reminded her in confusion.

'I was scared. You've always been my closest friend. We were young then too; just imagine how disastrous it would have been if we'd got together and then split up? I couldn't have lost you then and I can't lose you now.' Her voice rose slightly in distress before she continued. 'I've been afraid to tell you how I feel. I'm terrified that you don't feel the same and I've now ruined our friendship. I know you're getting married and it's probably not fair to just drop this on you, but I have to. I can't live with the regret that I didn't at least try. I can't move on until I've told you exactly how I feel. I'm in love with you, Jack.'

'I really don't know what to think, Amber. I don't know what to say to you,' Jack announced guiltily, his face blank.

Amber winced. He didn't love her back or he would have said it. As she'd feared she'd put him in a difficult position and now she'd spoiled everything. How would they ever move on from this?

'It's okay, Jack. It's not your fault if you don't feel the same. I'm sorry to have told you like this. I don't know when the right time would have been. It's taken me too long to realize my true feeling until it's too late—'

'Natalya,' he interjected.

'Yes, I know you're in love with Natalya,' she said, her throat dry as she attempted to swallow.

236

'No, Natalya is here. She's just walked in behind you,' he said with an anxious frown, standing up and waving her over.

Amber stood up too, intending on leaving. As much as she was mortified and heartbroken that Jack didn't love her back, she was also glad she'd finally told him. She wanted to point at Natalya and say to Jack that it was no surprise he couldn't even meet her for coffee without her showing up. Could he still not see? Maybe he didn't care? Either way, it was time for her to go. She spun round to face Natalya's suspicious, vexed gaze. 'Hi, Natalya. I was just leaving.'

Natalya ignored the comment and looked at Jack with a hard glare. 'I thought you were at your mum's house?' she accused him. 'When I went there though she told me you were here.'

'Yes,' Jack said in a timid voice clearing his throat. 'I just wanted to check that Amber was okay.'

'Which I am,' Amber added quickly as she put her coat on. 'I'm going now, so he's all yours. Goodbye, Jack,' Amber managed to say, before swiftly walking to the exit.

When Amber reached the safety of her car she breathed out slowly. Then tears formed in her eyes and she sobbed. Had she now lost Jack for good? What was she going to do now?

Chapter 30

'You look amazing,' Grace complimented Rachel as she admired her long electric-blue gown. They'd both had their hair done for the ball and Rachel had opted for a messy side bun with several loose braids intertwined. Her floor-length dress was backless, showing off her creamy, smooth skin and she looked stunning.

'Thanks,' Rachel replied gratefully. 'So do you. I love your black dress,' she told her. 'It must have cost a fortune.'

Grace smiled thinking about Simon who had generously purchased it for her. She laughed good-naturedly. 'It's a shame we don't have any men to go with tonight, isn't it? All this effort and we have no dates.'

Rachel looked uneasy suddenly. 'Yes, I know. It's a shame, but never mind.'

'Have you spoken to Amber?' Grace enquired.

'Yes, we're meeting her there. She's still upset about Jack of course and I had to encourage her to come out, but I think she'd putting on a brave face so we'll have to cheer her up.'

'Yes, the poor thing. I wonder what will happen between her and Jack now? I really hope it doesn't ruin their friendship; it would be such a shame.'

Rachel nodded in agreement before Grace's phone beeped,

signalling that she had a text message. Her heart sank when she saw it was only from her sister finalising Christmas day plans. She hadn't spoken to Simon since their shopping trip when he'd left her in a mood, and the truth was that Grace was worried about him. About them. She was afraid he was going to give up on her. She wished he was going to the ball tonight more than anything; it really wasn't going to be the same without him and he was right, why was she so afraid to tell people she was giving him another chance? She wanted him there. As much as she knew she would have an amazing night with just the girls, she felt guilty that she wasn't inviting him knowing that all her colleagues were taking their other halves. Would Amber and Rachel really mind if he came along? She was torn between just leaving things, or sending him a last-minute message in the hope that he could join her. Even if it was for just some of the evening so she could spend some quality time with her friends; was it really a big deal if she broke the pact? It was most unlike her to ever be disloyal to Rachel and Amber, but Grace wanted her marriage to work and she knew her friends would understand that. He wasn't just some random man she'd started dating; he was her husband. Simon had been trying really hard too, she had to give him that. He'd been making such an effort that she couldn't imagine him just switching back to the man he was when she'd left him.

As Rachel applied more lipstick while they waited for the taxi, Grace made up her mind and quickly tapped a message into her phone to Simon. He probably wouldn't be able to make it anyway.

Simon, if it's not too late, please come to the ball? I do want people to know about us. I want to take you back, move on and give things another go. Tonight won't be the same without you and I can't imagine Christmas without you either. I just hope this message isn't too late? Xx

'Are you texting Amber?' Rachel asked, intruding on Grace's worried thoughts that Simon wouldn't want to go now or had most likely made other plans. 'Tell her we'll meet her by the bar if you are. We can't have her getting stuck with some of the dull work lot.'

'Yes, I'll tell her,' Grace lied, before hitting the send button on her phone to Simon. She really liked living with Rachel and had to admit she would miss her, but Grace also couldn't wait to have Simon back in her life everyday where he belonged. She was excited about their future together. She quickly wrote a message to Amber to tell her where to meet them and then looked out of the window when the taxi sounded his horn.

Fifteen minutes later and they were walking inside the venue, which Tidemans had decorated beautifully. It seemed that no expense had been spared with white twinkling fairy lights covering little artificial trees, a large Christmas tree in the corner of the dance floor, little figurines to decorate the bar area and even a set of three brightly-lit reindeer by the entrance.

'Wow, very Christmassy; I'm impressed,' Rachel noted as she walked into the room.

They found Amber propped up at the bar with three glasses of Kir Royale.

'Cheers girls,' she smiled widely, handing them their drinks as they approached her. 'I haven't been here long luckily. I'm glad to see we all stuck to our word and are each other's dates. It's couples galore everywhere,' she pointed out with a quick roll of her grey eyes, looking round the room.

Grace looked at the floor guiltily and quickly checked her phone. No message from Simon. She felt half relieved and half disappointed that he wasn't going to make an appearance at least for a few hours.

'So how are you feeling about Jack now?' Rachel asked Amber. 'Have you heard from him?'

'Nope, not a word,' Amber said, her chin held high to show

she didn't care, but Grace could see from her glistening eyes how much she was hurting deep down. It was obvious that Amber was just putting on a brave face. 'I don't expect to either. I just have to face it; I told Jack that I loved him and he didn't say it back to me. He's in love with Natalya and I'm too late. I have to just move on. Get over it. Plenty of people find that their love is unrequited; I'm not the first and I certainly won't be the last. I'm a big girl now and I can take it.'

'Of course, you'll be fine. It's okay to be sad about it though you know,' Grace said gently, squeezing her arm softly.

'Not tonight girls,' Amber replied, looking as though she was forcing herself to be ebullient. 'Tonight is all about us having fun. Here's to being single at Christmas,' she said in cheerful tones. Grace noticed her smile was strained though.

They clinked glasses together, Grace feeling more dreadful by the second. Perhaps she should text Simon that it wasn't a good idea to come after all? He still hadn't replied though so there was probably no need. Besides, it would only appear strange if she now asked him not to come. Imagine if he had already left? She would be making things worse than they already were. She had no choice but to leave it.

'Perhaps we should do some shots?' Grace suggested, getting into the spirit. She might need them if Simon showed up. Amber nodded, picking up a drinks menu and Grace looked at Rachel who looked somewhat distracted. 'Up for it?'

'Mm? Yes, of course.' Her eyes danced round the room. 'Shots sounds great, you know me.'

They downed several shots at the bar, laughing at each other's grimaces as they did so.

'Let's dance!' Amber declared energetically. She was always the first one on the dancefloor and pulled Grace's arm, who in turn pulled Rachel's. If Grace was being dragged to the dancefloor, then so was Rachel.

'Oh really?' Rachel moaned dubiously as they reached the

empty floor. 'You know I can't dance. I would have planned some moves if I'd had known.'

'Just relax!' Grace laughed at Rachel's stiff routine of moving from side to side.

Amber found it hilarious and starting swinging Rachel round, making them burst into fits of laughter.

'I'm proud of you both,' Amber stated loudly over the music.

The song stopped and another started which they weren't familiar with so they shrugged at each other and walked over to three empty chairs, Grace and Rachel sitting either side of Amber.

'Proud?' Grace repeated.

'Yes,' Amber nodded, her eyes glistening. 'You've both been through a hard time and come out the other side. Grace, I admire how brave you were to realize you weren't happy and actually do something about it. Just imagine how many people remain in unhappy marriages, plodding along in life? But you didn't. You made a change to stop it heading that way. It's a brave thing to do.'

Grace nodded. What Amber was saying was true. She was also glad she'd made a stand and done something about her relationship. Otherwise Simon might never have changed. It had been a risk splitting up with him, but one that Grace knew she had to take. She would hands down have rather been alone than with Simon the way he was before.

'I think being single has made me realize how important friendships are,' Grace announced, looking back over the past few months. 'I can't thank you girls enough for being there to support me, and if there's one thing I've learnt, it's actually that we need to continue our nights out together. Whatever happens in the future, girl time is a must.'

'That's the best thing I've heard you say in ages,' Amber grinned looking pleased. 'Rachel, you too have been amazing. You handled what happened with Mark and Bianca with dignity and maturity.

I'm not so sure I could have done the same. Honestly, you're so strong.'

Grace nodded. 'She's right, Rachel, you really are strong. You've also always been so meticulous at planning everything in your life and since you've split with Mark, I think I've noticed a change in you. You seem to have mellowed slightly, don't you think? Maybe not with cleaning and keeping up to date with your washing—' she laughed good-humouredly, thinking how tidy and organized Rachel was to live with '—but generally speaking.'

Rachel smiled at her friends widely. 'Thanks, and yes, I guess I've just realized that things don't always turn out how you think, but that's okay. I've learned that it's a bonus to have someone to share your life with, but it's not a necessity. So long as I have you two and my other friends and family, then I'll be okay. I've enjoyed dating so much more than I thought I would. I know I haven't been out with tons of people, but still. The not knowing what's going to happen and who I may meet. Getting dressed up for a date and feeling nerves again, it's exciting. It makes me realize that what I had with Mark wasn't passionate or enthralling. Sparks didn't fly. I just thought he was a safe bet. I loved going out with you two as well. I can't thank you enough for being there for me either; I honestly don't think I could have done it without you,' she said, getting teary.

'Don't cry, you'll start me blubbering.' Amber flapped her hand in Rachel's direction. 'And these false lashes certainly don't need tears to start making the glue come off tonight. Let's all get a drink and cheers to us. To being single at the best time of year. Even though I know that Grace is probably getting quite serious with Steve and perhaps doesn't count.'

Grace just smiled, unsure how to answer.

'In fact, before we get that drink we need to dance again. I love this song!'

Grace rolled her eyes at Rachel good-naturedly as they waltzed back over to the dancefloor behind Amber.

243

Thirty minutes later they were standing by the bar.

'What's up with you?' Amber asked Rachel curiously. 'You seem to be in another world.'

'Me?' Rachel replied, her mouth twitching apprehensively and her eyes darting from the entrance and then back to them. 'What makes you say that? I'm fine. All good. Nothing new to report here. Nothing new at all.'

Grace frowned at her wondering once more what was up, before Amber's eyes grew wider.

'Hey, is that Nick? What on earth is he doing here?' she wondered in bewilderment. 'Seems you have a stalker, Rachel,' she snorted. 'He must have given your name on the door to be allowed in; who actually does that when they haven't been invited?'

Rachel looked abashed and Grace instantly knew that Nick wasn't a stalker at all. Her tense expression said it all: Rachel had planned for Nick to come.

'Oh yes,' Rachel said in a wan, shaky, voice looking disconcerted. Her gaze flew from Grace to Amber before she closed them quickly and took a deep breath. 'Okay, so there's something I have to tell you...'

'Why on earth is he here?' Amber said in exasperation. 'Doesn't the man have any pride to just turn up uninvited and ruin your Christmas ball?' She looked incandescent as she narrowed her eyes in Nick's direction who was looking round, obviously trying to find Rachel.

'Me and Nick are giving things a go,' Rachel said quickly. 'I was going to tell you both. I was supposed to tell you when I got here but it seemed to be really fun it being just the three of us, Amber, I didn't want to admit I'd broken our pact.'

'But he's *married*?' Grace reminded her, wrinkling her nose at the thought of Rachel happily taking part in an affair. Her mouth pressed into a hard line. How could Rachel take him back?

'It's a long story,' Rachel said.

'Rachel, an affair ruined my parents' relationship. It's the reason

I haven't seen my father since I was five up until now. How can you have forgiven him? Are you mad?' Amber was horrified.

'It's not what you think,' Rachel replied defensively. 'They've separated. They're no longer together; he hasn't been with Claire for over a year.'

Grace was astonished and pleased at the same time. This was *good* news. Rachel hadn't been caught up in someone else's marriage after all. Perhaps she would find happiness in love? She really did deserve some luck, and as she watched Nick's eyes light up as he walked over to Rachel, she had a good feeling about it. He looked her up and down in awe and kissed her lightly on the lips before turning to them.

'Good evening girls. Nice to meet you both; Rachel has told me lots about you. You all look stunning this evening,' he said genuinely.

Rachel couldn't stop smiling at him; she looked over the moon at his arrival and Grace was really pleased for her.

'Nice to meet you too, Nick,' Grace shot him a welcoming smile.

'Yes, hi,' Amber flashed him a natural smile too, and Grace could see she had already forgiven Rachel for breaking the pact. She obviously cared more for Rachel's happiness, which was radiating from her.

'Drink anyone?' Nick offered kindly.

They declined, still having some of their drinks left and Nick made his way over to the bar.

Rachel clenched her jaw and made a face. 'I'm so sorry I broke the pact girls, but when Nick asked to meet up with me tonight I just really wanted to see him before Christmas. I was so happy he didn't lie to me, and as much as I just wish he'd told me his story from the start, he has his reasons. I won't go into it now, but I hope you're not annoyed with me. I'll still stay with you all night I promise; you know you girls will always be my priority.'

'Don't be silly.' Grace was the first to answer her. 'We completely understand you wanted to see him and I think it's great you're giving him another chance; no one's relationships are straight-forward anyway.'

'Yes, just enjoy yourself and spend time getting to know him more.' Amber smiled gaily. 'As if we would ever be annoyed with you,' she told Rachel to reassure her.

'Thanks girls.' Rachel looked pleased with their response. 'In that case, I may just go and join Nick at the bar so he's not alone. I'll be back soon.'

Amber and Grace smiled at each other as Rachel walked away looking as though she was floating in the air. It was clear to see how smitten she was.

'I really hope it works out for them,' Amber stated sincerely with a cheerful smile.

'Yes, me too,' Grace replied, her mind elsewhere. If she was honest, seeing Rachel laughing at the bar with Nick was making her pine for Simon even more. If only she had told Rachel and Amber about seeing him again then he would be there with her. She couldn't deny she was having an amazing night with her friends, but if he had been there too it would have made the night perfect.

'Do you remember last year when Jack and Simon fell over at the end and Ed from menswear looked at them in disgrace?' Amber chuckled.

Grace giggled at the memory. 'What about when Jack got stuck talking to boring Mike? That was hilarious. You had to go and rescue him in the end, pretending you wanted a dance even though there was no one else on the dancefloor.'

They both laughed and then became silent, deep in thought. Grace looked round at her work colleagues. They were nice enough, but there wasn't anybody she was interested in talking to. She missed Simon and Jack being there like they normally were. She checked her phone again, disappointed when she saw the blank screen. Simon obviously wasn't coming and, even though she should have been happy that he wasn't in case Amber felt left out, Grace felt regretful about how she'd treated him and prayed to God that he still wanted to give things a go.

'I'm just going to the loo,' she told Amber over the Christmas music blaring out, who was looking at her phone.

'Shall I get us some more drinks?' Amber suggested, waving her empty glass.

Grace nodded and made her way through the growing crowds to the entrance where it was quiet. She didn't actually need to go to the toilets and had just told Amber that so she could be alone. She had a sudden urge to speak to Simon and check things were okay between them. She dialled his number from her mobile, hoping he'd answer. When he didn't, she tried again.

'Grace?' came the familiar voice at the other end of the line.

'Simon. How are you?' Grace asked. 'Did you get my message about this evening?'

There was a long pause. 'I did, yes,' he replied seriously.

'And?' Grace's heart was beating faster with every second. She wasn't used to Simon being mysterious about the way he felt.

'I'm just so confused,' he replied honestly. 'We've been getting on amazingly well, haven't we? You've repeatedly told me you're not ready to tell anyone about us, and that you didn't want me accompanying you tonight and now this? Now you're asking me to go to your work ball, with no notice whatsoever. You only told me the other day I wasn't welcome.'

Grace closed her eyes for a moment. 'I know, Simon and I'm sorry. I'm unsure why I didn't want you to come before. It was because of the pact I made, it was because I was scared…' She broke off desperately. Was she really losing him? Had Simon finally had enough of her being so blasé about their relationship?

'I've heard all that before, Grace,' he replied gravely.

'I'm sorry, Simon. I know I should have just been honest with everyone now. Please don't tell me you've given up on us. You're right in saying that things have been great between us and the truth is, I'm the happiest I've ever been. I love you, Simon. I love you more than ever and I want you to move back in with me. I'm ready to tell the world we're back together and to make a go of things. I want to be with you over Christmas. It won't be the same without you. I really feel like this time it will work. I'm so sorry I'm finally saying all this on a phone call. I know it's probably not good enough...' She broke off ruefully.

'No Grace, I'm sorry, but it's *not* good enough,' he said before the line went dead.

Grace swallowed hard, her eyes burning hot with tears. She'd blown it. She was astonished and devastated that Simon didn't want to know any longer. He'd been so lovely to her and this was all her fault. She wiped her eyes and took a deep breath before freezing when she heard a voice from behind her.

'It's not good enough when you can say all this to my face.'

Grace span round, her face bursting into a smile as she stared at Simon standing in front of her, his eyes twinkling in amusement. Her insides turned to jelly.

Grace tapped his arm playfully. 'You scared me. I really thought that you'd had enough and didn't want to know me anymore,' she announced forlornly.

'It would take more than a little bump in the road to get rid of me.' Simon gave a light laugh. 'I would never not want to know you, Grace. How can you not see that? I love you more than anything in the world. You're everything to me,' he said, gripping her into a tight hug. 'And just look where we're standing—' his eyes flicked upwards '—right under the mistletoe.'

Grace couldn't contain her smile as she leant towards Simon and kissed him tenderly on the lips. 'I want you to move back home in the New Year,' she said with certainty.

'Thank goodness for that,' he chuckled. 'I've certainly had enough of Paul and his mess.'

Grace exhaled in relief, delighted that Simon had made an appearance after all. She couldn't wait to tell the others that they were back together and she was giving Simon another chance. She instantly felt her spirits lift knowing that he was with her, but as they made their way through the busy dancefloor, Grace couldn't help but worry about Amber feeling left out.

She glanced over and saw Amber, Rachel and Nick chatting on the edge of the dancefloor.

'Just give me a moment,' she asked Simon with a reassuring smile. 'Get a drink and then come over.' She pointed towards the bar and Simon gave her an understanding nod of the head and quickly pecked her cheek before walking off.

Grace walked over to where the others were standing.

'Finally,' Amber exclaimed, holding out Grace's drink. 'I almost drank your one as well while I was waiting. Why have you been gone so long?'

Grace felt a slight colour coming to her cheeks and was glad that it was dark and they wouldn't be able to see. 'Amber, I'm really sorry, but I also have a date here tonight,' she told her, quickly glancing at her shoes. 'You see, I didn't know that Rachel was bringing Nick, and I kind of asked him on the off-chance, thinking deep down he wouldn't come anyway, even though I wanted him to. I'm really sorry, but I've broken the pact as well.'

Amber rolled her eyes in mock-annoyance. 'Oh for goodness' sake Grace, don't be so ridiculous. It really doesn't matter; I'm starting to wish we'd never made this stupid pact to remain single. *Some* people just don't know how to stick to a promise,' she stated, glancing at Rachel and then Grace, but she was smiling to show she didn't really mind. 'I'm pleased for you both, really I am. How could I be annoyed when you both seem so loved up? I'll be fine playing the gooseberry, I should get used to it.' She laughed.

Rachel frowned. 'Don't say that, Amber. You can have any man you want and you know it. I thought you preferred being single anyway?'

'So did I,' Amber said seriously. 'But I'm not entirely sure I'm so anti-relationships anymore. Realising my love for Jack has changed the way I feel about everything.' Her tone changed to a much brighter, enthusiastic one. 'Anyway, Grace, let's meet him. Where is this Steve you've kept hidden for so long?'

'Yes, I can't wait to see him,' Rachel joined in excitedly.

Simon approached them then, standing beside Grace and holding her hand.

'There is no Steve,' Grace explained, holding onto Simon tightly. 'Girls, I want you to meet the man in my life, Simon. Simon and I are going to give things another go.'

Grace had to bite her lip from bursting out into laughter. Rachel and Amber's astonished expressions were quite the picture.

Chapter 31

'Oh my God!' Amber's jaw almost hit the floor. 'So you've been seeing Simon for all this time and you never told us?' She was flabbergasted. How had Grace kept this a secret? They usually told each other everything.

'Hello again, girls,' Simon looked a little awkward and kissed them politely on the cheek.

'Sorry Simon, I'm glad to see you,' Amber added quickly. 'I'm just so surprised, that's all.'

'I'll leave you girls to talk for a bit.' Simon smiled kindly.

'I think I'll join you,' Nick said, before introducing himself and shaking his hand. They walked off towards two chairs at the other end of the room.

'I can't believe it.' Rachel shook her head, her eyes wide. 'I really thought you had a new man. What happened? How come you're back with Simon? I thought he made you unhappy; you seemed so sad before you broke up with him,' she said looking incredulous.

'He's been really different since the split,' Grace explained, her cheeks pink with pleasure. 'Honestly, I can't explain what a change there's been. It's like the old Simon is back, the man I fell head over heels in love with. I owe it to him, to myself even, to give our marriage another shot. I don't think it's a decision I'll regret; I love him.'

Amber was ecstatic for her friend and shot her a huge smile. 'Good for you, Grace. I don't blame you at all for giving him another chance, especially if he's changed like you say he has.'

'Yes,' Rachel agreed. 'All that matters is that you're happy.'

'I am,' Grace gushed, looking blissfully joyful, 'I really am.'

Amber gazed at her friends; she was really pleased for both of them. So what if they had broken their pacts about being single at the ball? So what if she was the only one without a date? It didn't matter. Not really. They'd both had a tough time recently and deserved a new start. Her own heart ached that little bit more though. Amber wasn't jealous; she was envious. She'd always been the single one, mainly out of choice and Amber usually loved the fact she wasn't in a relationship at Christmas time. Bars were always buzzing, packed with singletons wanting to celebrate and have fun. This year, her heart just hadn't been in it though. As soon as she realized that her heart belonged to Jack, Amber could honestly say she hadn't even thought about another man. The sad thing was, as much as she knew it was a long shot that Jack was going to feel the same, a tiny part of her had hoped that he would turn around and say he loved her too. She hated herself for that glimmer of hope. That little glimmer that kept telling her that once, he *had* tried to kiss her; maybe that meant something? But of course Jack wasn't going to forget all about the love of his life, Natalya, just because Amber had now decided she loved him, was he? He probably saw this whole thing as an issue he was going to have to deal with. Amber couldn't bear it.

She was mortified that she'd told him, yet felt she'd had no other choice. She couldn't have lived with herself. She'd been thinking over the last few days that she was going to pack up and go away somewhere as soon as possible. Dubai had been top of her list and she'd contacted an old school friend who lived there to see if she could stay with her. After New Year's Eve Amber was going to leave for a bit. She'd give Jack some space and she simply couldn't bear to watch him with Natalya. She needed to clear her head and didn't want to feel angry every time Natalya ruined her day. The only issue was her father who she'd just re-connected with, but she was certain he'd understand. Besides, she'd only go for a few months or so and perhaps he could visit if he really wanted to see her? She knew her mother had always wanted to go there. Then there was work; Amber had no idea what Judy, the boss at Tidemans, would say about her leaving. But Amber was a make-up artist, and as sad as she'd be to leave Tidemans, she knew she wouldn't find it hard getting another job somewhere else. She could always freelance too or try to work in TV or film or for an agency. Her mind was made up.

'What will you do about Christmas?' Rachel asked curiously. 'Are you still going to see Jack on Christmas Day?'

Amber pressed her mouth into a straight line as she thought about how mortifying it would be to watch him snuggling up to Natalya as they played board games.

'I guess I have to just act as though everything is normal. As though it's all fine. Perhaps I won't stay for too long, I don't know. I'll come up with an excuse as to why I have to leave.' It was certainly not a day she was looking forward to and that made her sad. Amber *loved* Christmas Day normally.

The rest of the night passed by fairly quickly. Rachel and Grace had made it their priority to spend time with Amber and she was grateful for that; she hadn't felt left out in the slightest and actually had fun in Simon and Nick's company. Grace was right about Simon; he did seem different around her, like he'd just met Grace recently and still found her mystifying and fascinating. She hoped he remained that way for Grace's sake, who looked just as smitten as he did.

Amber downed the last of her prosecco, noticing that the room was emptying out, and decided it was time for her to leave too. It had been a good night, but she still couldn't shift the sad feeling she had in the pit of her stomach and she was tired. Besides, slow music had started playing and there were a few couples dancing. Amber didn't want to get in the way of Grace and Rachel from doing the same.

After kissing her friends goodbye and promising them she'd let them know she got home safely, Amber put her cream faux-fur coat on and made her way outside, shivering as soon as her bare legs hit the cold, frosty air. She was walking towards several parked black taxis, when she spotted a familiar figure in the distance, looking in her direction. Had they been waiting for her?

'What are you doing here?' Amber asked sharply in astonishment.

Natalya looked at Amber icily with intense eyes. 'I came to warn you away,' she told her. 'I knew you were in love with Jack from the very start.'

'Go away, you absolute nutcase,' Amber fumed, pulling a face and brushing past her, but Natalya pulled her back. As Amber stared into Natalya's huge pupils, she realized that gone was the sweet, friendly girl she'd met weeks ago at Tidemans when she'd come in to get her make-up done. She'd been replaced by this jealous, possessive creature in front of her. 'How did you even know where to find me? Are you stalking me as well as Jack now?'

'I knew tonight was your Christmas ball,' she said, a nasty edge to her voice. 'Jack told me ages ago that he always comes with you. Before you decided you were going alone with those friends of yours. I noticed when I looked into the ballroom that they didn't do the same in the end. Poor little Amber all alone,' she said vindictively.

'What do you actually want? I don't understand. To warn me? To rub it in my face and tell me that Jack is yours, is that it? I know that. I don't think you're right for him at all, but that's down to Jack. To come to my Christmas ball and wait outside in the cold is pretty weird if you ask me, Natalya. You seem even more odd than I thought.'

'I *love* him,' Natalya rebuked, a wild look in her wide eyes. 'How dare you try to take him away from me!' she shrieked.

Amber looked around, embarrassed that Natalya was starting to cause a scene.

'Calm down,' she said in hushed tones. 'What did Jack tell you anyway?'

'He didn't need to tell me anything. I just know; I've always known,' she stated, blinking several times.

'Well, I can't help how I feel,' Amber replied indignantly, her eyes downcast.

'But you've known him for years,' Natalya shot back. 'Why now? Why now that he's engaged to me do you have to want him?' she demanded furiously.

Amber opened her mouth to answer, but no words would come. She didn't have an answer as to why. Perhaps she would be angry too if she was in Natalya's position? It still didn't excuse her craziness though.

'He doesn't love you,' Natalya laughed wickedly. 'He feels sorry for you. He's in love with me. He told me he's never seen you as anything more than a friend.'

Amber swallowed hard, feeling as though someone had kicked her in the gut.

'Well, I'm leaving anyway,' she declared, feeling beaten. 'I was going to wait until after Christmas, but I don't see any way I can spend it with you, so I'm going to go as soon as possible. Jack's all yours so just relax. Be grateful to have someone like him.'

'Where are you going?' Natalya asked in disbelief, like it was too good to be true.

'Dubai,' Amber replied. 'Far enough away for you? Not that my whereabouts has anything to do with you.'

Natalya exhaled looking satisfied and nodded slowly. 'I think that's for the best.'

'I'm sure you do,' Amber shot her a sarcastic smile. 'Take my advice. If you love Jack, if you really and truly love him, then let him breathe a little, Natalya. Jack has chosen to be with you, so let him live and go out with his friends without checking up on him the whole time. Give him the space he needs, trust me.'

'Like I could ever trust you,' she replied tartly.

'Bye Natalya. Take care of him for me,' Amber said sadly, before jumping into the black taxi at the front of the queue. 'He's a great man,' she muttered. Then under her breath she said in sorrowful tones, 'The very best.'

Chapter 32

Christmas Day

'Happy Christmas,' Grace sang to Rachel as she made her way downstairs to the kitchen and passed her a mug of coffee. 'Or would you prefer some Buck's Fizz?'

'Merry Christmas,' Rachel smiled widely at her friend. 'And no, the coffee is fine. It's a little early for a Buck's Fizz,' she giggled. She glanced at Grace. 'You look lovely. What are your Christmas plans?' she asked.

'Simon is picking me up in around an hour and we're going to my sister's house for the day. I'm looking forward to it. What time are you going to your parents' house? Love the Christmas jumper by the way,' she laughed.

Rachel was wearing a jumper with an image of Rudolph on the front. His large, red nose stuck out of the jumper, flapping up and down as she walked.

'Family tradition.' She gave a light laugh. 'I'm probably leaving around the same time as you in about an hour.'

'So you have time for a bacon sandwich?' Grace enquired, checking the bacon in the oven.

'Definitely. I'm starving.'

Grace quickly went into the lounge and collected Rachel's present from under the tree.

'Shall we do presents?' she asked, as she walked back into the kitchen.

'Yes, let's,' Rachel replied, before disappearing for a minute. She came back holding a bright red box, which she handed over to Grace at the same time Grace handed over her present.

'Thank you.' Grace smiled, delighted to see the perfume set she'd been going on and on about over the past few weeks. 'I'll wear it today. I love it.'

Rachel was pleased with her silk pyjamas too. 'Wow, thanks Grace. These are great.'

'I've noticed you're in need of new ones.' Grace smiled warmly at Rachel, thinking how much she was going to miss not living with her again. She belonged with Simon though, especially after what she'd just found out.

As if reading her mind, Rachel turned and faced Grace.

'Grace, I've been thinking. Obviously now you and Simon have made amends, you're very likely going to want to live with him again, aren't you? Which is perfectly fine and I completely understand, of course. I just wanted to let you know I've been looking at renting somewhere on my own. Nick has suggested this lovely little apartment close to where he lives and I plan to see it the day after Boxing Day.'

Grace cleared her throat. 'Yes, I've been meaning to talk to you about this. I don't want you to think I'm kicking you out or anything, because I love living with you. It's been so nice having you here and it hasn't even been for long. Don't feel like you have to rush finding somewhere; Simon will wait as long as I tell him to.' She flashed her a friendly smile.

'Thanks Grace. I know, I've loved living with you too, but it will be nice to get somewhere on my own and be independent. I'm sure Nick will be over quite a bit too though I certainly don't plan to rush into things. I'm not going to put any pressure on myself and just take each day as it comes.'

'Good idea,' Grace replied. 'You two make a great couple and I really think things will work out. What's he up to today?'

'He's seeing Noah this morning, which will be lovely for him, and then spending the rest of the day with his family. I think now he's told Claire he's not willing to be manipulated any longer and will take her to court, she's started to become a little easier to get along with. I think he's just going to show he won't be controlled any longer. I know being with Nick is going to come with lots of drama, but so long as I'm happy then I think it's all going to be worth it.' Rachel's lips curled upwards at the thought of him.

'Yes, I'm sure it will be,' Grace replied kindly. 'How do you feel about meeting Noah?'

'A little nervous, I'm not going to lie,' Rachel said. 'But I love children and hope to have my own one day. I just hope he likes me,' she said fretfully.

'I'm sure he will,' Grace told her confidently.

An hour later and Grace was kissing Rachel goodbye. No sooner had Rachel left, Simon arrived outside beeping his horn.

Grace couldn't contain her excitement as she made her way over to the car.

'Happy Christmas. You look amazing,' Simon said, his face lighting up as she sat next to him.

Grace had opted for a festive red embellished jumper and had spent time making sure her make-up was perfect. She appreciated the compliment and kissed him hello. 'Merry Christmas, darling.'

As Simon drove to Grace's sister's house, she suddenly felt a little nervous about giving Simon his gift. She didn't want to hand it over in front of the others; it was private, between them. She felt like she would burst if she didn't give it to him that very moment.

'Simon, pull over. I want to give you your present.'

'What now? Here in the car?' Simon looked baffled as he indicated to pull the car over.

'Yes.' Grace almost laughed, imagining his face when he opened it. 'You'll see why in a moment. It's a bit personal, between us.'

His frown lines deepened. 'Okay,' he said. 'Let me quickly get yours out of my bag in the back then,' he said, reaching over.

'I'll open mine first then,' Grace said, kissing him again as he handed her a beautifully wrapped present. He'd made a real effort, she could tell.

Grace thought back to the previous year when she had bought a pair of jeans from the shops in the sale just before Christmas and when she'd shown Simon, he'd said uninterestedly, 'I tell you what, I'll give you the money for them and that can be your Christmas present.' Grace hadn't been impressed.

Now in the car she was opening a lovely gift, and she gasped as she opened a box containing a beautiful diamond necklace and matching bracelet.

'Oh wow, Simon, they're absolutely gorgeous. Thank you so much,' she said gratefully.

He obviously hadn't held back this year and Grace couldn't believe how happy she felt at the change in him. But she knew that nothing could ever beat her gift to him.

She handed him the blue box, her hands a little shaky. Grace's heart was thumping wildly in her chest and she didn't know whether to laugh or cry as he opened it.

Simon held the stick out in front of him, a look a sheer bewilderment on his face.

'What's this?' he asked looking up at her. 'It can't be, Grace, can it?'

Grace was holding her breath, studying his stunned expression, her eyes feeling hot with tears.

'Is it really true?' Simon asked in astonishment. 'Are you really pregnant?'

Grace nodded and laughed, tears falling down her face as Simon held her tightly in his arms.

'Yes, Simon. You're going to be a father.'

He pulled back and stared at her with wide eyes, his face filled with awe and pleasure.

'Oh my goodness,' he whispered, before his face exploded into the biggest grin. 'This is the best news ever, Grace! I can't believe it,' he said, kissing her passionately on the lips.

'Me either!' She laughed again, and he joined in as they both sat there blissfully happy crying tears of joy. 'I only found out a few days ago. I was wondering what to get you for Christmas when I realized I was late. I felt silly doing a test, but something told me that this time it was different. All those times we tried unsuccessfully and then when I wasn't even thinking about it, it's happened. We're so lucky.' She beamed. 'Blessed.'

'The luckiest,' Simon agreed. 'This will go down in history as the best Christmas ever,' he announced with a beatific expression etched on his face.

Grace couldn't agree more.

Chapter 33

'I still think you've gone stark, raving mad, Amber,' her mother said, her voice a squawk as she narrowed her eyes, looking incredulous. 'I can't believe I'm doing this on Christmas morning. Honestly,' she huffed.

Her mother was driving her to London Heathrow airport. Amber had decided on Christmas Eve as she sat at home feeling sorry for herself that this year, she was going away for Christmas. She couldn't wait another day and the thought of spending time with both Jack and Natalya made her feel sick with worry. She couldn't, and wouldn't, do it. She was going to Dubai and would rather spend the whole day on an aeroplane where no one would look at her in pity, like she imagined Jack would, or with daggers, like she knew Natalya would. At least she was safe and unreachable on a plane. At least she was far away and could attempt to forget her sorrows.

'Say there isn't a flight? You'll have to come all the way back again. This is probably a complete wasted journey; you should have booked online. Do you want me to wait to see if you can get a ticket? That's probably the best idea, isn't it?'

'My wi-fi was playing up and I couldn't seem to get online,' Amber explained, blinking in frustration at her mother's negativity. 'Besides, I'll just wait until a ticket becomes available so really no need to wait. I don't mind.'

'They'll whack the prices right up, I guarantee it.' Her mother tutted disapprovingly. 'And call me selfish, but I was hoping to spend Christmas Day with my only daughter; we usually have such a laugh together with Diane and the family. Please, tell me why you're really running away? It's to do with Jack, isn't it?'

Her mother wasn't stupid. She knew this was erratic behaviour. It was typical Amber behaviour to run away when things went wrong. Perhaps she was more like her father than she realized? She'd called him the night before and explained about her sudden departure saying her reasons were personal. He had promised to visit if she decided to stay in Dubai for long and wished her a Merry Christmas.

Amber ignored her mother's question and looked out of the window, deep in thought. She wondered how Jack would take the news that she was going? Would he be relieved? She sure as hell knew that Natalya would. This would make her day.

'Are you going to tell me why you're going Amber, or not?' Her mother's tone softened. 'Today won't be the same without you. I'm going to miss you not just being upstairs while you're away.'

'Sorry Mum, I won't be gone forever. Yes, you're right too; it's to do with Jack,' she admitted. 'Let's just say that you were right about my feelings and let's also just say that he wasn't on the same page. I can't go today, it's just too painful. I need to clear my head and get away for a while.'

Her mother nodded understandingly. 'If it makes any difference, I think he's making a mistake,' she told her gingerly.

'Thanks Mum, but it doesn't. Jack obviously doesn't see it that way,' she replied in a small voice. 'You can't help who you love, can you?'

As they arrived at Heathrow, her mother looked at her sadly. 'I'm sorry things didn't work out this time, Amber. But I still have a good feeling about the two of you; I always have done.'

Amber rolled her eyes as she hugged her mum goodbye.

'He's marrying Natalya, Mum. And I'm going to Dubai. I need to move on and so do you.' She pulled away and gave her mum a loving smile. 'Can you give these gifts to the others? I bought them a while back. I even bought Natalya something, being the good friend I am.' She sighed, suddenly feeling nervous and alone. She didn't mind travelling on her own as she'd done it countless times, but it felt unusual because it was Christmas Day. 'Have a lovely Christmas, Mum. Send everyone my love, won't you?'

Her mother blinked away the tears. 'I will do. I wish I could change your mind, but I know better than to try. You've always done things the way you want, even from being a little girl. Stay safe sweetheart, and Happy Christmas.' She gripped her into a tight hug once more and squeezed her.

'Bye Mum,' Amber said, feeling as though something was lodged in her throat. It wasn't too late to change her mind. She could run after her mother and go back home with her head held high, but she knew she wouldn't.

Amber took a deep breath, looking at the jolly faces around her. Everyone was full of Christmas spirit and Amber seemed to be the only miserable person. It just didn't feel like Christmas today; there seemed to have been a massive build up and now Amber just felt like a deflated balloon, empty and lifeless. She walked over to one of the desks to enquire about tickets to Dubai. She knew her mother was probably right and it was going to cost a fortune seeing as she was buying at the airport, but Amber didn't care. Whatever the cost, she was leaving.

'Can I help you?' the kind looking red-haired lady asked her as she approached the desk.

'Hi, I was just wondering if you had any tickets to Dubai flying out today?'

'Today?' the lady repeated, checking her system. There was a short pause as she perused the screen in front of her. 'We have one seat left on our Emirates flight departing at one-thirty today...'

'I'll take it,' Amber interrupted her. She didn't care that she would have to wait. So long as there was a seat, she could go.

'It's £945,' the lady explained, pulling a slight face at the high price.

Amber bit her lip hard as she thought about how long it took her to earn that kind of money. She was thankful she'd been able to save some money over the years; it wasn't much, but it was enough to get by while she was out there until she started working.

'Okay,' she heard herself answer. 'I'll take it. I want that ticket.'

'Amber, stop,' she heard a voice say.

Amber squinted her eyes at the lady in front of her who was looking behind her, perplexed. Had she just imagined that voice?

'Cancel whatever she's booking,' Jack said, marching over with authority. 'She's not going anywhere,' he said robustly.

Amber felt herself become flustered at Jack's sudden arrival.

'Jack, what on earth are you doing here at the airport?'

'I can't let you do this, Amber,' he said, almost angrily. 'You can't just run away.'

'I'm a big girl, Jack, and I'm going,' she told him obstinately. 'There was really no need to come. You should be with Natalya.' She continued to look for her credit card in her purse. She was completely shocked that Jack had turned up, but there was no way he was stopping her departure. He must have felt more sorry for her than she realized.

The red-haired lady looked uncertain. 'Look, why don't I give you two a few moments to talk about it,' she said, staring at them blankly for a few seconds. 'I really think that's best. Now if you don't mind stepping to one side...' She gesticulated for Amber to move over and the couple behind her wasted no time in stepping into her place.

'Jack, what are you doing here?' Amber said impatiently with a theatrical sigh. 'I don't need your sympathy. You should be with your family today, not wasting time with me here. This isn't what I wanted. I'm not an attention seeker and was hoping to just get away without any fuss.'

Jack looked at her intensely. 'Merry Christmas to you too.'

Amber clicked her tongue and looked away, colouring slightly. 'Happy Christmas, Jack. I'm sorry, I really didn't want to spoil everyone's day by doing this.'

'Well, you have,' Jack said tetchily. 'You've ruined mine.'

'I'm sure you'll get over me not being there for just one year,' Amber told him, feeling shaky at his presence.

Jack's eyes narrowed. 'Why do you have to be selfish and just run off, Amber? You didn't even tell me you were going,' he said resentfully. 'I only heard first thing this morning from my mum that you were leaving.'

'Are you kidding me?' Amber said defensively. 'After what I said to you, you haven't said a word to me. You haven't called me or texted me, so why on earth would I assume that you cared? I didn't ask you to come all the way here, Jack. You could have just called and said goodbye…'

'You know I care,' he interjected stubbornly, 'and if I'd have called, you probably wouldn't have answered anyway. I know what you're like. It wouldn't have made any difference.' He stiffened and his jaw set.

'I don't know what you want to me to do or say. Sorry if I've ruined your Christmas Day, I really am. But I'm leaving for Dubai for the foreseeable future.'

He fell silent.

Amber continued, 'Now you'd better be heading back to Natalya. I'm sure she'll be fuming when she realizes you're gone. She's very likely on her way here right this very second. I'm surprised she's not already here.' She looked over her shoulder, half expecting Natalya to jump out from somewhere and throttle her.

'Oh, just shut up,' Jack closed his eyes momentarily.

266

Amber felt annoyed. 'No, Jack, I won't shut up. Like I said before, she never lets you do anything and it's ridiculous. She's going to turn up here, I just know it, and then you'll really be in trouble. She'll go absolutely ballistic. Do you know she even came to my Christmas ball to warn me away? Who does that? She's lost the plot, I swear, she's—' She broke off, gasping as Jack pulled her close to him and kissed her hard on the mouth. Amber couldn't breathe. It took her a moment to actually realize what was happening and she pulled away, breathless. 'Jack, what are you doing?'

'It was the only way to get you to shut up,' he said breathlessly. 'There *is* no Natalya,' Jack looked up at her and smirked. 'I broke up with her two nights ago. You were right about her, Amber. I think I always knew it deep down. Perhaps not at the very start, but I could see what she was like and I knew it wasn't healthy. I guess I just ignored her strange ways, hoping they'd go away. She was my first real serious relationship and I think I didn't want to believe it was over.'

Amber wanted to smile from ear to ear, but she was concerned about something. 'I don't want to be a rebound, Jack,' she said timidly, taken aback by what had just happened.

He gazed at her in adoration, as if he'd always been waiting to tell her what he was about to. 'You could never be a rebound, Amber. I've always been in love with you.' He laughed. 'I thought you knew that? After you turned me down that time, I promised myself I wouldn't attempt it again. I may have acted like it wasn't a big deal, but I could never have handled the rejection again. My sixteen-year-old ego was very bruised that night, let me tell you, and since then, I've never been brave enough to tell you how I really feel. Not until you ever showed me some kind of sign that you loved me back.'

'But you never said it back to me when I told you the other day?' Amber was confused. 'Why didn't you tell me all these things then?'

'It came as a surprise and I think I was too shocked for words. That, and the fact that I was still in a relationship with Natalya who showed up moments afterwards. I had to speak to her first. I couldn't tell you I've always loved you when I was still in a relationship with someone else. When I was *engaged* to someone else; you know I'm not like that.'

Amber couldn't resist a grin. She felt elated by his words.

'I'm scared, Jack,' she admitted. 'I'm scared we're going to ruin what we have if it all goes wrong.'

He rested his soft hands either side of her cheeks and looked into her eyes making her feel as though she was in a dream.

'I'm terrified too,' he confessed in gentle tones. 'But I'm more petrified of not giving this a go. I'm a lot more scared of losing you to Dubai. I love you, Amber. I've always loved you; it's been so hard to keep it in and watch you date guy after guy when I felt this way, but I didn't have a choice. I forced myself to move on and forget about the idea of us. I thought being with Natalya would mean my feelings were switched off, but they weren't. My feelings are still very much the same.' He smiled at her once more and she kissed him, her insides flipping over as she did so.

'What did Natalya say?' she whispered moments later, not wanting to bring her up again.

'Well, as you can imagine, she isn't very happy. But as luck would have it, when I told my friend from work, James, who introduced us that we'd split, he told me that Natalya had cheated on me several times anyway. She denied it at first, but eventually came clean and said she did it because she thought I must be doing the same. She's begged for forgiveness, but at least now she may accept that we will never be getting back together. I'm sure she'll move on.'

It didn't surprise Amber in the slightest that Natalya had cheated on Jack; she'd been so insecure that Amber actually felt a little sorry for her. Despite everything, Amber hoped Natalya managed to find some kind of happiness one day.

'I'm sure she'll move on too,' she replied hopefully. 'Eventually.' She rolled her eyes knowing that it was likely Natalya wouldn't go down without a fight. She could handle it though. So long as Amber had Jack by her side then she could handle anything.

'Right, let's go and enjoy our Christmas Day.' Jack held out his hand and Amber took it like it was the most natural thing in the world. She wondered why she hadn't realized her feelings for Jack sooner. It just felt so right between them, as though they had been made for each other all along and Amber knew that this was the start of something that would last forever. She would spend the rest of her life with Jack, she was certain of it.

'I can't wait,' she said happily and they practically skipped back to Jack's car.

Chapter 34

Rachel listened to what her mother was saying in shock. It was hard to take her seriously with her flashing Christmas jumper and hat, but what her mother was telling her wasn't as amusing as her outfit.

'So they've split up, can you believe it? Mark has left Bianca even though she's pregnant. Honestly, what a complete mess. Thank goodness you're out of the equation. Imagine getting a girl pregnant after having an affair and then walking out on her when it's not quite as exciting as before?' her mother said, showing her distaste.

'How do you know?' Rachel asked.

'I bumped into Mary Harper in the supermarket, remember her? She's best friends with Bianca's mother,' she explained as she dried up another plate. 'Bianca isn't that bothered by all accounts. She said it wasn't working out and she'd rather bring the baby up alone than with him. She doesn't know what she's let herself in for, let me tell you that now. Babies, as cute as they are, are hard work. Especially alone.'

'I can't believe it,' Rachel said, stupefied. 'He said he was leaving her because the excitement had gone?'

'Well, Mary didn't exactly say that, but I guess that's the reason, don't you? Never happy, that man; always after something else. He'll end up alone, you mark my words.'

'It could be for a number of reasons,' Rachel said thoughtfully. 'I knew they weren't compatible, but I really thought that they'd last somehow, especially seeing as a baby is involved.'

Her mother was right; it was all one big mess. Rachel wished she didn't feel sorry for Bianca, but she couldn't help it. She guessed because she no longer cared about them being together, because she'd finally accepted it, she couldn't hate her any longer. In fact, she didn't even feel angry about it anymore. Not entirely. All her thoughts were taken up with Nick and what could happen between them. She constantly found herself daydreaming and fantasizing about him. Rachel just pitied Bianca's situation; it wasn't easy for any woman to bring up a child alone when it was unplanned. She wondered how Bianca would cope. Mark's mother would be absolutely livid with her son for walking away, she knew that much.

'Well, it's nothing for you to worry about now, is it?' her mother said protectively. 'I think you handled yourself marvellously, and now look how happy you are meeting that lovely new man.'

Rachel felt a slight colour coming to her cheeks. 'It's really early days, Mum. I want to take things nice and slow. I'm not rushing into anything this time.'

After the Christmas ball, Nick had stayed at Grace's place for the night with her and the following day they'd gone to Rachel's parents for breakfast because he'd wanted to meet them. It felt amazing to get their approval after they told her what a lovely man they thought he was. Normally if a man had wanted to meet her parents so soon it would have put Rachel off; after all, who usually wanted to meet the parents? But with Nick it was different. She *wanted* her parents to know that she'd met someone. Someone pretty special too.

The loud, buzzing sound of the doorbell startled both Rachel and her mother and they glanced at each other in wonderment at who could be visiting them on Christmas Day.

'I'm not expecting anyone, are you?' Rachel's mother questioned in puzzlement, her brow furrowed as she put down the tea towel that she was holding.

Rachel listened out to who it was at the door as she sat drinking her tea, surprised when her mother called her name out.

Her heart leapt as she spotted Nick standing at the door and her mother looking delighted with a beautiful bunch of flowers he'd obviously just given her.

'It's Nick, darling,' she beamed brightly. 'Look at these stunning flowers he's bought me, aren't they lovely?' she gushed, smelling them with a huge grin.

'Nick, Happy Christmas,' Rachel said, unable to resist smiling widely at him. She leant forward and kissed him. 'Do you want to come in? I didn't realize you were going to come over.'

He flapped his hand. 'No, thanks for the offer but I can't stop. I just wanted to give you your present and to be honest, I couldn't bear the thought of not seeing you today; even if it's quickly.'

Rachel took the gift, feeling on top of the world. How wonderful it was to hear words like that when Nick had been all she'd been able to think of all day.

'Thanks so much. Have you seen Noah?' she asked.

'I've just dropped him home to Claire. I'm off to see my family now as they're waiting for me. I told them I had to quickly pop over to see my girlfriend and I'd be straight over,' he said casually.

Rachel's heart skipped a beat as he said the words. 'Your girlfriend?' she ventured.

Nick's cheeks reddened slightly and he looked at his shoes in discomfiture. He gave a brittle, nervous laugh and looked up at her in hope. 'Well, aren't you?'

Rachel giggled. 'Is this *the* Nick Cunningham, who's usually so confident and self-assertive, asking me to be his girlfriend on my doorstep?'

He screwed up his face tightly, like he had a toothache. 'Yes.'

Rachel burst into laughter and leaned in for another kiss. 'Of course I'll be your girlfriend. No need to look so worried.' She gazed into his eyes. 'Providing there are no more ex-wives or other children you haven't told me about?' she asked in mock seriousness.

He raised an eyebrow. 'I'm pretty sure I've told you about them all now.'

She kissed him again.

Rachel was giddy with happiness; what a very merry Christmas this was turning out to be.

Epilogue

'I'm so glad we got to meet before New Year's Eve,' Grace said, pouring the tea from the teapot into the three china cups on the table. 'Did you both have a lovely Christmas?' she asked interestedly.

'Obviously mine was very eventful,' Amber told them dreamily. 'I honestly thought I'd be sunning myself in Dubai by now. Who would have thought I'd rather be here, more excited to be making plans to go to the cinema tonight with Jack?' Her face was radiant with joy.

'I think it's so romantic that he went to the airport to get you,' Rachel told them, her eyes glittery. 'It's like something out of a film.'

'Or just like that episode of *Friends* with Ross and Rachel,' Grace pointed out. 'What about you with Nick turning up on Christmas Day asking you to be his girlfriend?' Grace laughed happily. 'I didn't think he had it in him.'

'I know, you should have seen him.' Rachel chuckled at the memory. 'He does have a really soft side to him. I never would have thought that when I first met him. I'm glad.'

'Perhaps seeing as things have worked out so well for all of us, we should be celebrating drinking wine instead of tea? Who's up for hitting a bar? It's kind of still Christmas, after all. We haven't had New Year's yet so it's still part of the festive period in my book,' Amber suggested, a mischievous glint in her eye.

Rachel had a faint smile on her lips. 'I'm in if you are?'

Their eyes swivelled towards Grace, waiting for her to agree and she looked away, her face suffusing with colour.

'I've kind of got something to tell you,' Grace started, her voice scratchy with nerves. This was a huge moment telling her friends. It was *big* news. 'Simon and I are having a baby. I'm pregnant!' she exclaimed, her face crinkling into a beam.

Rachel and Amber seemed galvanized.

'What? You're pregnant?' Amber's mouth popped open. 'No way!'

'Oh wow, congratulations!' Rachel's voice was a high-pitched squeak.

They both stood up to hug her.

'I'm so happy for you, Grace. This is what you've always wanted,' Amber pointed out, a cheerful expression on her face.

'I know, I know; we're both thrilled with the news. We can't wait to be parents. It's early days still, but I just can't keep the news to myself. Besides, you'd never have believed any reason as to why I wasn't drinking.'

'You'll make great parents,' Rachel said giddily. She lifted her mug of tea. 'Cheers.'

They clinked cups, giggling.

'Perhaps it wasn't the season to be single after all?' Amber said doubtfully.

Grace agreed. Maybe for some it was the best time to go out with no commitments and have fun, but for them, Christmas had brought them love and happiness, and what a magical time it was.

Acknowledgements

Firstly, I would like to thank the lovely Charlotte Mursell at HQ. I'm so grateful that firstly, you loved the book and have been so passionate and enthusiastic about it and secondly, you've been such a wonderful and helpful editor to work with! None of this would have been possible without you.

To my agent, Hannah Ferguson, who has always stuck by me and been so patient with my attempts; I got there in the end! Thank you for believing in me. I would also like to give a huge thanks to Joanna Swainson, who was covering for Hannah who was on maternity leave when I got this book deal.

Thank you to the talented Anna Sikorska who designed this book cover; I loved it as soon as I saw it.

Thanks to all the team at HQ who have worked on this book and made it happen. I'll always be pinching myself that I'm in such a lucky position to have my novels published.

Thank you to my family for putting up with me always being on my laptop, and thanks to my lovely mum for babysitting my children whenever I've needed to work.

Last, but certainly not least, I would like to thank anyone who has read this book. I really hope you've enjoyed it. Feel free to tell me your thoughts or just say hello on Twitter @lauraziepe or Instagram @lauraziepewriter.

Dear Reader,

Thank you so much for reading my book, *'Tis The Season to be Single*. I really hope you loved reading it as much as I did writing it.

After deciding to write a Christmas-themed novel, I thought a perfect, festive setting for the characters to work was a department store. I used to work in one myself part-time when I was seventeen, and I remember the continuous Christmas songs, joyful faces and flashing decorations always really got me in the holiday mood. I currently work as freelance make-up artist, so it seemed like the perfect idea that the three friends in my book worked for a make-up brand.

This will be my third published book now, and I count myself as incredibly fortunate to be able to have a job that I love so very much. For me, writing doesn't feel like working, and as the famous saying goes, 'if you find a job you enjoy doing, you will never have to work a day in your life.'

I know there are tons of books out there to choose from, and again, thank you so much for choosing mine to read. I love hearing your thoughts and feedback so don't hesitate to leave a review on Amazon or contact me @lauraziepe on twitter or @lauraziepewriter on Instagram. Please look out for my next book, which is set in summer, or check out my previous novels which you can find on Amazon.

Laura x

Dear Reader,

Thank you so much for taking the time to read this book – we hope you enjoyed it! If you did, we'd be so appreciative if you left a review.

Here at HQ Digital we are dedicated to publishing fiction that will keep you turning the pages into the early hours. We publish a variety of genres, from heartwarming romance, to thrilling crime and sweeping historical fiction.

To find out more about our books, enter competitions and discover exclusive content, please join our community of readers by following us at:

🐦 *@HQDigitalUK*

📘 *facebook.com/HQDigitalUK*

Are you a budding writer? We're also looking for authors to join the HQ Digital family!
Please submit your manuscript to:

HQDigital@harpercollins.co.uk.

Hope to hear from you soon!

ONE PLACE. MANY STORIES

ONE PLACE. MANY STORIES

If you enjoyed *'Tis the Season to be Single*, then why not try another delightfully uplifting romance from HQ Digital?